B.H.

The Bells of San Carlos
and Other Stories

G·K Hall &C°.

Also by Max Brand
in Large Print:

Clung
The Border Bandit
The Cross Brand
Dr. Kildare Takes Charge
Dr. Kildare's Crisis
Dr. Kildare's Search
Fighter Squadron at Guadacanal
Free Range Lanning
The Galloping Broncos
The Hair-Trigger Kid
The Lightning Warrior
The Long Chase
The Longhorn Feud
Marbleface
Murder Me!

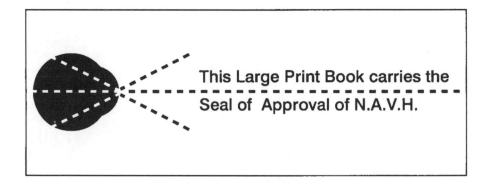

This Large Print Book carries the
Seal of Approval of N.A.V.H.

The Bells of San Carlos
and Other Stories

Max Brand

*Edited and with a Foreword
and Headnotes by Jon Tuska*

G.K. Hall & Co.
Thorndike, Maine

Acknowledgments for previously published material appear on
page 6.

The texts of the stories in this work adhere as closely as possible
to the original typescripts by Frederick Faust and are published
here as their author wrote them.

Published in 1998 by arrangement with
University of Nebraska Press.

G.K. Hall Large Print Western Series.

The text of this Large Print edition is unabridged.
Other aspects of the book may vary from the original edition.

Set in 16 pt. Plantin by Juanita Macdonald.

Printed in the United States on permanent paper.

Library of Congress Cataloging in Publication Data

Brand, Max, 1892–1944.
    The bells of San Carlos and other stories / Max Brand ;
edited and with a foreword and headnotes by Jon Tuska.
        p.   cm.
    ISBN 0-7838-0121-1 (lg. print : hc : alk. paper)
    1. Large type books.   I. Tuska, Jon.   II. Title.
[PS3511.A87B44   1998]
812'.52—dc21   98-2816

A

Contents

Acknowledgments 6

Foreword 7

Cayenne Charlie 11

The Bells of San Carlos 139

Between One and Three 165

The Gift 257

Acknowledgments

"Cayenne Charlie" by George Owen Baxter was first published in *Western Story Magazine* (2/22/30). Copyright © 1930 by Street & Smith Publications, Inc. Copyright © renewed 1958 by Dorothy Faust. Acknowledgment is made to Condé Nast Publications, Inc., for their cooperation. Reprinted by arrangement with Golden West Literary Agency. All rights reserved.

"The Bells of San Carlos" by Max Brand was first published in *Argosy* (4/30/38). Copyright © 1938 by Frank A. Munsey Company. Copyright © renewed 1966 by Jane Faust Easton, John Frederick Faust, and Judith Faust. Reprinted by arrangement with Golden West Literary Agency. All rights reserved.

"Between One and Three" was first published under the title "Mountain Madness" by George Owen Baxter in *Western Story Magazine* (8/26/22). Copyright © 1922 by Street & Smith Publications, Inc. Copyright © renewed 1950 by Dorothy Faust. Copyright © 1996 for restored material by Jane Faust Easton and Adriana Faust Bianchi. Acknowledgment is made to Condé Nast Publications, Inc., for their cooperation. Reprinted by arrangement with Golden West Literary Agency. All right reserved.

"The Gift" by Max Brand was first published in *Western Story Magazine* (12/24/21). Copyright © 1921 by Street & Smith Publications, Inc. Copyright © renewed 1949 by Dorothy Faust. Copyright © 1996 for restored material by Jane Faust Easton and Adriana Faust Bianchi. Acknowledgment is made to Condé Nast Publications, Inc., for their cooperation. Reprinted by arrangement with Golden West Literary Agency. All rights reserved.

Foreword

Max Brand is the best-known pen name of Frederick Faust, creator of Dr. Kildare, Destry, and many other fictional characters popular with readers and viewers worldwide. Faust wrote for a variety of audiences in many genres under numerous pseudonyms. His enormous output, totaling approximately thirty million words or the equivalent of 530 ordinary books, covered nearly every field: crime, fantasy, historical romance, espionage, Westerns, science fiction, adventure, animal stories, love, war, and fashionable society, big business and big medicine. Eighty motion pictures have been based on his work along with many radio and television programs. For good measure he also published four volumes of poetry. Perhaps no other author has reached more people in more different ways.

Born in Seattle in 1892, orphaned early, Faust grew up in the rural San Joaquin Valley of California. At Berkeley he became a student rebel and one-man literary movement, contributing prodigiously to all campus publications. Denied a degree because of unconventional conduct, he embarked on a series of adventures culminating in New York City where, after a period of near starvation, he received simultaneous recognition as a serious poet and successful popular-prose writer. Later, he traveled widely, making his home in New York, then in Florence, and finally in Los Angeles.

Once the United States entered the Second World War, Faust abandoned his lucrative writing career and his work as a screenwriter to serve as a war correspondent with the infantry in Italy, despite his fifty-one years and a bad heart. He was killed during a night attack on a hilltop village held by the German army. New books based on magazine serials or unpublished manuscripts or restored versions continue to appear so that, alive or dead, he has averaged a new book every four months for seventy-five years. In the United States alone nine publishers now issue his work. Beyond this, some work by him is newly reprinted every week of every year in one or another format somewhere in the world. Yet, only recently have the full dimensions of this extraordinarily versatile and prolific writer come to be recognized and his stature as a protean literary figure in the 20th Century acknowledged. His popularity continues to grow throughout the world.

The stories I have collected for this book do not appear in chronological order. The organizing principle, instead, is the expansiveness of Faust's imagination when it comes to the Western story as a form of literary art and the fecundity with which he would vary his themes, examining problems and dilemmas of the human condition from numerous disparate viewpoints. In another sense these stories fit together as episodes in a great saga, very much after the fashion of Homer in the Books of *Odyssey*. No matter how much editors or his agent might tell Faust that he was writing stories that were too character-driven, he could never really change the way he wrote. In order to write, he was fond of saying, I must be able to dream. As early as 1921, writing as George Owen Baxter, Faust had commented about Free Range Lanning in "Iron Dust" that Lanning "had at least picked up that dangerous equipment of fiction which enables a man to dodge reality and live in his dreams."

Brave words! Yet, beyond this, and maybe precisely because of the truth in them, much that happens in a Western story by Frederick Faust depends upon an interplay between dream and reality. There will come a time, probably well into the next century, when a reëvaluation will become necessary of those who contributed most to the eternal relevance of the Western story in this century. In this reëvaluation unquestionably Zane Grey and Frederick Faust will be elevated while popular icons of this century such as Owen Wister, judged solely in terms of their actual artistic contributions to the wealth and treasure of world literature, may find their reputations diminished. In such a reëvaluation Faust, in common with Jack London, may be seen as a purveyor of visceral fiction of great emotional power and profound impact that does not recede with time.

The stories collected here, early or late, have all been restored where necessary by comparing the author's manuscripts with the published versions. They are set in that land Faust called the mountain desert, a place for him as timeless and magical as the plains of Troy in the hexameters of his beloved Homer and as vivid as the worlds Shakespeare's vibrant imagery projected outward from the bare stages of the Globe. Faust was not so much mapping a geographical region in his Western stories as he was exploring the dark and bright corridors of the human soul — that expanse which is without measure, as Heraclitus said. For Faust, as for his reader, this experience is much as he described it in 1926 for Oliver Tay in what became *The Border Bandit* (Harper, 1947): ". . . He was seeing himself for the very first time; and, just as his eye could wander through the unfathomed leagues of the stars which were strewn across the universe at night, so he could turn his glance inward and probe the vastness of new-found self. All new!" In these explorations of the inner world Faust's fiction can be seen to embody a basic principle of the Western story, that quality which makes the Western story so vitally rewarding in world literature, the experience of personal renewal, an affirmation of hope through courage, the potential that exists in each human being for redemption.

Cayenne Charlie

"Cayenne Charlie" was Faust's title for this story published under the byline George Owen Baxter in *Western Story Magazine* (2/22/30). The same issue carried the fourth installment of a serial by Max Brand that Faust had titled "Destry Rides Again" and which Frank Blackwell, editor of *Western Story Magazine*, changed to "Twelve Peers." Fortunately, when Dodd, Mead & Company published the book version in 1932, Faust's title was restored. This novel has never been out of print since it was first published.

The year 1930 marked a period in which Faust was experimenting more daringly than ever before with the conventions of the Western story, varying his structures and themes. While it is true that *Destry Rides Again* follows much of the action of the closing Books of *Odyssey*, Faust's story is not totally faithful to the source since Harry Destry, unlike Odysseus, does not complete his revenge against those who betrayed him. In "Cayenne Charlie" Faust violates a basic rule in the narrative structure of fiction: he does not introduce his principal character until almost halfway through the story! The stratagem works in this case precisely because such a tardy introduction shifts the thematic emphasis of the story in a significant way. Just as Harry Destry's abandonment of his revenge before it is completed reflects an essential change in the kind of human being he has become and therefore of what is expected of him, so Charlie Bird cannot perform many of the traditional functions of a Western hero because the pattern of expectation has been disrupted by this belated appearance.

I

"Young and Old"

A man who united many virtues in one person was Alfred Clark, and he never had a better chance to exhibit them than when he was talking to his niece, Dinah. She was tall, strong, graceful, imperious, beautiful, and cruel. Alfred Clark was short, weak, awkward, humble, ugly, and charitable.

She was young enough to feel that knowledge was absolute and that she had her share. He was old enough to feel that knowledge is comparative and that he had not cornered the market. She was rich in prospect and would have a million or so when she reached twenty-one. He had been a humble, toiling lawyer all his days.

She had always been the first choice at every schoolhouse dance in the county, the first invited to every celebration, the first girl that every new-comer fell in love with, and the last he proposed to. Because, like a star, she was not only shining, but seemed distant — not in her manner, which was adapted from the ways of wild mustangs, but in herself. Men like to feel that a wife will be a possession. Nobody was apt to feel that way about Dinah.

Alfred Clark never had been retained in a big case, never had convinced an important jury, never had even so much as raised a family. He was fifty years old. He was five feet three inches tall. He hardly could begin a sentence without saying: "Excuse me."

His brother, Tom Clark, had been the exact opposite of Alfred in everything. He had been the bad boy of a bad town. And he had spent the strength of six feet of bone and muscle for thirty years without accumulating a penny. Alfred was always the good example, and Tom was always the good time.

Then Tom married a little gentle, trustful, un-worldly girl who had inherited a good many thousand acres of valueless land. The land was not valueless because it was poor in quality, but because it was poor in situation and environment. That is to say, it was in a true hole-in-the-wall country which was filled with free-hand artists with a running iron. It was a truly democratic country where a herd of cows belonged to the first comer and where men killed a cow to eat a steak.

Tom went up into those wild highlands and brought order out of disorder. He killed three men in the first year and gathered around him for 'punchers a gang of ex-criminals, ex-yeggs, long riders, rustlers, and jailbirds. He knew them by heart. They understood Tom, his fist and his gun. That became a happy ranch, a busy ranch, and a ranch that turned out dollars fast enough

14

to make the head of any man swim. But, great as he was, before his death Tom began to be known as the father of Dinah Clark.

When he lay on his deathbed — a certain brutal scoundrel named Tabasco Joe had shot him full of holes, though in a fair fight — Tom Clark had named his far-off brother, Alfred, as the guardian of his daughter during the year and a half which would pass before she reached her twenty-first year. He was to manage the estate, in the meantime, at a generous salary. Tom had not even thought of Alfred for twenty years. And when Alfred came West, the 'punchers wished that he had not remembered on his deathbed.

But the wishing of the 'punchers was nothing compared with the wishing of Dinah. She never saw him mount a horse without wishing that he would be pitched off on his head. She never saw him enter a buckboard without wishing that a wheel would come off as he was going downhill.

For when she wanted to go out for a ride, there had to be a chaperon. When she went to a dance, Uncle Alfred also attended and sat in a corner with a bright, patient eye. She could not begin a dinner with chocolates and end it with soup. She could not go to bed at three and get up at five. She had her daily life flavored with old wives' maxims and her nights were poisoned with bad dreams. She could not speak ten words without having her grammar corrected. One might have thought, after living for a time with Uncle Alfred, that schools really were worthwhile!

However, she had her revenge. So did the 'punchers.

That hand-picked bunch of thugs was dear to the heart of Tom Clark. The same will which made her brother the manager of the estate for a year and a half also forbade him to discharge a single member of the old crowd except for shooting from behind. The will was known to all the men, and they took advantage of it. For this unsympathetic Easterner who did not know how to use a pair of spurs or swing a rope, they shirked their work; they let the place run down; and when a friendly rustler appeared on the horizon, instead of blasting him into another world with plentiful gunpowder and good lead, they winked at him askance. The great Clark herd began to diminish.

Alfred Clark talked to them in assembly. He talked to them one by one. He implored them in the name of Tom Clark. He did everything that he could. He turned from iron-gray to gray-white. But nothing would do. He could not handle these men; but these men could handle him. They soldiered on the job, and the more they soldiered, the more Dinah smiled on them. She was what counted, in their eyes, and she wanted nothing so much as to have her uncle throw up his hands and pronounce this a bad job. He would not do it.

Quiet, grave, gentle as a lamb; there was in him the same streak of iron that had appeared more visibly in his brother. He stuck to his guns, though they were guns of silence and reflection. If he could not stop the wagon from rolling downhill, at least he could apply a brake that jarred on everyone's nerves. In the meantime, he strove to uphold and maintain the business methods of his brother.

One of Tom Clark's best moves had been to go south every year and, crossing the Mexican border at the town of Libertad, he would gather up many hundreds of Mexican cattle, undersized, composed of bony backs and gaunt stomachs and hanging heads. These he drove north, and in three months they had fattened in the rich mountain lands of the ranch where water ran in every valley and the grass was as green as a cowman could wish. These half-priced skeletons, at the end of three months, sold for as much per pound, in Chicago, as the finest Durhams. They were smaller parcels, to be sure, but they had the necessary beef and sold at the same rate per pound.

This system never had failed to net him more than a hundred percent. In addition, it supplied every year with an excursion into the land of high adventure. Tom Clark had looked forward to this excursion. So had the 'punchers. So had Dinah. In their own way, Mexicans know as much about the art of living as the French. At least, they understand that tomorrow may take care of today. So, to Tom Clark, and his daughter, and his men, the annual excursion to Mexico was like a trip to fairyland.

This trip was made by Alfred Clark, pursuing the old traditions. But everything turned out wrong. He had taken with him every man who could be spared for the drive home. Dinah went along also, though against his better judgment. But, when he came to Libertad, the town which had loved his brother as a great god looked at him over the tip of a Mexican nose — than which nothing is more supercilious.

The prices they demanded for cattle were outrageous. It seemed for the moment that Yankee gold meant nothing to them. And Alfred Clark meant less than nothing.

When he got some cattle into the corrals, thieves broke in and stole them. He never knew what to do. He was in despair. He never could fasten blame on anyone.

That was the reason he talked to Dinah on this night. She was almost the first person in his life who had touched his pride. He had vowed, after a few days, that he never would appeal to her even for information. But his honesty determined him to throw pride to the winds on this occasion. It was for her, after all, that he was working, except for that salary that would cover a transient year or two and then send him back to an old business newly ruined.

He sat in a chair in the corner of the room, next to a little window that looked down on the moonlight of the street. He sat quietly, except that now and then the leg which was crossed on top of the other swayed up and down. One could not tell whether this were impatience or a mere flexing of the muscles.

Otherwise, he sat immovable. He always was cool. This night beaded every brow but that of Alfred Clark. He was pale, dry, and smooth, as usual. Except when now and then he raised his brows wistfully, like a child.

Dinah could not keep still. She walked up and down the room restlessly. She knew that she was in the wrong and, therefore, she was angrier and more sulky than ever.

"I've had to surrender," said Uncle Alfred.

"You mean that you're going to throw up the job. Too bad!" she said hopefully.

"No," he replied, "I'll never throw up the job."

"I don't know what you mean, then."

"I mean that I'm failing at the work, and I've decided to ask you for your help."

"Humph!" said Dinah.

"Do you think that you could work with me, Dinah?"

"I dunno," she said. "What about?"

"Don't know," he corrected. "You blur your letters, my dear."

"Yeah?" said Dinah. "Wacha want me to do, Uncle Alf?"

"Alfred," he said, "is better. We have not known one another very long, Dinah."

"Yeah?" said Dinah. "Well, whacha drivin' at . . . Uncle Alfred?"

"I have bought cattle every day since we came to Libertad. And a day or so after buying, most of those purchases are stolen."

"You mean that I steal 'em?"

19

He paused a moment. Then his foot swung once, up and down. "Practically," he said.

"Yeah. You mean it?" said Dinah. "I'm a thief, then!"

"No, you're young."

"Bein' young," said Dinah, "seems to have meant about everything else before now. But it's the first time that you've said that it means bein' a thief." He made another of his thoughtful pauses. She never could tell whether those pauses meant that he was trying to think of something to say or whether he was trying not to say too much. "Stealing? Why I'd be stealing from myself!" she broke out.

"Exactly so," said he. "Stealing from yourself in order to spite me."

II

"Uncle and Niece"

This was such a degree of frankness that she looked suddenly at him, wondering if, after all, he might belong to her own world. She decided, after the glance, that he could not.

"Let's have it out," she said, for she loved a fight as much as had her famous father.

"That's what I intend to do," he answered surprisingly.

"Go on, then," said the girl, squaring her jaw.

"You want me to get out," said the lawyer.

"Yes, I do!" she said, willing to meet him on any ground that he chose to select.

"I'm in the way, here."

"Yes, you are."

"Your way, and the way of the cowpunchers."

"Yes, in the way of everybody and everything!" agreed Dinah.

"If I were gone, you could do as you choose."

"Yes, I could. And a good job I'd make of it."

"Running around unchaperoned?" he said.

"What sort of a girl do you think I am?" she asked.

He swayed his foot again. "A young girl, my dear," he said.

"Leave the 'dear' out and just make it young," she said.

"Willingly."

"You think that I'd do everything wrong without you?" asked Dinah.

"No. But you'd be apt to do the important thing wrong," said her uncle.

"And just what is the important thing?"

"Your marriage."

"Humph! You figger that I'd take a no-account 'puncher?"

"Yes. Probably."

"You gotta nerve," she said. "I gotta say that."

"I'm an old man," he said.

"Well, you're old, all right. But I'm not asking you for a fist fight, if that's what you mean."

"My dear, don't you think that young as you are, and old as I am, we might be friends?"

"Well, I'm a friendly sort. I won't bite."

"Dinah, you've been going hand in hand with these 'punchers."

"They were good enough for Dad."

"Of course they were, because he was man enough to handle them."

"Yeah, he handled 'em, all right."

"When they shirked, he found out why. He punished them with his fists."

"Of course he did!"

Uncle Alfred bundled up a puny fist and considered it carefully.

"That's a thing I couldn't do," he said.

"Yeah," she said, "I guess you wouldn't go far

22

down that road, Uncle Alfred."

"But you, Dinah, could easily do what I cannot do. You could keep the men all in order."

"Whacha mean by that?"

"They love you for your father's sake, and for your own. They could not possibly be unfair to you, as they are to me."

"Out here, Uncle Alfred, you gotta understand that men that ain't satisfied the way they're treated go grab a gun and start trouble."

"I never fired a revolver in my life," he said.

"Get a riot gun, then."

"The only weapon that I can think of using with them is a discharge, and your father's will forbids that."

"Well, you want me to go in and handle the boys? Drop down on my knees and beg 'em to be good?"

"I'm asking you to help me . . . yes. You'd know the best way, if you cared to give your mind to it."

"Would I?"

"Yes, I think so."

"But I'll tell you. There's only one right way. That is for you to barge off back East and leave us all alone. We did pretty good before you came out here!"

"You had your father here then."

"We could chance it without him. You don't understand the men and you make a lot of trouble. You don't understand me, and that makes more trouble still. What good is wastin' all your time? Pay yourself for the clean year and a half, and let the place rip. Will you?"

"No," he said. "That I cannot do."

"Then you can be your own chief mourner."

"You mean that you definitely won't help me?"

"I dunno why I should, the way that we've been chums."

"Mind you, my dear! I've gone as far as I can go to get your help."

"Yeah. I'll say that you've done that."

"You have me practically beaten," he said, raising his voice a little because of a noise in the street.

"Yeah?" said the ungracious girl.

"You have me practically beaten, but still I won't quite give up. I am going to try for another day to find some way of solving the problem. If I fail, I shall step out, because it bleeds me to the heart to see my brother's estate dissipated."

"Look here," said the girl, coming to him suddenly and putting her hand upon his shoulder. "You're pretty off me, ain't you?"

"Let me see. If I understand what you mean . . . no, I'm not entirely disgusted with you, Dinah. I remember that you're young."

"There've been younger," she said. "But I wancha to know that you'll lose nothing by it if you pull out. You've stuck to your guns long enough. There's no use in getting yourself shot down at your guns."

"No?" he said.

"No. You won't lose your salary."

He watched her steadily for a moment, according to his custom.

"I won't apply for salary that I haven't worked for," he told her gravely.

"You got me wrong," said the girl. "I didn't mean that you're a cheapskate. . . ."

He raised his hand.

"What a good thing for you, my dear, if you could have two or three years of proper schooling."

"Oh, I don't care what kind of English I use," she said. "I want people to understand what I'm talkin' about. That's all. I'm no Willie Shakespeare. I don't aim to be."

At this, when she was expecting a stinging retort, he was simply silent again, and his silence embarrassed her more than any words could have done. Finally he said: "Will you let me tell you how much faith I have in you, Dinah?"

"Yeah," she said. "That'd be a new line. Let's hear it."

"I'm convinced that when you've grown up, you'll be ashamed of this whole episode. I have that much faith in the good that's in you."

"Thanks a lot," she said, very dryly.

"But the end of this talk is that you won't try to influence the men for me?"

"I'm only a girl," she said. "How can I handle men?"

"With two words you could have the lot of them in hand, as you know."

"Could I?"

"Yes, I think that you could."

She was sullenly silent. The truth of what he said was too apparent to her. She grew angrier. She knew that everything she had done and said had been wrong, in her treatment of this little withered uncle of hers.

"Very well," Uncle Alfred went on, "you won't help me. I can't help myself. I shall have to look about for new levers to lift the old load. It may be that I shall find them. If, at the end of twenty-four hours, I have not found the right chance, as it appears to me, I shall leave, refund the salary that has been paid to me, and leave you the mistress of your own destiny."

She could not help the gleam of joy that flashed into her eye, though she protested: "But the salary . . . why, Uncle Alf, you can have ten times the salary. It isn't the money that I so much as think about, you see."

He raised his hand and, at the same time, the uproar in the street became so great that the last of her words was not audible, but her meaning had been clear, and his gesture which dismissed any such idea. He stood up and leaned at the window.

As he raised his hand, she had been starting forward, overcome suddenly with a generous re-morse and a willingness to be more than fair; but when he turned toward the window, thereby clos-ing the interview, her pride stopped her. She merely went and leaned at the window beside him, looking down toward the street.

Most of Libertad seemed to be there.

They could count the bright uniforms of a dozen gendarmes. The crowd filled the narrow sidewalks and overflowed into the street, and down the center, accompanied by a heavily armed guard, marched two mules, with a man thrown over the back of each.

These burdens were lashed hand and foot, and bound so that they could not stir. One of them seemed unconscious. His head dangled; his long red hair flopped with each step of the mule that bore him. And as the procession passed, there were loud whoops and shouts from the crowd. They yelled; they danced; they frantically waved their arms.

And repeatedly Alfred Clark could hear the word "gringo" over and over again.

One gringo, or two? That red hair certainly seemed to fill the part.

"It sounds as loud as a revolution, doesn't it?" asked Alfred Clark, very willing to turn the subject of conversation from the dispute.

She did not answer him, but leaning from the window she called in a voice as strong as a man's: "Hey, Harry!" She repeated the call.

On the sidewalk beneath a brown-faced 'puncher looked up to them. He was one of the biggest, strongest, wildest, and most troublesome of all the Clark cowpunchers. At the sight of the girl, his scowling face broke into a great grin of welcome.

" 'Lo, Dinah," he said.

"Hey, what's the big news?"

"Aw, a ruction."

"C'mon up and let's hear," Dinah suggested.

"Sure. I'll be up in a minute."

The girl drew back from the window and looked with a frown at her guardian.

"Is it all right for me to talk to him?" she asked.

"Certainly," said Alfred Clark, and sat down to wait.

III

"Gran' Ol' Party!"

When Harry broke into the room, grinning broadly in pleasure at this chance to speak to the girl, he saw Clark and paused for a whole half second in the middle of his stride and the middle of his smile. Swiftly a dark scowl took the place of the grin.

"Well, what is it, Dinah?" he asked bluntly.

He was big enough to fill a door — or break a hangman's rope, thought Alfred Clark. He had a long, narrow brow, with greasy black hair cataracting out over it, and the line of his hatband was indented visibly all around his head. All his face was darkest bronze, a little shadowed in the unrazored parts of it. He looked like a villain.

Alfred was convinced that he was at least as bad as his looks. Yet there was no man in the world, apparently, that young Dinah Clark liked better than this forty-five-year-old brute, with his jail record, and his list of dead men!

She was smiling already at him, frankly, expectantly. It seemed that the poor child had no taste in men, whatever. A fine thing if his brother's ranch should pass by marriage into the hands of this thug. He began to regret that he had made his promise to leave within twenty-four hours, unless he could find what he called new levers.

"Hullo, boss," said Harry, with a mere side-glance at Clark. "What is it, Dinah?"

"Give your feet a rest, Harry," she said.

"Yeah, I don't mind."

He did not wait for his hostess. He slumped into the most comfortable chair.

"What's up in Libertad?" Dinah began.

"Trouble!" said Harry.

She did not shrink. Her smile only became gladder.

"What kind?" she asked.

"Fists."

"That's all?"

"Naw. Rough-an'-tumble. Knives. Then some clubs and guns to finish off."

"Thought I heard some shooting. Dead men they were packing by?"

"Pretty near," said Harry. "I been and seen the most outstandingest scrap that I ever looked at in my life."

"Yeah? Let's hear it."

"Why, I was up to that cheap dump at the end of the street. That one with what they call a golden lion over the door. It looks a pile more to me like a sick cat."

"Yeah, me, too. What gotcha there?"

"Busted," Harry said.

And he cast an ugly eye askance at his boss.

"Why, I'd always stake you, Harry," said the girl. "G'wan, though! What happened? Starting at the beginning, who busted you?"

"That slick Ben Clay. Me sitting tight with a full house, he comes four measly treys over me and grabs three months of my life."

He chuckled, without regrets.

"He's stackin' 'em, I figger," he said. "But that ain't the fight."

"No, it ain't," said the girl.

Alfred Clark writhed silently in his chair.

"Well," Harry said, "I slope into that cheap dump and look over the supply of wines and liquors, which they ain't none too fancy, and while I'm tastin' and tryin' out, preparin' for a bust as big as one dollar ninety can give. . . ."

"Sounds like a bargain sale," said the girl.

"Yeah, don't it? But in that joint you're sold before you start in buying."

"G'wan, Harry, let's hear the fight."

"Why, you'd a-laughed. In sashays a big gent with a black head of hair longer than goat's wool, and he leans on the bar and takes a look around him. Mean, what I mean to say. Looks around him and don't say nothin'. And the barkeep, he bows and smiles and looks real friendly, like he was meetin' a rich uncle that ain't got no heirs. And he takes a good slant at the gent and wheels out some special liquor in a special bottle and feeds it to him by hand."

"Like raisin' a calf, it sounds," said Dinah, tucking her feet under her as only women can do. "G'wan, Harry!"

"Yeah, I'm goin' on. Blackie, he stands around

31

and absorbs a couple or three shots, like drops spilled on extra-dry blottin' paper. All the time, he looks around over the edge of his glass and asks questions of every face in that joint. I'm five years past the age of charity fights."

"G'wan, Harry! It sounds good."

"Yeah, and it was good, what I mean. He's big, this gent. You'd wanta survey him. You wouldn't wanta guess. He's got slopin' shoulders that make me feel like a boy again, and he can scratch his knees without bendin' over at all. Nobody offers him no business except the bottle, which he don't slide no change over the counter for it, neither. Hard-boiled. That's his first name, and the only name he's got, I reckon. But pretty soon, whacha think?"

"I dunno. G'wan, Harry!"

"Why, pretty soon, somebody kicks the doors open, and there stands a red-headed gent that needs surveyin', too. Not for weight. He wouldn't budge no scales at more'n a hundred and seventy. But the sporting editors say that's big enough to lick the biggest. Anyway, it wasn't weight that needed the surveyin' in him. It was the nacheral fire that brimmed over in him and leaked out at his eyes. You can guess some men by the load they can lift, and others by the wood they can burn. This here, he looked like he could burn a whole ton and not get the frost eased out of his fingertips.

"He looks around him, too. Not mean, like Blackie, but smilin'. But when the smile comes to me, I grin back. The rest, they was lookin' at the floor. Greasers, mostly.

" 'Why if it ain't old Jerry!' says he. 'C'mon and have a drink with me!' says he. 'If it ain't old Jerry that used to work in the mines with me! How many times we been to the same prisons, Jerry, boy? C'mon and we'll talk it over.' This listens, to me."

"Yeah, I bet it did," said the girl. "I like the sound of this one."

"Yeah, sure you would, but you'd like him better if you had asbestos ears. I'm expurgatin', honey. And doncha make no mistake about it, either.

"I sashays up to the bar and we have a drink. I put mine down, sort of glad of the burn of it. Red-head pours his out on the floor.

" 'Hog wash!' says he.

"Then he translates it into Mexican. Whacha might call a free translation . . . more free than translation, too.

"Then he looks down at the bar, and he says: 'I never seen a black-headed sucker that didn't know his likker. We'll try that bottle.' And dog-gone me, if he don't take it out from under the nose of that black-headed bear!

"I stepped back in time to miss the fist of Blackie as it shoots over the shoulder of Red-head. The whiff of it, only, was enough to make me wish that I was home in bed.

"What does the Reddie do? Aw, he steps in kind of easy and graceful, like he was askin' his

33

best girl for a dance, and he soaks Blackie three times on the jaw with home-made uppercuts, the kind that mother loved.

"Blackie goes back on his heels to think it over. Then he rocks forward with a yowl, and lets loose fourteen wild cats and a big bear to tear Red-head to bits.

"Red didn't tear.

"He just glances around in the middle of them claws and paws. And while he steps, he's hitting. He puts a mask of red on Blackie, and still he's laughin'. Blackie fought like he wanted to murder the world, but the kid, he just seems to be eatin' ice cream and hearin' the latest song on the funny-graph. He never stops talkin' neither.

" 'Uppercuts is the latest fashion, Bubbie,' says he, 'but they ain't in it with overhand wallops.' And he leans over and pastes Blackie four times in the face without no return.

"Blackie, he goes crazy. He rushes in and gets a stranglehold.

"Then Red-head, he explodes. What I mean to say, they ain't no other word. He blows Blackie offen the floor, hits him five times in the air, and lands on his face when he comes down. But by that time, that bright little bartender has got himself a brand-new idea, all to himself.

"He goes to the door of the shop and blows a whistle.

"When he turns around, Red is explodin' the other six chambers. He picks up bottles and heaves them through the mirror. He crashes a pair of chairs through the windows. He scatters that crowd like a riot gun, and I wonder whether I'd better try to eat a hole through the floor, or climb the chandelier. And all the time, mind you, Red ain't mad. He's only enjoyin' himself, and always talkin'.

" 'Take that for luck,' says he to a big bohunk, shooting his fist clean through his middle section, as we'll call it for politeness. 'And here's a handful of spare change,' says he, crackin' the jaw of another.

"Then in comes a charge of gendarmes. There is too many people lyin' around to make guns good diplomacy. They club their guns and six of them goes for Red.

"He's busted the windows open, but he don't go to dive through 'em and make a getaway. He just laughs and hollers *¡Viva Méjico!'* And then he dives into that crowd of gendarmes. He splits it like water. He gets up, wadin' in mud. And then the second section of gendarmes comes in and takes him behind.

"They puts him down. They beat him limp. They cover him with gore. And the last thing I hears from him is: 'Gran' ol' party, boys!'

"Yeah, what I mean, he was lovin' it all the time!"

"Did they kill him?" cried the girl. "The brutes! The cowards!"

"Kill him?" said Harry. He leaned back in his chair and laughed so loudly that Alfred Clark gritted his teeth. "Say, whacha think?" asked Harry.

"If they beat him over the head . . . ?"

"Sure they done that. But listen, honey, d'ja ever hear of killin' Inja rubber with clubs?"

IV

"In Jail"

The conclusion of Harry's story was brief.

"They grab Red and sling him over the back of a mule. They grab Blackie and they put him there, too. They take Red to slough him in the hoosegow, and they take Blackie to try to bring him back to life. If they give that Red hard labor to do, he ought to turn out enough to keep the whole State of Chihuahua from turnin' a hand for the rest of his life. I'll tell you what kind of a man, Dinah . . . the kind that your father would've loved!"

She nodded, her eyes bright. "What will happen to him?" she asked.

"Aw, I dunno. Nothin' more than he can stand, anyway, and I guess that's all that matters."

"I'll go to see how he's treated in the morning," said Alfred Clark.

They were both so surprised that they turned to look at him in silence. Then Harry said: "Make you feel at home to hear about him, boss?"

He left immediately afterward, and Clark went off to bed. He lay that night for a long time with his thin hands crossed beneath his head and his weary, patient eyes staring up into the darkness for a solution to his problem. None came. He had loved his brother with a devotion that twenty years and three thousand miles had not dimmed in the slightest, but he decided, calmly, bitterly, that he had attempted a thing that he could not carry through.

When he wakened in the morning, he found that the sun was barely up, but the heat of the day seemed already beginning. He was dizzy with it when he went down to the street, and there found house *mozos* and store servants throwing water onto the dust with buckets. They contributed enough to lay the dust for a few hours, and to insure a good, hot, steaming middle of the day. That was all their labors amounted to. He smiled faintly as he watched them.

He had breakfasted in the dining room, served by a heavy-eyed villain who wheezed from tobacco-choked lungs with every breath that he drew. Breakfast over, Clark went out onto the street and rolled and smoked a cigarette. With a great uproar, a drove of cattle went past him. He watched the hollow sides, the red-stained eyes, and the long, polished horns of these animals, knowing perfectly that just such a consignment was what he needed to complete his business and then start north. But he knew, also, with a surpassing bitterness that he never could hope to put the deal through with such men as burdened his hands.

He thought of discharging the whole gang and taking on a crew of Mexican workers. That is to say, he would continue board wages to the old hands of his brother, but he would relieve them of all duty. This scheme, however, he instantly saw would not hold water. Nothing would please the banished men more than hanging about to do what harm they could. Inside a day he could promise his new hands at least half a dozen hard gun fights and, if that did not decide them to leave their new positions, the following day would be still worse.

Finally, he decided that he would ponder no longer. He was glad that he had set a time limit, and that the time was short. But that evening, he would be a free man.

Free for what? To return to his closed law office. To open his business to a dispersed clientele. To find that they had already shifted their work and their confidence into other hands. And, for this sacrifice, he would receive from his niece nothing but scorn, and a lasting ridicule. He would become a standing and classic example of the ridiculous tenderfoot!

He was a calm and patient man, as has been said before, but these thoughts aroused his temper until he gritted his teeth together. So he strolled down the street and came to the jail. It was part of the municipal building, which was built on a scale at least three or four times as great as Libertad ever could need. The large and liberal hand of graft appeared in its dimensions and in the cracks which seamed its walls. It looked as though one good gale would blow it into a heap.

But when Clark saw the barred windows of the jail portion, he remembered the promise he had made the evening before — that he would look into the condition of the gringo prisoner in this foreign jail.

He was particularly stimulated, because most vividly he recalled the faint little smiles which had been exchanged between the girl and Harry. They had very little faith, obviously, in his performance of such a promise. He wondered why. At the entrance to the jail he found out.

A slattern guard with the look of a murderer and the manner of a dyspeptic listened to his request to see the white prisoner and sneered openly. He looked over Alfred Clark from head to heel, and then laughed in his face.

"We are busy cleaning house," he said. "We have no time to waste on sightseers, *señor!*"

Alfred Clark grew angry, which was a rare thing for him.

"Should I have a letter of introduction?" he asked.

"Yes, *señor*. A letter from your president, perhaps?"

Mr. Clark bit his lip. "Do you know of Abraham Lincoln, *señor?*" he said.

"Are you a cousin of his?" asked the guard.

"I have a letter from him," said Clark, and passed a five-dollar bill into the hand of the guard.

The latter continued to sneer, partly because he felt that a sneer was always dignified. At least, it prevented laughter. With a sneer, therefore, he took the five dollars and pushed it contemptuously into his pocket. With a sneer he opened the door, and gave a careless jerk of his head which invited the gringo to enter. And still he smiled to himself a small, secret, evil smile, as though there were apparent to him many things of which the American could know nothing.

He called an underling, and directed him, more contemptuously and sneeringly than ever, to take the visitor to the cell of the red man, and let him talk for a few minutes. Five minutes would be enough. Then he turned his back on Clark and disappeared.

The latter was taken down the hall into another room which was fitted up in an old-fashioned way as a jail. That is to say, there were a series of rooms built with brick partitions which were quite thick, and into the face of each door there was let an opening screened over with steel bars. It was a most inefficient and carelessly run jail, and yet it gave forth an atmosphere of depression and of eternal gloom as strong as anything this visitor ever could remember feeling.

He was taken to a corner cell.

"We should have thrown him into the dark one!" said Clark's guide. "But you see! We are kinder to Americans than they are to us!"

He pointed to this example of Mexican kindness, and the accurate eye of Clark listed it. Mentally he also jotted down a double list somewhat as follows. Missing: from the coat, a sleeve, and all the front buttons; from the shirt, all buttons also, as well as the collar; from the trousers, half of one leg; from the feet, both boots, and most of one sock. Added: to the coat, several tears in a free and liberal pattern; to the shirt, a large, greasy, black smudge across the breast, and incidental rips, together with some streaks of red; to the trousers, the pattern which one would have expected a vigorous wild cat in the prime of life to have created; to the feet, half a dozen cuts of minor importance; to the face, a large purple swelling on each side of the jaw, near to the point; to the left eye, a circle of purple, relieved with cunningly-worked shades and gradations of green and black, obviously hand-painted; to the right eye, one rich, sweeping, and almost eye-closing mass of blue-black, glistening, and rich to see — this eye, furthermore set off and relieved, as it were, by a good, broad-mouthed cut running beneath it; to both cheekbones, large, discolored lumps; to the forehead and throat, big scratches, as though made by the clutches of a drowning man; to the nose, a perpetual blush, and a swollen condition that made it as large as a pear, and red as such a pear in October.

This prisoner was sitting on the edge of a bunk, loaded with irons. His feet were anchored to the floor by the weight of what must have been at least a hundred-pound ball of lead. Two pairs of irons were fitted about his ankles. His arms, likewise, were confined together before him by two sets of handcuffs. Yet he had managed to roll for himself a cigarette and was now smoking it.

"Hullo, partner," said the redhead. "Look at the picture they painted on me! Then tell me what you think of it. I can only feel it. I can't see."

"You look as though you've had a rough time of it," said Clark with much sympathy.

"Aw, a little stormy," said the redhead. "Nothin' much. When you get into a hurricane, you gotta expect high waves."

"I want to know how they're treating you here."

"Me? They're treating me about average for a Mexican jail. They ain't much, you take them by and large."

"You've been in them before?"

"Yeah. I've been broke pretty often in Mexico. And jail is better than the pavement, I suppose."

He laughed, and his voice rang with perfect freedom and sincerity of mirth. The guard, not wishing to miss anything, edged closer and scowled at them both.

"Can I do anything," asked Clark, "to make you more comfortable?"

"How d' you break into this party?"

"I'll tell you," Alfred Clark said. "I was in a situation where I wanted to smash and dash and break things up in general and, when I heard what you had done, it was a relief to me even to know that another man had managed what I really had needed to do. I couldn't have enjoyed hearing about that riot more if you had been in a ring, with my money on you!"

The prisoner laughed again.

"Well," he said, "I know what you mean . . .

a time when you wanta claw things up, and can't. I had a broke leg, once, and had to lie around and listen and wait for three dog-gone months before I could dare to put my hands on a big sap of a Canuck lumberjack. So I know whacha mean!"

V

"Cayenne Charlie"

All at once it struck both of them as amusing that there should be anything in common between the pair of them — so diverse were they from one another. They chuckled, and the guard looked suspiciously from one to the other.

"There's nothing I can do for you, then?" asked Clark, rather unwilling to leave this stimulating presence.

"No, not a thing."

"You don't know whether or not they will keep you in for a long time?"

"I dunno," said Red. "I don't care much what they intend to do. I'll leave when I get ready."

"You mean that you'll escape?" asked Clark, staring again at the irons.

"Sure," said Red. "Why not?"

"I should think those bracelets would be enough to keep your interests inside the jail."

Red laughed again. "These here things?" He shrugged his shoulders. "They won't hold nothin'."

"And the ankle irons, too?" inquired Clark.

"Well, they're harder. But it can all be managed pretty dead easy. I'm just restin' here an' gettin'

45

my strength back, as you might say, and pretty soon that puffy feelin' will be out of my face. I hate to have my head all swelled up, because it makes the next bang I get so darned much more painful."

Clark paused.

"I shouldn't ask questions," he said. "But I'd really like to know how you can do these things."

"Sure, and I'll tell you," said the prisoner. "Anybody can slip handcuffs . . . anybody that'll practice foldin' his hands for a while, because you can make the measure around the thumb and palm less'n the measure around the wrist."

"But when you've slipped the wrist irons, there still remain the manacles on the legs. A hundred-pound lump of lead isn't a dream, I take it?"

"Why, I just unlock those irons, when I've got my hands free."

"Have you a key?"

"Yes. I gotta key that'll fit into most locks, the kind that they got in this here neck of the woods. It's a stiff bit of watch spring."

"Do they let you keep it when you're searched?"

"They never find it. I keep a snag tied in my hair close to my head, and in that snag there's the watch spring. It catches on the comb every day, but it's worth the trouble."

"Well, then, I'll believe that you can do as you say and get rid of the irons, but it seems to me that you're not a great deal better off at that point, because you'll still be inside of this cell. You'll have a lot of thick walls between you and free-dom."

"Yeah," said Red. "I dunno what I'd do about it. But I reckon that I could pull the bricks out of that wall like blocks out of a play house. Or the bars on that door, there, would likely come out by the roots pretty easy. Anyway, I'll have a try one of these days."

"I think you're using the jail as a sort of hotel?" suggested Clark.

"Why, kind of," said the other.

"I'd like to know your name," said Clark.

"Charlie is my name. Bird is my last moniker. And Cayenne is what some puts in front of the whole job."

"Cayenne Charlie Bird?"

"That's the lineup. What's your shingle say?"

"It says Alfred Clark. Cayenne, I'd like to give you a hand, but if I passed you some money now, they'd certainly take it away from you."

"Sure they would. Unless I murdered 'em while they were doin' it. Whacha mean by a hand?"

"Well, suppose you tell me what you would do with fifty dollars?" asked Clark, amused.

"Yeah. You wanta know? I'd take fifty dollars and send twenty-five to my ol' mother what is declinin' slowly to an unhappy grave, if you foller what I mean. And I'd send twenty-four dollars and a half to my poor wife, which is hungerin' with her five little children. Then I'd take the last fifty cents and I'd spend twenty-five in buyin' soap and a washrag. And the last twenty-five I'd spend on a comb and brush and borrow a couple of toothpicks. Then I'd pull my belt tighter and start the long march across the desert . . . on foot . . . to reach my near and dear ones."

He paused with a grin and a yawn.

"That touches my heart," said Clark. "You're a married man, are you, you rascal?"

"Me?" said Cayenne Charlie. "Nope. I ain't got a family except when I was talkin' just now. I dunno how it is, but every time me and some girl set the marriage date, along comes some trouble and I step into a jail instead of the holy bonds, as they call 'em!"

"Has that happened often . . . engagements, I mean?"

"Oh, I dunno. Maybe five or six times."

"Hasn't left you with a broken heart, Charlie, I hope."

"Fact is," said Cayenne Charlie, "that my heart has been broke so often that it's all just one big mend, now. And there ain't anything tougher than a knot, you know. It's just turned into one big knot with the pain and sufferin' that I've had on account of women, Mr. Clark."

The latter chuckled.

"I'd really like to let you have that fifty if I thought it would help you out," said he.

"Make it twenty-five," said the surprising Cayenne, "because that wouldn't look like such a big party to me."

"I'm leaving Libertad this evening," said Clark. "Where can I put the money for you?"

"You're leaving? You can't put it anywhere. There is noses in Libertad that would smell twenty-five bucks through three feet of armor plate, I tell you! Nope. If you got that much money to spare, I'll call on you for the cash."

"You'll break the jail today, you mean?"

"Well, why not? Sure I will. I'll call at Mr. Clark's room at the hotel."

"You will?"

"Yes."

"With the police force on your heels?"

"Not them. I was pretty gentle with 'em, last night, but I bet half the crowd are stayin' in bed for a week and the other half, they wouldn't follow me to free drinks."

He grinned in much enjoyment of this state of affairs, and Clark grinned also.

"I'll expect you at eight o'clock. There is a ten o'clock train, but I'd like to have a chat with you before I start back north."

"I'll surely be there at eight," said Red.

"Good-bye till then."

"So long, Mr. Clark."

Little Alfred Clark got out of that jail with a shiver in the center of his spine, for he felt that he had broken the law so largely that it would never be the same again in Libertad. It was sapped and snapped and broken, and no mistake, once Cayenne Charlie broke loose and started for the hotel. It seemed that more than mere man would be required for the stopping of him.

Then Clark walked back to the hotel and found

his niece Dinah up and ready for business. Harry was with her.

Straightway she plunged into the discussion.

"You're quitting the job today, Uncle Alfred?"

"Yes, that's true."

"Well, what time today, if you don't mind telling us."

He resented the "us" hotly.

"There's a ten o'clock train leaving Libertad this evening," he said.

"Are you going to keep in the saddle until then?" she asked.

For a moment, he doubted her completely. That is to say, before this talk, he always had felt that her cruelty, her unfairness to him, really were expressions of the difference in background which made her a Westerner and him an Easterner. But now it seemed to him that her restless indifference to him, her manifest eagerness to get him out of the way, simply indicated a callous and wicked spirit. So he hesitated, filled with thought, before he answered her.

"You know, my dear," he said, "that I'm using this last day not to resign, but to cast around me for some lever, as I told you before, which might enable me to handle this affair of yours. I am almost beaten, but not quite. But you see that I cannot very well give you a signed and sealed promise that I shall depart at ten, and at the train say good-bye to you and all your business."

"Oh, of course," she said. "I want you to have a good break, too, and all that. But at the same time, it's another day gone, Uncle Alfred, and if you'd let . . . us . . . go ahead now with the cow business, we'd be that much quicker through in Libertad. And then. . . ."

"Who will be your manager?" he asked her.

"Oh, Harry, of course," she said.

Harry's face swelled with joy and with pride.

"Thanks, Dinah," he said.

She chuckled. "I guess you guessed it before," she said. And she slapped Harry powerfully upon his shoulder.

This exhibition of familiarity between her and such a heavy-handed, low-browed brute of a cowpuncher chilled the sensitive soul of Alfred Clark.

"He'll be your foreman?" he asked, trying to keep the distaste out of his face.

"He will," said the girl.

She almost went on to ask, pertly, if the choice were to his taste, but checked herself just in time. Clark, however, knew perfectly what was in her mind.

Then he said coldly:

"Naturally I'd like to please you, Dinah. Naturally I'd like to please your new foreman, or manager, or whatever you may call him. However that may be, there is no doubt that I must stay with my present position for one more day. After that, you and your manager will have a free hand."

He went off, expecting that remorse surely would touch the girl. But he was wrong, for she spoke not a word to call him back.

VI

"A Voice from a Corner"

By the end of that day, the head of Alfred Clark
was buzzing and aching. He had been turning
and twisting in his thoughts for twelve hours to
try to reach some solution, find some way of
cutting the Gordian knot. He could not. His
hands were helpless, and still he had not found
the lever with which he could budge the mass of
weight. He felt that he was forsworn if he failed
to live up to his contract with his dead brother.
But better be forsworn than undo the work of his
brother's entire life by letting the ranch go to ruin.
He had no longer much hope of stirring the girl.
There was only one last weapon he could use.
Up to this point he had tried reason and logic.
He felt that he would go still farther and try the
power of sheer appeal.

Therefore, after supper, he asked to talk with
her alone. But she said: "It'd be a lot better if
Harry came along, and one of the 'punchers, too.
Say Buddie Vincent, eh?"

Buddie Vincent was the youngest man on the
place. He was the last to be employed by Tom
Clark. He was the wildest soul, the hardest fist,
the quickest temper, and the fastest gun. He

could run faster, jump farther, hit harder, ride better, sleep longer, eat more, work more, than practically any man in the Southwest. He was the famous Achilles of the Clark outfit. He was the most insolent, outspoken, discourteous puppy that Alfred Clark ever had known. It seemed an unnecessary insult to have him present at such a conversation as this, and Alfred Clark said so.

"I should think you and I could talk alone, Dinah," he said.

She looked at him with hard, sullen eyes.

"I think the men have a right to know where we all stand, and there's no better way than to be present through some sort of a representative when we're having our last talk."

"You've grown so grammatical, Dinah," he said, "that I hardly know you. Well, then, let it be as you will. I don't seem able to carry even the smallest point."

That was the reason why he had to talk with three instead of with one. They came up to his room. It was very hot. No wind stirred. The heat still was radiating up from the walls of the nearer buildings, and they stuck to the cheap, moist varnish of their chairs.

It was not a pleasant place for conversation. A suitcase lay on the bed. A raincoat was folded neatly on top of it, with a pair of magazines for train reading also at hand. Signs of departure always are unpleasant.

Alfred Clark could understand clearly why the girl wanted not only one but two men with her.

In this company, she was fortified against him. He could not make a remark which possibly might break down the power of her defense. But he decided that he would shake her if he could. He struck right at the heart of the matter.

"Now, Dinah," he said, "I'm sorry that you haven't had the courage to meet me alone."

Dinah was fairly staggered by this opening gun. But young Buddie Vincent, furious at the attack, flashed out: "She don't want nobody cryin' all over her shoulder!"

Clark waited a moment and looked at the girl. But she did not correct her myrmidon. Only, gradually she flushed.

"Do you like that?" asked Clark of the girl. "Is that the sort of language that you approve of? Tell me, because I'm interested."

"Buddie spoke a little out of turn," she said. "No reason he should be kicked in the face for that, though."

"I can see now," said Clark, "that I've come here foolishly. I've lost before I begin talking. The judge is you, Dinah, and your mind is poisoned against me by cheap, bitter, sectional prejudices. And you have a corrupt jury, as well. They're bought out before the trial begins."

"I dunno how much of that lingo we gotta stand!" burst out Buddie.

"Oh, leave him be! He's makin' his grandstand play, now," said Harry.

"Aye," said Alfred Clark. "I've tried to appeal to you people in every way that I know about.

I've tried to convince you that I'm just and reasonable, and good-natured, and fair-minded. Now, heaven forgive me for believing that all normal and sane humans must respond well to such treatment. I've been wrong. I came out here expecting to find the great, big-hearted, noble West . . . running a bit to flannel shirts, not very fond of razors or grammar but, nevertheless, honest, decent, faithful, brave, and true to what good men and women ought to be. And, instead, I've found miserable jealousy, cruelty, unfairness, and a general desire to bully and ruin a man too old and feeble and untrained to fight back but who, if he could meet you with your own weapons, would gladly fight you one by one until either he was shot down, or he had taught you all your lessons. Brutes that you are, like brutes you should be handled!"

He had started fairly mildly, he thought. But his temper mastered him as he went on, until at the end he was no longer responsible for what he was saying. He felt his indignation mount higher and higher. He felt certain that he was right.

"Let me hear from you, Mister Manager!" he said. "What offenses have you to charge against me?"

All three of them had been overwhelmed by the first outburst they had heard from his lips. Gradually, Harry recovered himself.

"I dunno," he said. "Fact is, we just never wanted you from the first. You didn't belong. You didn't know cows. You didn't know nothin'.

55

What right had you on the place?"

"A contemptible conspiracy, I call it," said Alfred Clark. "This very moment you know that you're all prepared to work together and pull together in order to finish off the Libertad business which you've prevented me from completing. By heaven, it makes my blood boil when I think of your cowardly attitude! Western men! Western women! If you're types of them, I can't describe the contempt I feel for you all!"

"He's talking a good deal," said the girl coldly, to her two men, "but he can't talk forever. Ten o'clock is gunna come sometime."

"Yeah. Ten o'clock," said Buddie Vincent.

The age and all the circumstances connected with Mr. Alfred Clark shielded him from the wrath of these cowpunchers, but Vincent looked at him with the cold, biting, snaky eye of a killer.

"I brought you up here," said Alfred Clark, "in the hope that I could move you by making an appeal to the celebrated chivalry and decency of the Westerner. I wanted to point out to you that the work that I have been trying to do is the work which was committed to my hands by the man whom you pretended to love so much. I wanted to ask you, almost on my knees, to help me try to execute his will. But I see that appeals are not in order. In your hard eye, Dinah, I can read the same message."

The girl stood up.

"G'wan, Uncle Alfred," she said. "Maybe you're partly right. Maybe we haven't given you the squarest break in the world. But certainly the best way now is for you to cut and go and let us try to wrangle our own affairs."

"Is that so?" said Clark. "That's the opinion of the rest of you, too?"

"Yeah, that's my opinion," came from both men.

"Very well," said Clark. "I'm one man, and I can't stand against all of you. . . ."

"Why not count me on your side, partner?" said a voice from a corner of the room.

Clark whirled about. The others also started up. There in the corner by the second window they could make out now the form of a man who was leaning his shoulders against the wall, his hands in his trouser pockets. He must have entered through the window with the silence worthy of a professional thief.

"Who are you?" asked Buddie Vincent, advancing a little.

"Why," said the stranger, "if it ain't ol' Buddie Vincent, that regular man-killin', hoss-bustin' 'puncher! If it ain't ol' Buddie Vincent, the riot gun and sharpshooter. Him that kills linnets on the wing at a hundred yards, and shoots the eyelashes off a wolf at half a mile. Why, dog-gone me, Buddie, but I'm glad to see you! How many men you murdered since I last seen you?"

He advanced into the light. It was Cayenne Charlie, his bruised and swollen face broadly smiling.

Buddie Vincent said fiercely, "I don't know

you. But I don't like your lingo and I. . . ."

"Buddie!" snapped Dinah Clark.

And Vincent stepped suddenly back.

In spite of himself, Alfred Clark could not help admiring the manner in which the girl had controlled that wildest of all young blades.

"Is this a stage trick?" she asked of Clark.

"This is Cayenne Charlie," said her uncle. "He's simply dropped in to arrange a small loan with me. Charlie, here you are!" He handed the money which had been agreed upon to the jail-breaker.

"Why, it's Red!" exclaimed Harry.

"I see you, old-timer," said Cayenne cheerfully. "I ain't met you yet, ma'am?" he continued to the girl.

"This is Dinah Clark," said her uncle.

"And you're the fellow who smashed things up last night?" asked the girl, measuring the other.

"No smashin'," said Cayenne. "There was just a little party up the street, and the police force of this here town got mixed in and warmed themselves up on me."

"How did you get free from the jail?" asked Alfred Clark, almost forgetting his troubles in the curiosity and interest with which he looked upon this youth.

"I got off the irons the way that I told you, pulled a tooth off that door, grabbed a guard by the throat, made him unlock the door of the cell, and then the door of the jail. Dropped him then with a good punch on the button, took his gun, and here I am, Mr. Clark, thankin' you very much for the money. I'd better breeze along. They'd slam you in the hoosegow, if they knew I was here."

"That's a chance I'd take," smiled Clark. "He had an appointment with me here," he explained to the others, "at eight o'clock. And that's the hour now, as you see. Good-bye, then, Cayenne, if you really have to go."

"I'm going," said Cayenne, "unless I can give you a hand in the business that you've got on deck here now."

"You give me a hand?" echoed Clark.

"I've been sittin' in on this conversation longer than you'd guess," said the other. "It looks to me like this bunch has framed you. Well, take me on your side. What's this business in Libertad? I know some of the ropes here!"

Alfred Clark gasped. He felt like throwing up both hands in wonder and delight.

"By heaven, young man," he said, "I think that you might help me."

"You!" snapped Cayenne Charlie, pointing to Harry who was slipping toward the door. "You stand tight. You ain't gunna sneak off and be stool pigeon, my lad!"

VII

"Red Bird Flies"

At the door, Harry turned.

"What sort of a showdown is this?" he asked. "Are you runnin' the hotel, Red?"

"I'm not runnin' the hotel," said Cayenne Charlie. "But I'm runnin' this room."

Buddie Vincent made a sound no louder than a whisper and reached inside his coat. Instantly, a bright revolver gleamed in the hand of Cayenne and covered the head of the youth.

"Right between the eyes is where you get it, son," said Cayenne, "if you so much as wink. Hoist up your hands, will you, and cool 'em off where the wind is blowing about more? You back up, Harry, and carry your arms wide of your hips. I'm watchin' you both. Sorry, ma'am, to make all this trouble. But these here boys of yours, they look kind of restless. That's all right, Buddie. Now you can put your hands down and rest easy!"

He had stepped to Vincent as he spoke and dexterously removed two guns from the person of the gunfighter, while the latter, groaning with helpless rage, kept his hands hoisted high.

"I'm going to have the heart out of you!" Vincent promised him.

"Sure you will," said Cayenne Charlie. "Set down and rest your feet, Buddie. Now you might try to recollect me, maybe. I'm the hobo that you hit with a chair up in Denver, just outside of town in that wayside tavern. But I don't carry any grudge. They got good jails in Colorado, and I enjoyed a mighty fine rest after the coppers hauled me in."

He sat down on the edge of the table. He had put away his gun. He had not disarmed big Harry, but instead merely kept a watchful eye upon him.

"Don't make a move, Harry," said the girl, perfectly calm. "Cayenne is having a good time. Let him have it till the gendarmes grab him again. Now, Cayenne, what's on your mind heavier than red hair?"

Alfred Clark was amazed by her good humor and her easy way. She seemed not in the least affronted by the wildness of this battered jail-breaker.

"I'll tell you," said Cayenne Charlie. "Me and my friend, here, are together. It sounds like you and the boys have been crowdin' him a little."

"What have you to do with that, Cayenne?" she asked, rather in curiosity than in anger.

"Why, I was just sayin' that we're together."

"Do you aim to help him play his hand?"

"No, I aim to get him a new deal."

"Where'll you find your cards?"

"Up my sleeve," said Cayenne.

"Don't talk to this hobo, Dinah," said Buddie Vincent. "I know the only lingo he understands."

"Be quiet, Buddie," replied the girl. "Cayenne is gunna be a hero if he can. How can you, Cayenne?"

"The boss, there, is down here for cows?"

"Yeah. That's right."

"And you and the boys have stopped him?"

"No. But the Mexican crooks have been stealing the cows about as fast as they came in."

"How could they steal 'em, if boys like Harry and Buddie were on their job in earnest?"

"I'm telling you the facts, Cayenne. You can do the sizing up."

"I size it up a crooked deal."

"That's your privilege. Now, where do you come in?"

"I come in easy. I know you got spot cash, Mr. Clark?"

"I have, Bird."

"Well, then, I know gents in this neck of the woods that'll give you a herd about any size you want, thirty percent under market price, and delivered right on the border . . . for hard cash. Does that sound to you?"

"He's out of the picture, Cayenne," said the girl. "He's leaving for the East in another hour."

"Are you leavin'?" asked Cayenne. "Or are you stayin' with me?"

"My friend," said Alfred Clark, "I made up my mind five minutes ago. I've been praying for some way of meeting these people on their own ground, with their own weapons, in order to make the ranch a go in spite of them. Cayenne, you dropped into this room out of heaven, so far as I'm concerned. Of course, I'll stay!"

There was a groan from Harry and from Vincent.

"Then let's put out part of the cards and see if they want to draw against our hand," said Charlie Bird.

"You promised me," began the girl. "And if you go back on the promise you. . . ."

"I promised you that today I'd make up my mind. Well, I've made it up. I stay!"

She was still cool, though a little pale.

"If you meant to sashay up to the ranch with this man for a big gun," she said, "you gotta remember that we have a place loaded down with fighting men. D'you think that he could handle the whole crowd, Uncle Alfred?"

"I think that he might be able to. They won't spill on him in one heap. That isn't Western sportsmanship, I believe."

"They won't need to," said the girl. "I simply warn you . . . if that man comes up to the ranch, there will be several funerals . . . and the bloodshed will be on your head."

"Grammatical again, Dinah," said her uncle. "It surprises me to see how easily you can speak correct English when it comes to a pinch."

"You think it's your turn to scoff," said the girl. "But we'll see about that. I'll tell you again, for the last time, that the ranch is my ranch, and the only people who have a right to say a word about the running of it are the men that Daddy hired and who helped him to build up the place. I can't see your claim to any position on it. I don't see why you want to be there."

"Out of stubbornness, if for no other reason," he said. "Your father appointed me. You've arranged to have that ranch go downhill until I leave. Well, Dinah, now I think that I have a lever in my hand, and I intend to use it. Cayenne Charlie, are you with me?"

"Up to jail!" said he, with a battered grin.

"That's all, then. I can't persuade the rest of you to change your minds and throw in with us, boys?" said Clark.

"No, I can't be persuaded," said Buddie Vincent.

"And that's the end of any chance to compromise?"

Dinah lifted her head with a jerk.

"You've decided on war," she said. "And war it is, then! Only . . . we'll never hit an unfair blow."

"No?" her uncle asked her with stern irony. "Your conduct thus far has been an example of that spirit, I dare say?"

Suddenly she trembled.

"I've been insulted over and over again in this room tonight," she said, "and I don't intend to stay and hear any more."

She turned on her heel.

"It ain't insults you need . . . it's a spanking," said Cayenne Charlie. "The kind that Pa used to deal out, with a good, hard-soled slipper. So long, folks."

The girl made no retort to this last remark, but went through the door hastily, head high. Harry followed her without a word. Vincent would have done the same thing, but Charlie called him back.

"You've forgotten something, old son," he said.

Vincent wheeled and came slowly toward the table, on which Cayenne had placed the two weapons.

Slowly and more slowly the gunman approached, until his face was not more than a few inches from that of Cayenne, who was leaning over the table, resting his fingertips upon the center of it. Both weapons were now in the grasp of Buddie Vincent. It looked to Alfred Clark as though there might be danger of an instant explosion of wrath and of weapons. But instead, as the pair confronted one another, he saw that Cayenne was whispering rapidly to the other.

Vincent, listening, set his teeth, seemed about to answer, and then gradually allowed his glance to drift away from Cayenne until it seemed as though he found something of the vastest interest outside the window. But Clark understood. In that low, tense whisper, Cayenne was inviting the other to come outside the hotel and there fight out the battle to the end in any way he chose — fists, or knives, or guns — however Vincent wished to come to a conclusion.

The latter gritted his teeth, and Alfred Clark

heard the sound; but this pressure proved too great for Dinah's champion to endure. His eyes wandered toward the window again.

"I'll settle you, all in good time," he said, and went out through the door, pausing a couple of times as though on the verge of whirling back on Charlie.

The latter mopped his forehead.

"I wouldn't've wanted that beauty on my hands," he said. "Not with the way that I'm smashed up now. About the cows, chief, it'll take a week to get things together. A week from today, you show at Santa Cruz of the Willows on the river. The cows will come in there at night. They ought to be across the river before the next morning. Me, I've gotta barge along."

He went to the window but, after looking out, he instantly stepped back.

"The boys've passed along the word," said Cayenne. "The gendarmes've got the hotel watched already. It's over the housetops for me!"

He left Alfred Clark before the latter could speak a word and, running noiselessly into the hall in his stockinged feet, Cayenne Charlie disappeared. Not without leaving an echo behind him, however. For no sooner had he reached the hall than there was a loud shouting, followed by three or four gunshots in rapid succession, then a noise of heavy falls, followed by frantic screaming of fear and pain.

What had happened? It was not Cayenne Charlie, at least. He would never have uttered such cries on the rack, even. Clark hurried out to investigate.

One gendarme had just got up from the floor and was staggering about with red running from nose and mouth, cursing, yelling, blinded still by the blow he had received. Other men were shouting and running in the distance, and doors slammed heavily, and then gunshots rang out beyond the building

But whether through other windows and down to the street, or over the housetops to another descent, Clark was confident that the redhead, like a bird, had flown freely away.

VIII

"All Quiet"

They lay a half day's march north of the river. That is to say, they had passed from Mexico half a day into "God's country." The great mass of long-horned cattle, with their fierce eyes and their scrawny bodies, had been bedded down for the night, and ahead of them and on either side rode three men on night watch.

Everyone seemed fairly contented. After crossing the river, at the long noon halt when the strength of the sun made traveling a doubtful virtue, Alfred Clark had gathered the men around him and he had made a speech.

He had said: "My friends, we've gone through a good deal together. When I came out here, I had a duty to perform that looked to you like an intolerable imposition upon you. You felt that you were able to run the ranch well enough and that any one among you . . . like Harry, for instance . . . would be amply able to manage affairs so that Dinah's interests would be well taken care of. As I saw it, I had a sacred duty to perform in executing the will of my dead brother. You felt that you were right. I felt that I was right. But I was not willing to cling to my post if it

68

meant the ruin of the affairs of the ranch.

"Now, through luck and the assistance of Mister Cayenne Charlie Bird, I've been put in the way of a stroke of business fortune which ought to more than recoup any losses that I have cost the affairs of Dinah so far. You may say these cattle have been stolen, and that they're shady goods. Perhaps they are. I don't know. Everything, so far as I could see, was perfectly regular, except that the sellers wanted their cash on the spot. Very well, I gave them their cash. Then my right to the cows . . . in Dinah's name . . . seemed well enough established. I was afraid that Cayenne Charlie, frankly, might have double-crossed me. He had not showed up at the time of the deal. He has not showed up since. I was afraid that he might be a rascal, and that he and the others might rush in and stampede the cattle away after they had the cash in their pockets. But this did not happen. As you know, we managed to cross the Rio Grande successfully. We have not lost hide nor hair of a single cow since the start.

"It is true that we have a distance to go, still. It is true that we go through a rough country, filled with rough men, where Judge Colt remains the highest authority of law. Nevertheless, I feel almost as secure as though we were now at the home ranch. For I believe that you men are going to work for me, realizing that I am not devoted to my own interests but to those of my niece, and I am convinced that all of you are devoted to her. I don't believe it is possible for a Westerner to strike a foul blow against an orphan girl.

"As for me, I don't pretend to be an expert in cattle. I don't know anything about the management of a ranch, except such little odds and ends as I have been able to pick up since I came to this country. Nevertheless, I have asked for advice, and some of my mistakes I may put down to the fact that instead of giving me the best opinions, some of you have given me the worst. Well, I'll overlook that.

"I believe that we know each other better, now. I have had bad ideas about you for a long time. I've often lost my temper. And you've lost your temper with me. But, if you'll stick by me and my niece, in one short year I'll be able to throw over the reins, she'll come to her majority, and then she can select her own manager. Perhaps from among you. It may be unmanly to appeal to you, but I can't help begging you to stand by the guns and not desert the ship in time of battle.

"Before my niece left me and went north by herself to the ranch, she told me that she thought I had crossed through the worst of my troubles the moment that I put the Rio Grande behind me. I don't want to give the impression that she is greatly interested in my welfare. That would not be true. She still looks upon me as an outlander, a tenderfoot, an intruder into the happy family of all of you. But she seems to feel less bitter toward me. She seems to be of a mind that at least I've demonstrated, through luck perhaps, a right to have half a chance to do my work. She seems even to believe," he could not help adding ironically, "that I am not really working for myself, but for her.

"Now, then, I can't help knowing that you rather resent the fact that, through the agency of Cayenne Charlie, I've had cows delivered at the rate of fifty percent of their cost. It is too good a stroke of business for a tenderfoot to put through. And the business is not put through, I'm aware, until I get the cows to the home ranch; and then it's only consummated if you all will help by riding range carefully and looking after the new stock so that we can deliver them fat and ready for a good market when the right time comes.

"I'm not going to ask for any show of hands. I only beg you to help me fight this thing through."

When he had finished this novel speech, there were no directly spoken comments, but there were grunts and noddings of heads, here and there. Only Buddie Vincent looked grimly down at the ground and said nothing at all. But Clark knew the secret rancor in the mind of that warrior and was not surprised.

On the whole he felt that his appeal had been successful, and certainly during the rest of that day the men went about their work with an apparent willingness.

He guessed, after the start, that the entire crowd had been amazed by his stroke of business, amazed that he was able to attach that furious and strange vagrant, Cayenne Charlie, to his fortunes, amazed that Cayenne had cared to live up to his contract by delivering the cattle as agreed beforehand. They were startled out of themselves. Or else their good behavior was simply the lull before a storm.

Now, as this evening settled in, he went out to see how the herd was lying, and found it rather comfortably placed and apparently serene. Now and then there was a grunt and an upward lurch as some young animal was touched by the angrily swung horns of an older one. One of these lurches was followed by a whole wave of rising backs, but these subsided, and the watchmen on guard circled around and around, walking or jogging their horses, and singing the low, endless, crooning songs which reassured the herd.

Clark could understand for the first time the fascination of the entire cattle business as he watched and listened, and saw the dull gleam of the starlight on the polished horns, and the bright glint of it, here and there, on the eyes of awakened sleepers.

The evening was very quiet. There was no wind. At any stir of the cows, a cloud of dust rose chokingly in the air and slowly settled, though a certain pungent and alkaline taint was never out of his lungs. There was the reek of the cattle, also. But what astonished him was that this vast mass of powerful life was submitting to the hands of so few weak men. There they lay, ready for the long journey to the grasslands, to markets, but leaving behind them young life which would grow in turn, and so would follow harvest after harvest, while God planted the grass and sent the rains which nourished it. Peace descended upon the soul of Alfred Clark.

He spent a while motionless in the saddle, except when his horse, grazing on a long rein, stamped or took a step for new grass. Then he went back to the camp wagon, where a small fire was maintained by the cook, with a great blackened coffeepot simmering constantly over the coal. The rest of the hands were sleeping, but the cook was there on watch. Sleep is never necessary for cooks!

He took some of the coffee, ladling it out with a long dipper, and sipping that bitter, hot brew and, munching soggy, sweet corn pone, he squatted on his heels, 'puncher fashion, and felt that life was not so bad, though the collar of his coat scraped and irked his sunburned neck. Other men had delighted in this life. He could delight in it himself, as a matter of fact. And, looking to the northwest, where the mountains rose in small waves against the stars, he felt as though he were already almost at the gate of success.

One of the night watch came in, dismounted, threw the reins, and poured a big tin cup full of the coffee. This he sipped greedily. He was a rawboned, sun-dried man named Chick Thomas. He was fifty if he was a day. His hair, nevertheless, was deep brown and his long mustaches swept down and out with never a hint of gray in them.

This great tall fellow possessed a certain style, Alfred Clark decided at leisure, with his slouchy, comfortable clothes, and the slight outward sagging of his legs, as if for strength and for the curve of a saddle. His trousers were tucked into his wrinkled boot-tops, a low-belted revolver dragged down from the right hip; there was a bandanna a little askew, the knot properly at the back of the neck; and upon his heels stood out the glistening lines of his spoon-handled spurs. Like the symbol of a belted knight, thought Alfred Clark.

He stood at ease, drinking the coffee. In some mysterious manner, without putting down the big cup, he was able to roll a cigarette. As he lighted and puffed it, he spoke. Alfred Clark had learned his lesson and rarely broached conversation with these rough men.

"Logie," said Chick, and nodded, as though that one word conveyed a deep meaning.

"Yes, Logan was thrown, this morning," said Clark. "That's a bad one . . . that piebald he likes to ride so well."

"Yeah, he was piled," said Chick. He added, after a moment: "Plenty!"

Mr. Clark said nothing. He waited. Just how to pursue the talk he could not guess.

"Logie's only forty-three," said Chick after a time.

"Is he that old?"

"Old? That ain't old. It's only ripe."

Chick Thomas swished the last of the coffee around and around in his cup.

"Look at 'em," said Chick.

He gestured with the cup to indicate the herd,

74

and Clark regarded them.

"They're very quiet tonight," he suggested.

"Sure," said Chick. "But I've seen lightning out of a clear sky."

"Actually?"

"Yeah. I mean golden balls of fire rollin' down the mountains. And overhead, a sky as clear as a girl's eye . . . before she starts goin' to dances, I mean."

Clark smiled. "I think they'll spend a good night," he said.

"Yeah. But thinkin' ain't cows. Cows, they don't think. Which reminds me of a story about. . . ."

Here a scream burst at them. It was distant, but so peculiarly shrill, and with such a pulse, that it seemed to run at them on wings and swell closer and closer.

Then a chorus of wild shouts broke out on the northern verge of the herd. The whole mass lurched to their feet. They spilled into groups and odd clusters, like iron fillings over which a strong magnet had been rapidly passed.

"Stampede sure as fate!" said Chick without emotion, and leaped into the saddle on his horse.

IX

"Stampede"

From the camp wagon came the cook, literally flying, not speaking a word, but throwing a saddle on a hobbled horse with wonderful speed. Yet it seemed still to Clark that there could be no serious trouble. There were not apt to be Indians abroad in these days. It seemed more like some foolish cowboy prank, such as he had seen before.

Then all doubts about its seriousness were set at rest. The yells continued, but they were broken and accompanied by a rapid rolling of pistol shots. With this, the entire herd swung about and bolted for safety — and safety in their eyes seemed to lie south, toward the Rio Grande.

Clark himself had mounted. He did not need to give a word to his horse. That strong-willed mustang flattened his ears and stretched out his neck as though to lower wind resistance, and began to run as though it were striving to blow the saddle off its back with the speed of its going. Certainly, it very nearly blew off the rider.

Poor Alfred Clark, never a good horseman, dangled on one side of the animal and then the other, with a sense that a starlit sea had risen upon the desert and was rushing at him with a vast and increasing roar. But by keeping one grip strong on the pommel and the other strong on the mane of the horse, he managed to get again into the saddle and find the dancing, swinging stirrups; he caught up the reins and prepared to slow down his mount. He might as well have pulled at the Rock of Gibraltar.

And then, looking back, he decided that the horse had been right from the first, and that he himself was little better than a fool. For not six steps behind him tossed a low-headed wave of which the lighted foam consisted of tossing, sharp horns, and glittering, fear-widened eyes, and the thunder was beaten out by the pounding of innumerable hoofs.

He freshened the grip of his knees, and gave the horse the quirt. But the best a horse can do cannot be improved. Who said that the horse is the fastest of animals which run on four legs? Here were mere cows running like the wind. They were not weighted down by sagging stomachs. They were tucked up as fine as racers ready for a championship race. They were fleet as so many antelope, and they were able to last for days — their wind had been built up in the long jog.

Fear jumped into the throat of Clark and choked him. He looked back again. He saw the cook wagon reel like a ship in a stormy sea. Then it toppled and disappeared. After that, he looked straight ahead and rode for all he was worth, bending over, not because he knew what the bending was for, but because he had seen other riders lean like that when they wanted to make good speed. Certainly the mustang seemed to quicken beneath him in this new posture. They flew on.

He looked back again and made sure that he was gaining on the herd, but only slowly; and, looking to either side, he saw a long dark horn of stampeding animals stretching out before the rest. He actually felt that these arms were stretching for him, and that he was a doomed man!

Then with whip and spur he urged on the mustang, keeping a short hold on its reins, and so, by sweet degrees, he heard the snorting grow fainter behind him, while the roar of the hoofs diminished a little, and the bellowing no longer seemed directly in his ears.

He looked back, and made sure that he was able to cross over the face of the herd to one flank. Then he remembered that he had heard of stampedes being broken and turned by shooting revolvers under the noses of the cows. He tried this, pulling out his Colt for the first time — he had worn it as a matter of mere fashion — and firing it four times into the air.

It did not make the slightest impression upon the cows. Perhaps he was too far away from them. At any rate, they seemed to come on faster than ever, and he pulled away to the side, across the wild front of the storm of animals.

He kept the mustang galloping, though as it ceased from full pace, the bolting herd gradually drew up. Then a dense cloud of dust rolled over them. It blotted out the northern stars. It choked the lungs of Alfred Clark.

What had happened, he wondered? What had started this rush? What malicious persons were those who had rushed at the head of the sleeping herd? Rustlers, perhaps!

He groaned and, as he groaned, he heartily cursed the West and all that it stood for in man and beast. The shining face of a varnished desk, that was the proper environment in which he should spend his days, and a good part of his nights. Not this mountain desert — this place of torment.

He heard the beating of hoofs. Chick Thomas was beside him.

"What's happened, Thomas?"

"Aw, they wanted a little exercise. I told you. Lightning out of a clear sky just. . . ."

A hundred steers burst from the flank of the herd and swept toward them. They rode for their lives, and afterward they were separated, and Alfred Clark rode on alone through the night.

His horse, he knew, might put its foot in a hole at any moment, and end his own life and that of his rider; but Clark kept on at a high speed, not because he thought he could do any good by remaining here, but because he knew not what else to do. And he almost wished that the end of his life and his worries could come at this instant. Life, after all, had not been especially sweet to him.

But still he rode on. He could guess that, as

the speed of the runners diminished, they would fan out and scatter. Even if the 'punchers wanted to do their best to save the herd and redeem the danger, it was probably true that half of the lot would be gone before morning. And in that country, filled with adroit rustlers, it would be very odd if they managed to recollect from the desert what malice or bad luck had spilled upon the face of it.

This was the end of his proud hopes. This was the final outcome of the good path upon which Cayenne Charlie had started him. This was the last upward step. He would have to throw up his hands and admit his failure.

He afterward thought that the herd was running even faster than in the beginning, when he saw out of the thickest night before him a mad rider who actually bolted straight in at the face of the fleeing ocean of cattle! One of the 'punchers gone insane? They were not likely to go frantic in the direction of serving him!

Moreover, to complete his bewilderment, behind this leader, who rode screeching like an Indian, came a string of four or five other silhouettes who yelled as loudly as their leader. Straight across the head of the herd they swept, shooting off their guns.

The center of the herd began to slow. It halted. It whirled into a tangle. The arms of free cattle upon either side continued to lurch forward, but these 'punchers, if such they were, swerved outward, and caught those horns at the tips, and bent in the flying streams. Never had Alfred Clark seen such wild riding, such utter abandon, such total recklessness of life and death. But the stampede was unquestionably stopped.

The rear of the frightened animals came up with a rush and packed the mass, in the center, unbearably close and hard. Then the whole herd expanded a little, and more and more. And it continued that restless milling, while the thundering voice of the frightened, bewildered animals seemed to be rolling up from the solid earth at the feet of Clark's horse.

He could see little. The cloud of the dust spread higher and higher and put out every star in heaven. It choked him to the bottom of his lungs. He kept passing a hand across his eyes, but only succeeded in rubbing the alkaline dust deeper into them, until he was more than half blind.

So he drew back his horse to a greater distance, so far that he was freed from the dust, except what lay in pockets made by the folds of his clothes. Now he could see the picture as a whole, and it was a grand one, with the dust cloud mounting up like smoke into the heavens, reaching, as it were, into the Milky Way; while from the earth where it rose, he could see the very dim silhouettes of the whirled cattle. They were not bellowing so much. They were sneezing and coughing more.

From this distance, he could see the action of the mass as a whole, also, and this consisted entirely of putting out a rapid arm, here and there

— a mass of cattle in full flight toward the distant river like cavalry rushing together at the word of command. But every time these charges were met by the adroit and fearless counter attacks of the 'punchers, who rode right in under the noses of the stampeding cows and fired off their guns.

So, finally, the last attempt ended, and gradually the milling ceased. The herd settled. Some of them sank down from sheer exhaustion, stifled by the dust fumes. Others finally grew calm enough to follow that example. The dust cloud rose, cleared. The whole picture was complete and, above them, only a dim stain against the stars. 'Round and 'round the herd now passed riders, singing strange songs which Clark could not understand — not a single word. The very tunes were different. He would not have called them music at all. He would not have called the rhythm an actual rhythm. But gradually it began to slide into his blood. It passed into his ears. It assailed his mind. It was a new world which he had found here in the desert, and wilder than all he had dreamed or heard of.

These were the men who had stopped the herd. Why? For their own benefit? Did they intend that they should gather the cattle up, when they were sufficiently rested, and hurry them off in a new direction? Suddenly he hit upon it. These were some of the originators of the herd, displeased with the direction which the rout had taken!

He rode straight in at that. He spoke to the first of those jogging, singing men, and got no answer;

but the one next behind seemed to hear his voice, and suddenly there was a loud, cheerful shout.

"Hullo, Clark! I been lookin' for you. That was a good game, eh?"

It was Cayenne Charlie!

X

"Night Herd"

They bedded the herd down where Cayenne
Charlie and his men had stopped the stampede.
What men they were!

By the little fire which presently was started,
Clark had a view of them from time to time. Of
the six, three were Indian half-breeds, the out-
cross being Mexican blood. Two were pure-
blooded Indians, gaunt as ravens and hardly more
cheerful. One was a Negro with a face like a mask
of comedy.

The old hands objected strenuously to these
people. Harry talked apart with Clark.

"You see how it is, chief," he said. "The boys
won't work and ride with a sketchy lot like these
fellows. What kind of a face would we have if
folks knew that we herded along with a lot of
half-breeds, and such?"

"Only through the pinch of the work," said
Clark, striking a happy line immediately. "Someone is trying to stampede the herd. We don't
know who it is, but they nearly succeeded tonight.
With the help of all of you, and Charlie's men as
well, we may be able to beat off an attempt. I
know that you boys will fight tooth and nail, and

it looks as though Charlie's men will, also. Well, we can't afford to throw such help away, can we?"

As he said this, he managed to keep his eyes openly and frankly upon the face of the other. But, for all that, he knew that Harry and his crowd certainly had connived, if they had not actually helped, at the stampeding of the herd. And the ignorant malice of these men amazed him. He had been of a mind, before this, to believe that mere pique at the tenderfoot and presuming outlander had made them act such a bad part; but now he began to think that the men in themselves were thoroughly a bad lot, perhaps well kept in hand by the great force of his brother, but now ready to run riot. His determination to stay with the work became fixed. He could not allow the place to be trusted to such a wild crew.

Harry went off, muttering, and Clark went to find Charlie, which was easily done by the loudness with which Charlie was singing.

"Charlie," he said, "tell me the straight of it. Are these old hands no good at all, or are they simply against me with a prejudice so great that they can't tell right from wrong?"

Charlie's answer was no help at all. He merely said: "I dunno anything about them. They may be as straight as a string. I dunno. The only thing is that right now they're makin' trouble."

"Do you think that they started the stampede?"

"Sure they didn't! They simply passed the wink to a gang of rustlers. That's all, and an easy way to figure it out. The rustlers come in and get the

85

cows, and the 'punchers are all sort of out of the way when the stampede begins. There you are!"

"In the East, Charlie, that sort of thing would be called plain theft. Now, tell me, just how should I look at it out here?"

"Why, I dunno again," said Charlie. "I ain't run with this bunch long enough to know all their brands. Out here, it'd be either hangin' or a joke. I dunno which. A joke, I mean, so long as the stampede was stopped."

"And tell me, Charlie, what made you follow us up with your men?"

"Suppose," said Charlie, "that you seen a sheep dog startin' out to run wolves, wouldn't you wanta foller along and keep an eye on him?"

Clark pursued the conversation no farther along this line. He switched to another vital question.

"These men you've brought . . . are they trust-worthy?"

"Yeah. They're mighty trustworthy, so long as you've got a gun over 'em and the fear of the bullet in 'em. Just now they'd rather get free with nitroglycerin than with me, but they might get over that. Those half-breeds, they need a pretty careful eye. Somethin' about the look of their necks seems to tell me that they been one day close to havin' 'em stretched with good new rope. I dunno. It just looks that way to me. The Negro is a Louisiana no-good. Mostly Louisiana Negroes is a good lot but, when they go wrong, they go mighty wrong. You hear me sing?"

"I heard you sing," admitted Clark, worried and amused. "What about the others?"

"There ain't much doubt about them. Gimme mostly pure Indian, pure Mexican, or pure American. But you start a-mixin' 'em, and you get trouble. Them half-breeds, they're so dog-gone dry that they'd burn in the rain. That's about the facts! No, that crowd of mine ain't much good. But they work cheap, and they fight cheap, and if any of 'em get plugged in the fightin', it's only a quicker trip to the end that they're already overdue at. No, sir, your gang might be a bad lot. But I know that mine are no good at all."

"Charlie, what's in your mind to do for me?"

"Well, I sold you this gang of cows . . . I mean, I sent the right lot to you. Now I'm gunna see that outfit delivered on your home ranch, and after that I take a vacation."

"I'll see that you have money for it, Charlie," said Clark.

"I got your money already," said Cayenne Charlie tersely. "And I don't want no more. Just wages and board for my scalawags."

"You mean to say that you'll not take a penny?" demanded Clark, feeling that he could not be hearing correctly.

"That's what I mean."

Clark gasped aloud. "Man, man," said he, "what's the meaning of it?"

"Well, I took from you the first handout that I ever took in my life. I never been a beggar before that day in jail."

"Hold on, Charlie! You mean that I insulted you by offering you. . . ."

"Naw, I seen that you was a tenderfoot. It come into me in a flash that here was a gent that wanted to do me a good turn and not get nothin' back for it. That's why I busted jail and come to look you up. I was sort of curious."

"Well," said Clark, "I don't know what I can say to you, Cayenne. You're treating me in a very big-hearted way."

"Aw, go to sleep," said Cayenne Charlie. "You'll need a rest to get you through tomorrow."

There was no doubt about that. Alfred Clark rolled into his blankets a few moments later and gave the bright face of the stars one bewildered glance; then he fell soundly asleep.

Cayenne Charlie continued his rounds at a walking pace, or sometimes jogging his horse softly. And sometimes, too, he would sing, though it was hard for him to keep his voice to a soothing pitch.

He was very happy. It was rare for him to have so many good times crowded together. There had been the good, soul-filling fight in Libertad to begin with; then the jail break; the pleasure of rounding up the six thugs, and finally the almost hand-to-hand battle with the herd upon this night.

This was about all that man could desire but, as he journeyed on around the edges of the big herd, he had a joyous feeling that more trouble lay ahead of him, and the foretaste was to him like the bouquet of old wine at the lips of one who knows.

He was not one who relished the intellectual processes of long thought but, rather, he liked to take each day in turn, without question and without doubt of the future. At this moment the center of his pleasant anticipations, however, was Buddie Vincent. If that man did not mean to make trouble, then Cayenne Charlie knew little of humanity.

He oddly enjoyed this jogging around the verge of the herd. Work of all kinds he detested with all his might, but this was not work. It was rather a mounting guard. Therefore, he enjoyed it to the depths of his soul.

After a time, he dismounted and walked, not that he wished to spare the horse, but because he was so fickle and changeable that nothing was apt to please him very long. He was walking in this manner when another rider came up and rode alongside, at such a distance that there was only a silhouette to be seen. And a voice addressed him in soft Spanish, pitched just loud enough to reach the ear of Cayenne Charlie Bird.

"*Señor,*" said the voice, "I know where you can find five thousand dollars."

"So do I," said Cayenne Charlie.

"You do, *señor?* Where, then?"

"In any bank."

"I mean five thousand you will not have to crack a safe to get."

"Well, then, tell me where."

"If you ride two hundred yards straight ahead, a man will meet you with a sack of money. Hard cash, *señor*."

"That's interesting. What then?"

"You take the money and keep on riding. That is all."

"Oh! I quit the herd. Is that it?"

"That's it, *señor*."

"Go back to the man who sent you," said Cayenne Charlie, "and tell him to take his five thousand and go to hell with it. I'm altogether too busy to be bothered."

The rider did not attempt argument. He simply jogged his horse away, and Cayenne Charlie looked after him as the outline melted away into the dark of the night with a calm soul, but a rising anticipation. Five thousand dollars at a throw was the sign of crime in a good big way, a way that might lead to much burning of gunpowder before long.

Cayenne remounted. He began to feel as though he needed to make his rounds at a faster pace, so as to keep in touch with all parts of the herd. When he came near the place where Alfred Clark was sleeping, the boy dismounted once more, however, and leaning over the sleeper he peered intently into the vaguely starlit face. A thin and weary face it was. He slept with his mouth a little open, and every breath he drew was a faint groan. Certainly his strength had been overtaxed, poor man.

Cayenne leaped into the saddle again and was off. He could not tell why his heart was melted by this withered little man. But it was as though he had encountered one who during all of his fairly long life had never lived though a single truly happy day. The very taste of time was soot and ashes in the mouth of Alfred Clark, felt Cayenne Charlie.

He thought of the careless band of 'punchers. He thought of the girl, Dinah, tall, handsome, strong as a man. And these were in the ring to fight against such a poor fellow as this?

Cayenne Charlie set his strong, white teeth, and the sound of the gritting could be heard far about him. And so he rode on through the night around the herd, humming softly to himself, and looking right and left. Sometimes he even turned sharply around in the saddle, because he began to suspect that a bullet might come toward him from any direction out of that bright and placid night.

The darkness deepened. Then he noticed that the stars in the east were growing dim, the mountains more black — and at last the soft gray of the dawn commenced.

XI

"Horses and Riders"

Seven of the entire herd were gored, or trampled to death, or died of fright and exhaustion. The rest were apparently unharmed, though a little wilder. And, in this order, without the loss of a single additional head, they made the long march through the rising hills beyond the desert to the Clark ranch. For seven more days they were on the road, but they reached the ranch without a single untoward incident of any kind. There was not even a brawl of any sort between one of Cayenne Charlie's men and those of the ranch. The latter in particular were strictly, if somewhat gloomily, polite.

Clark, amazed and delighted from day to day with the lucky progress of the drive, began at the end to wish for a little action of some sort. This seemed an unnatural silence. He wondered how Dinah would take the arrival of the herd. All doubts on that head were banished the instant they came through the southern pass into the big amphitheater which composed the ranch. Its treasure was water, which ran in three or four streams, not overlarge, down the sides of the valley and joined in the center in the Clark River.

Their peculiar value was that they ran all the year long, not like some of those living and dying rivers of the lower plains. The upper slopes were dark with woods; the lower stretches were softly undulating; and here the cattle grazed, growing fat almost too soon. Which was the reason that Tom Clark had conceived the yearly drive from Mexico.

Coming through the southern pass, with the dust of the drive blowing back upon them, Dinah broke through the windy mist and came in upon them riding a beautiful, slender, bay gelding, a fiery four-year-old with the grace of a wildcat and much the same disposition; but Dinah got him alongside long enough to shake the hand of Alfred Clark.

"You've done it, Uncle Alfred!" she cried. "I've been sitting up here shaking my head, all this time, but here you are. I'll tell you what. I take off my hat to you. I've been a silly, sulky fool, and you're a man!"

There was no hidden meaning, no secret smile. She looked at him with radiant eyes and his hand still tingled from the grasp of hers.

"Why, Dinah, why, Dinah . . . ," he began. Then he said with his own modest smile: "It looks as if the war might be over, my dear."

"You betcha!" said Dinah. "It's a dead war. Uncle Alf, you've beat the game, and you've beat me, and I'm with you to the crack of doom! That's all!"

It was all, apparently, according to her way of

thinking. He could see that as far as she was concerned, this one success had banished the past. There was something in her manner that, for the thousandth time, reminded him so sharply of his brother that his heart ached. But it was a pleasant sorrow, this time.

"It isn't I who get the credit," he confessed. "The herd was brought together by Cayenne Charlie. And it was on a ruinous stampede when Charlie and his men came up and stopped them again."

"And who brought Charlie inside the fold?" she asked, showing no surprise at the news which she heard. "You did, Uncle Alf, and therefore you get the credit. Hullo, Harry. This looks like the best bunch we ever got up from Old Mexico, eh?"

"It's a good bunch," said Harry. "Good enough, I reckon."

"Yeah . . . you reckon and you know. How you boys gettin' along with Charlie?"

"Why, pretty good. Good enough to please you, Dinah, I hope."

"Now, whacha mean by that?" she asked him bluntly.

"I dunno. Nothing, maybe."

"Look here, Harry, doncha go to getting deep with me, will ya? What's bitin' you, Harry? Mad at me?"

"Why, no," said Harry. "Of course not."

His horse lurched away, and Harry let it go. The girl looked after him with a pucker of her brows.

"He's sore all the way through," she decided. "But let him get over it without nursing. He's all right, but he ain't the only man in the world. Hullo, Cayenne! Glad to see you. What's the news with you?"

"The news is that cows'll raise the dust, and the wind'll sure blow it. You look like you been eatin' three squares a day. Where'd ya get that wildcat, anyway?"

He jerked his hand toward the horse, and Uncle Alfred looked on bewildered. With such ease and speed did the young men and women of today glide from subject to subject. Where were the men of yesteryear, silent, embarrassed, giggling foolishly in the presence of women? The brazen brow of Cayenne Charlie was undisturbed.

"This is a prime good one," said the girl.

"Yeah. Good to bust your neck," he said. "He's a side-windin' fool, ain't he?"

"How'd ya know that?"

"I knew a first cousin of his once, I take it. He busted three ribs for me, gettin' introduced."

"Yeah?" said the girl. "But this here is silk, what I mean to say."

"Slippery like silk, maybe. You better watch that baby, Dinah. He's gunna pile you, one of these days."

"Oh, he ain't so bad. You just gotta watch his ears a little. Try him. He steps out like a dancer."

"These here rocks look pretty hard," he said. "I'd rather try him in the spring, when things is softer."

"Lookit him!" said the girl to Alfred Clark, laughing. "He's trying to pretend to be afraid!"

"It ain't pretending," said Charlie. "They's too much whites in his eyes to please me. But slide off and I'll take a chance."

She dropped to the ground and handed him the reins, holding his own roan mustang by the bridle. A Roman-nosed brute was this, with the build of an Indian pony — mostly stomach, and very little legs to him. The girl regarded this brute for a moment, then prepared to mount.

The gelding, in the meantime, was spinning in a circle to embarrass his would-be rider, but Cayenne Charlie found his time and was into the saddle with a bound. His feet fell into the stirrups instantly, and the next moment the bay was trying to bump a hole in the blue of the sky. Cayenne sat him with great ease until he saw the girl swinging into his own saddle.

"Hey, quit it!" he said. "That ain't a lady's hoss! That's nitroglycerin with a tight cork in the bottle. He'll blow up and bust!"

The roan, obediently as it were, immediately exploded. There was no other word for it. He seemed to disappear in an unjointed, spinning mist of striking and kicking legs. He whirled; he leaped; he sunfished. He began to spin like a top. And the girl presently, inclining farther and farther to a level, at last shot from the saddle.

Alfred Clark cried out in an agony of fear as she pitched headforemost upon the hard ground, rolled over and over, and then lay still. But Cayenne Charlie reached the spot before him. He got off the gelding and ran to her just as she suddenly sat up.

"You gone and busted something now!" said Cayenne Charlie, his face stern and white.

"No," she said. "I just got a mite dented, I guess. He's got a punch in him, that little old Solomon-nosed runt of a roan of yours."

"Stand up!" said Cayenne fiercely.

"Gimme a chance for my head to clear. I never seen the earth go around so fast before."

"Stand up!" repeated Cayenne. He took her beneath the armpits and jerked her roughly to her feet.

"You gone and busted something!" he repeated savagely, standing back from her.

She reeled, reaching into thin air for support.

"No, I'm all right!" she gasped.

"You ain't broke a leg or a hip, anyway," he decided critically. "How's your arms?"

"I dunno. I ain't got much feeling, just now."

Her clothes were torn in twenty places. Her hat hung on one side. Her hair streamed down. She was covered with dust. Her mouth was black with it.

"I guess maybe he didn't crack you," said Cayenne. "You're made of Inja-rubber, the same as me."

"Catch up that roan again," she commanded. "I loosed up on him too much, that time. I'll ride him till he hollers for home and mama, this round."

He caught her by the shoulder and shook a finger in her face.

"You listen to me, d'ya hear?"

She was so surprised at this unprecedented tone that she gaped at him, unable to speak.

"You hear me?" he repeated roughly.

Alfred Clark was sufficiently horrified by this procedure to grow hot and then cold.

"Well, what is it?" asked the girl. "Leave go of my shoulder. I'm not having a free-for-all with you, Cayenne."

"The next time I tell you to lay off of something," he commanded, "you do what I tell you. You hear me talk? You oughta be turned over somebody's knee and spanked. That's what I mean. A dog-gone nuisance is what you are!"

"Who are you to give me lessons in manners?" she asked him furiously. "Where'd you go to Sunday school?"

"You hear me talk. That's all I mean," Cayenne reiterated. "I don't want none of your talk back, either. You hear me?"

"I got no cotton in my ears," said the girl. "But who elected you judge? I never heard such a line."

"Look here, Cayenne," broke in Alfred Clark, "there's really a limit past which I can't allow you to speak to my niece."

"You can't, eh?" asked Cayenne with sinister lowering of the brow.

To Clark's amazement the girl, also, turned upon him.

"Aw, leave Cayenne alone, Uncle Alf," she

said. "Yeah, he's right, and I'm all wrong, as usual. That was a fool play for me to try out his horse. I might've known it was dynamite. And I'm going to be black and blue for a week."

"Serves you right," said Cayenne Charlie. "I hope you have to eat off the mantelpiece for a week, too."

"You've rode me long enough," said the girl angrily. "Let me alone, will you?"

"You chucked a chill in me that'll wake me up at night for a month," he said. "I thought you was busted. . . ."

The memory seemed to overcome him. He made a very wry face, and rubbed his hand hard across his puckered forehead.

"Hey, Pedro!" he called out to one of his own followers.

"¡Si, señor!"

"Go fetch up that old gray mare, will you?"

The mare was brought. She was a weary old cartoon more than a horse.

"You climb into that saddle," said Cayenne Charlie. "I'm not gunna have no more nerve shocks out of you!"

The girl gasped. So did Alfred Clark, but a moment later he was seized by a still more profound emotion. For, beyond the belief of his eyes, she actually was climbing obediently into the saddle.

XII

"A Lesson in Riding"

He was not the only one to feel amazement. All the men of the ranch knew the spirit and dominant will of the girl too well. They had been hiding their smiles beyond bronzed hands while they looked on and listened to this odd curtain lecture which he was giving to Dinah Clark. They expected — well, what everyone of them, at some time or other, had received from this wild young creature of the mountains. They had barely been able to swallow their rising laughter until the critical moment of the explosion came.

Now, as she mounted, they gaped widely at one another. It was a thing to be seen, but not to be believed. She who rode nothing but Thoroughbred steel and fire — behold her jouncing away on the bone-breaking trot of the old gray mare!

Alfred Clark himself, bewildered, continued near them, and saw Cayenne Charlie close at the side of the girl. Doing what? Instructing her in horsemanship! She who prided herself on her qualifications in that direction. She who had appeared at bucking contests, and ridden in the races of every rodeo within two hundred miles.

"You spent some time in the saddle," said Cayenne, "but you never had no teaching."

"No," she said humbly. "That's true."

"Now, you listen to me!"

"Yeah. I'm listening, Cayenne."

"You mind what I say. I never seen a more fool thing than the way that you turn out your toes. Is that any way to get a grip on a horse?"

"I don't know," she said. "I don't suppose it is, Charlie."

"You wanta turn them toes in. Doncha forget it!"

"No," she said meekly, "I won't."

Her uncle stared at her. He was convinced that there ought to be hidden mockery and mirth in her eye. Yet, behold, it was as wide and listening as the eye of a child.

"Now, I'll tell ya something," went on the mentor.

"Yes, Charlie," she said.

"When a hoss begins to spin like that, what I mean . . . the way he done, back there. . . ."

"Yes?" she said.

"You don't wanta bend over to keep close to him."

"No?"

"No. I tell you, no! You sit up straight. The straighter that you set up on a spinning hoss, the better it'll be for you. That keeps you the hub of the wheel, where there's less motion."

"Yes, I can see that."

"You're too proud to pull leather, it seems?" he went on with a sneer.

"My dad never raised me to pull leather," she said, and actually flushed under the savage criticism of Cayenne Charlie.

"You ain't talkin' to your dad," he said. "You're talkin' to me!"

"Yes," she said.

"One of these days, you're gunna go sashaying out on a high-steppin' hoss and, when you come back, it's gunna be on a door. You're gunna get piled, and you're gunna get plastered, what I mean!"

"Do you think so?"

"Say, do you think I'm talkin' for my health?"

"No, for mine, I suppose."

"You keep right on supposin', and you'll suppose right. Now, I was talkin' about pullin' leather."

"Yes, you were."

"You forget what you've learned before. When a hoss begins to pitch, you pull leather. You hear me?"

She was silent.

He went on angrily: "Why, you act like you was a bronc peeler! You got your head up in the air like you could ride a hoss! Why, the part of the country that I come from, the little kids ten years old, they'd laugh pretty nigh till they died, to see you settin' up there in the saddle. They would need no saddle, to ride better'n you do. And you go out and stack your neck on what you know, and you don't know nothin'. I never seen nothin' like it! You've been spoiled."

"Yes, Charlie," she said, "I'm afraid that's true."

"Now, when a hoss begins to stand on his head the next time, will you reach for leather?"

She hesitated.

"Yes," she said at last.

And her uncle rolled his amazed eyes up at the listening sky.

"Well, that's pretty good. You can see sense when it's painted all in capital letters," Cayenne said. "Which leather would you reach for, Miss Buckaroo? Peeling a bronc, which leather would you grab?"

"Why, for the pommel, I suppose."

"You would, would you?"

"Yes. Is that wrong?"

"Wrong? Well, it couldn't be wronger. That's how wrong it is. Listen to me!"

"I'm listening, Charlie."

"It's the cantle that you wanta lay your hold on. You hear?"

"Yes."

"Grabbing the pommel, that just sort of leaves it to your arms. And what sort of muscle have you got?"

She looked at him with a flash of pride. "I can chin myself five times in a row," she said.

"Well, listen to that!" said Charlie, with sneering admiration. "She can chin herself five times in a row. Dinah, I can chin myself thirty-five times in a row, but I wouldn't go to grabbing the pommel. I'd take the cantle. And I've pulled leather.

103

Yes, and I'll pull it again maybe."

He qualified that statement with the last hesitant word, which his pride could not help inserting.

"Keep a pull on everything but a sunfisher," he said, "and belt that baby while he's in the air. It makes him think that maybe they's wasps the minute that he gets off the ground. Belt him low, so's the lash will bite his stomach. No hoss likes to have his stomach cut."

"I'll remember," she said thoughtfully.

"Yeah. And you'll see, too. I'm gunna show you, if you got any bad actors."

"We have plenty. I don't suppose you've been piled very often, Charlie."

"I been piled on every inch of my head," he answered deliberately. "I've been slammed on my shoulders, on my back. I've broken both legs three times. I've been dropped every place, and the worst place is flat on your face, believe me. It sort of makes you sit up and think. But don't you go riding the high steppers till you've had a few more lessons!"

She sighed, and Charlie Bird muttered: "I've gone and got all heated up. I've made a fool of myself, I guess?"

"No, you haven't at all," she told him earnestly.

At this, he lifted his head and turned his still-battered and discolored face toward her.

"You're all right," he said gently. "You don't let a gent down when he's up in the air, like I've been. I've said a lot, I guess."

"You've said a lot of sense," she replied.

"I'll tell you how it was," he confessed. "When I seen that brute spinning, and seen you leaning out in the saddle, all I could look at was the rocks. I said to myself that you was a goner. . . ." He stopped short, and took a great breath. "Well, thank heaven!" said Cayenne Charlie.

Dinah said nothing. She looked straight before her, but it was plain that she was moved.

"Well," said Cayenne Charlie at last, "you're dead game. I never saw a gamer!"

At this her head turned as quickly as a bird, but at once she looked back straight before her.

Alfred Clark felt that he had heard enough surprising things, but he was not prepared for what followed.

"As a matter of fact," said Cayenne Charlie, "I still must make some explanation, because now I begin to remember some of the things that I said in the heat of the moment."

Was this the language of the hoodlum, the tramp, the waster, the battle-loving Cayenne Charlie?

The girl did not seem to be surprised; she listened with her head canted a little.

"I had a sister," said Cayenne Charlie, "who loved horses . . . as you apparently love them. She had had her falls, but still she seemed to believe that the ground would always receive her softly. And she liked to see a hot Thoroughbred come out of the stable door on his hind legs, walking like a bear with a couple of grooms dangling in the air from his bridle reins. That was what she considered a good beginning for a day's riding. Then, one day, the horse came home without her."

Here he fell silent and tilted his head back, as a man will do who finds it a trifle hard to breathe freely.

"Was she young?" asked Dinah gently.

"She was fifteen," said Cayenne Charlie. "She seemed older, she was so gentle. But sometimes she seemed like a child, she was so gay."

He paused here again, and obviously because he found speaking difficult.

"We loved her," he said, "beyond words to tell you of it."

At this, he paused, and looked guiltily to one side; or was it merely in thoughtful remembrance? And the girl, drawing her horse nearer dropped a hand upon his arm.

"Thank you, Charlie," she said.

He did not seem to hear her. He reined his horse with a sudden jerk and bawled out: "You, there . . . you, Pedro, you wall-eyed, lantern-jawed, thick-lipped, black-faced, wooden-headed rummy, doncha see them cows spilling off the trail? Why doncha wear glasses, you dummy?"

Pedro did not wince. He merely said, with a smile: "*¡Si, señor!*" and galloped with speed to correct the line of march.

But Alfred Clark looked at the girl, and in no other direction. Certainly the mask of rudeness and the ruffianly way of Cayenne Charlie had been cast completely aside, and the uncle wished in some way to read her mind to see how she had been affected. He did not have long to stare. He could see, at a glance, that her lips trembled, and that her gaze was fixed straight before her, and that there was a brimming moisture in her eyes.

At this, his heart turned cold. He muttered to himself: "He's going to bring more trouble than all the others. I wish to heaven that I'd never gone to see him in the jail of Libertad!"

XIII

"Trouble Ahead"

The home guard met them. They reached the old camp in the early evening and here there was quickly trouble in the air. For Harry wanted the cattle to be scattered at once so that they might graze, whereas Cayenne Charlie insisted that they ought to be kept bunched and under guard.

Harry caused this debate to be made a regular showdown between him and the new man.

"All I wanta know," he said, "is Cayenne the foreman, now?"

"He's not the foreman," said Alfred Clark.

"Then, will you say what we're to do with the cows? They're dead beat. They been on the trail for a long time, and they oughta have a quick chance at this grass. We're gunna have a storm up this way, too, and it's likely to hit us tonight. You can see the way the clouds are bankin' up high on the north mountains, there. They're likely to let out wind, and thunder, and lightnin', and it's better for the cattle to have a chance to scatter around and get bits of shelter."

This seemed reasonable enough. Clark looked at Cayenne Charlie, and found that the latter was scowling darkly at Harry from under bent brows.

"Whacha up to, Harry?" he said. "What's your game, I'd like to know?"

"It's gunna be this way, is it?" said Harry gloomily. "Every time I got an idea different from Cayenne's, he'll wanta fight about it, will he?"

"I don't think that follows," said Alfred Clark. "What's your side of the case, Cayenne?" Cayenne could not speak for a moment, so keenly were his eyes fixed upon the old boss of the ranch.

"My idea," he said, "is that these here cows need a good rest, and they ain't gunna get it if they're wanderin' around in batches in a country where they never been before. A cow is a lonesome critter and likes its own home pasture and, if you turn 'em loose scattered, without no guard to ride 'em close, they're gunna have a miserable time of it. By the mornin', you'll find some of 'em scattered over every part of the valley, and you can take my word for it!"

There was a sullen viciousness in the manner of the other as he replied: "All right. You take his word for everything and let me slide. I'm new in this here valley, I reckon!"

He turned on his heel and marched off, without waiting for the official answer of Alfred Clark.

"He's soaked full of poison," said Cayenne Charlie. "But that's nacheral. He ain't had this party organized just to suit him."

"Charlie," said Alfred Clark, "I think that we'd better humor him, unless you can depend on the men you've brought along with you."

"I can't depend on nothin' about 'em," said Cayenne Charlie. "They was all right on the road. But when it comes to stayin' here in the valley with all these thugs around, my boys feel kind of nervous. Harry and Buddie Vincent and the rest have passed the word around that the regular thing here in Clark Valley is the slicin' of the throats of greasers and such, and my boys, they believe it. Before mornin', there won't be a hide or a hair of 'em in sight."

"And you, Charlie?"

"I'm here as long as there's any action . . . if you still want me."

"We'd rather have you than all the rest. You can't promise us a long stay?"

"No. Not a promise."

"Charlie, there's another thing that I want to talk to you about."

"Fire away."

"It's not an easy thing to talk about, but perhaps I'm old enough to do it safely. It's about your past."

"Yeah? What about it? I don't mind talkin'. I'll give you a list of the jails that I've slept in."

"I don't care a whit about the jails," said Clark. "You've been jailed for breaking the peace and a good many heads. You've never been jailed for theft or a killing that wasn't in a fair fight."

"Who told you that fairy story?" asked Charlie blandly.

"It's not a fairy story. It's the truth. Otherwise, you would have thrown in with the crooks and got this herd together just in order to take it away from me again."

"You tell me about myself," said Cayenne cheerfully, "if you don't like the yarn I tell."

"I think I can," said Clark. "You were raised in a good home. Your parents were rich, or at least they lived as if they were rich. You had what you wanted as soon as you named your want."

"Go on," said Cayenne. "You make me feel better and better about myself and the way I was raised. I was a gentleman, maybe?"

"You still are," said Clark quietly, "under the skin."

Charlie Bird, hardening his glance to a point, probed at the face of Alfred Clark. "Now, what in hell do you know about me?" he asked.

"Nothing except what you've told me, and a little that I've heard and seen for myself."

"Such as what?"

"This, for instance: that you speak perfectly good English when you choose to do so."

"Ah?" said Charlie Bird. "And when was that, if you please?"

"This very moment, for one. And another when you were talking to Dinah about your sister's death."

Charlie bit his lip.

"You were off guard," said Clark. "So was she. And every word that you said sank deep in her mind, I'm afraid."

"Afraid of what?" asked the wanderer sharply.

"You've dropped into Dinah's life like a hawk

out of a blue sky. She never has known anybody like you. You're a hero, in her eyes, and loaded with romance. To conclude, she's a wild, impressionable young girl."

Cayenne Charlie grew a dark and dangerous red.

"I'm tryin' to foller you, old son," he said. "Just go soft and slow."

"I've said all that I intend to say, Charlie," went on Clark. "I've told you before that I believe you're a gentleman. Well, I think I can trust you. I want you to look at Dinah, look at yourself, consider the future . . . and then act accordingly."

Cayenne, though about to answer, changed his mind and remained silent.

At last he muttered: "I'm on parole. Is that it?"

"On parole to your own sense of honor, Charlie. You'll have plenty of time to think things over this evening, and if you think then that it's best for you to go . . . well, much as we need you here, I'd be glad to have you do what you think best."

With that, he left Charlie and went for Dinah, who readily agreed with him that Harry should have his own way in the handling of the cattle, at least for a time.

"He'll go straight and come to time," she insisted. "Harry's not a bad one, but he's jealous, now."

"He is," said Clark, "and so are all the old hands. You've been their guiding star and the post they tie to. Because of you, they've felt that they owned this valley and the cows in it. Well, they see that you're drifting away from them. They hate Cayenne Charlie with all their might, and I don't suppose that you can really blame them for it."

"Why should they hate Charlie? What's he done?"

"He's made them into a herd of fools. And worse than that, he's treated you like a four-year-old child . . . and you've shown that you like that sort of treatment."

She flushed hotly. "Why are you coming over me now, Uncle Alf?" she said.

"Well, are they wrong?" he asked brutally. "Wasn't it plain to them as it is to me that this fellow Cayenne Charlie has turned your head?"

"Rot," she said.

"Is that an honest answer?" he demanded.

"No," she said. "I'm pretty dizzy, all right."

"And dizzy about young Cayenne Charlie?"

"Yes, I am. I never saw such a fellow. And a man of some background, when he dares to show it. He's come a long way farther down in the world than most people ever climb!"

"I agree with you," he said. "I only wonder whether he'll ever stop sliding. I'm not giving you advice, Dinah. Only this much of it, at least: the more the old hands see you smiling at Cayenne Charlie, the sicker they are going to become of their work, the valley, and you. They're apt to leave."

"Did they expect me to marry one of them?" she asked furiously.

"Would that have shocked you so much, a week or two ago?"

"What are you driving at?"

"Suppose that Buddie Vincent, with his list of dead men and his handsome face and pleasant manner, had asked you for the tenth time to marry him and. . . ."

"Did he dare to tell you that he'd asked me before?" cried the girl, crimson.

"I'm a very dull-eyed old uncle, Dinah, but I didn't have to be told what a blind man could have guessed. You weren't really horrified at the idea of marrying one of those bold, dashing fellows, and making him the king of this round table, with all the other 'punchers about you as paladins around the big chief? It seemed a pretty romantic life to you, didn't it? Something to look forward to?"

"Well, perhaps it did." She confessed it suddenly, with a snap of her fingers. "You make me feel that I've been a fool, Uncle Alfred!"

"No, but you've been pretty young, and you're not much older, today. Mind you, I'm not advising. I'm not criticizing. I'm simply pointing out what appears to me a good political attitude for you to take."

"Tell me one thing."

"Whatever I can."

"Has Charlie ever said anything to you?"

"No, not a word."

"Did you say anything to him?"

"Yes, I did."

"Good heavens! What?"

"Nothing to hurt his feelings, or yours. But something that may make him do a little thinking. Which I hope you'll find time for, also."

"Of course I shall!"

He left her. Harry was instructed that the herd was in his hands for that night, and received the word with a cynical and sneering silence.

Alfred Clark sat in silence at the head of the long table and listened for the usual riot of noise. But there was not a word. And even the knives and forks seemed to be plied softly. No man looked at any other man, but down into the face of his plate. And very surely Alfred Clark knew that there was dark trouble ahead for them all.

XIV

"They've Gone!"

It was the wildest night that Clark ever saw. There was always more or less wind up there in the mountain valley except when the noon heat poured its weight down from the sky. But on this night the wind rose up in its might. It flowed against the house like a river in spate.

Cowpunchers might sleep on a night like this, but not Alfred Clark. He lay for a long time awake, telling himself that there was nothing to be nervous about, though the place quivered and shook violently. But after a time there was a dizzy heeling of the house. He could have sworn that he felt the windward side lift and then settle slowly back against the pressure.

This got him out of bed in a hurry and he ran shivering to the window. What he saw amazed him. He had been conscious of a steady, loud, angry roaring which he had taken naturally for the voice of the wind, but now he saw that the Clark River was flooding its banks! There had been gusts of rain, like musketry to be sure, but certainly not a sufficient downpour to account for this rising of the flood. He rolled his eyes, bewildered, to seek for a cause.

There was ample moonlight to enable him to see the entire valley on this side of the river. For though the south wind brought throngs of clouds across the sky, they were not sheeted solidly from horizon to horizon. Instead, they went in fleets and in single masses, cruising with an incredible speed. They swept so close above the house that he could see the hulls of these torn and ragged craft, and then at a little distance they rushed on with the moon making their upper sections as translucent as sails.

These argosies of moisture sailed full tilt to the northeast and there gathered, and wrecked in dense masses upon the slopes of Mount Fortune. It had its name from the scores of men who had wasted precious, bitter years prospecting among the shams and pretenses of its narrow veins which always pinched out to nothing as soon as they were worked.

He could see the lofty, glistening head of Mount Fortune, but its great shoulders and all its body were lost under ten thousand cloaks of darkness, for there the clouds piled in ranks and in thunders. Now and then lightning jerked through the masses from head to plain and showed the long tresses of the descending rain that fairly touched against the foot of the mountain.

That was the source of the Clark River's rise. Yonder on those great slopes the rain must be bucketing down in close showers and in solid masses, and it was no wonder that the river ran as white as milk and brimmed its banks. He heard a booming report, wind-muffled, but very like the explosion of a gun. Again and again it was repeated. It could not be a gun battle in the bunkhouse, a thing which he had more than half expected for that night, with Buddie Vincent, Harry, and the rest closed into one room with terrible Cayenne Charlie. A gun fight would have meant a continuous rattle of weapons for one brief moment. But this was like the regular firing of a cannon. Then he saw the source.

The big swinging door at the near end of the largest barn had blown free from its fastenings. There was some pool in the air currents that, when it had been blown wide with a crash against the side of the barn, caught it on the recoil and sent it staggering back in place, to be hurled open again by the impatient arm of the wind a moment later. He watched this for a moment with amazement. Not because of the force of the wind — whose force was apparently lessening every moment — but because no one left the bunkhouse to put the door on latch again. And yet the bunkhouse was infinitely nearer and the clamoring must have kept everyone awake there. He was in the midst of his puzzling over this when a light, quick knock came at his door. He opened it on Dinah, fully dressed.

"There's something wrong, Uncle Alf," she said.

"The wind, you mean?" he asked her.

"That door of the barn, slamming. If there were

any men in the bunkhouse, they certainly would get up and close it."

He listened to her, hearing the words but failing to grasp the full import at which she hinted.

"If there were any men in the bunkhouse . . . ," he repeated. "But, of course, it's full of men, Dinah!"

"Well, then," she said, "they're tied hand and foot, or else they'd go out and fix that door."

She insisted on it calmly, and gradually a sense of horror came over him.

"I'll go and see," he said.

"I'll go with you."

She closed the door. He huddled into some clothes, and hastily went downstairs, buckling a revolver about him and hoping that he would not need it. Yet he felt oddly convinced that this was the end of something.

He found the girl waiting for him just outside the door of the house in the broad sweep of the moonlight, for no cloud shadows were passing at that moment. The wind had fallen a good deal, and still was dropping, though it was strong enough in separate gusts.

"You stay here, Dinah," he told her. "I'll look into this business!"

She shook her head.

"I don't want to stay here in the house alone," she told him frankly. "I'll go along."

He was glad enough to have her. They went straight out to the bunkhouse, Clark carrying a lantern and, when they showed the light of it through the open door, it gave back to them a scene of the wildest confusion.

The clothes which had hung on the walls had been thrown down, and not by the force of the wind, for the door opened to the lee of the storm. Old chests and bags had been opened also, and part of the contents had been scattered here and there.

The girl looked at this scene of confusion for a single instant and then said: "They've packed up their best belongings and got out. Let's see what's left in the horse corrals."

"But Cayenne Charlie . . . he wouldn't be apt to leave with them," said Clark.

"Cayenne Charlie was probably put out of the way," she said.

She was so calm about it that he glanced sharply at her, and then he could tell, even by the moonlight, that she had turned blankly white.

"We'll go off to the shed where his own men were," said Clark. "Probably he changed his mind and went to bunk with them."

"He'd never change his mind. That would have looked too much like the white feather," she declared.

They went accordingly to the shed which had been assigned to Cayenne Charlie's nondescript crew but, when they pushed open the door, they found not a soul there.

"They've gone, too," said the girl, "but not with the other precious lot. The men that Daddy trusted so much . . . that I believed in. . . ."

She hurried straight off toward the horse corrals, big enough to serve as pastures also, in a certain sense, and there they saw a number of animals lying down, close to the shelter of the barn, while a few stood disconsolately, facing the wind, miserable, glistening with the rain that had fallen.

"I don't see Chick's Baldy," she said, "and he was caught up yesterday, I know. No, Baldy's not here. And that dark-pointed chestnut that Cleve Daniels always liked. He's gone, too; and he was here last evening when I came out to take a slant at the horses. No, and the little black mare is gone . . . they've cleaned out, Uncle Alf. They've cleaned out and stolen horses to get away on!"

Both of them remained looking at the tall rails of the corral fence as if into the future, finding it dreary enough.

"But Cayenne Charlie . . . somehow, I can't imagine that he would be beaten," Clark muttered.

"What chance?" cried the girl passionately. "What chance would even he have against a gang of murderers and cut-throats, and sulky, cruel, selfish cowards? That's what they were. I can see it now. Daddy could handle them. But he was the only one!"

"We'll go back to the bunkhouse," said Alfred Clark. "They certainly haven't gone away without leaving some message for us."

He led the way, the girl following with a fallen head; as though all faith in humanity had been stolen from her in this moment of disappointment. When they came to the bunkhouse again, they went in, and going inside the door, the confusion was doubly confounded.

The whole floor was littered. Beds had been ripped up, perhaps because some of the treasures of the 'punchers had been sewed into the sacking, and the straw was scattered, lifting and rustling in the draft. Old magazines lay about, fluttering their time-yellowed pages. Old boots with rumpled tops, shoes whose soles had been worn through, battered hats, dunnage bags sometimes only half emptied, tattered shirts, underwear — all the garb of cowpunchers lay heaped and tangled about them.

Alfred Clark, with an odd feeling of walking a deserted battlefield, moved slowly here and there until it seemed to him, with a start, that he saw the body of a man lying face downward on a bunk in the corner of the room.

It was a ghostly thing to see. He pulled out his revolver and raised the lantern. Beyond doubt, it was a man, and even at the distance he could see the great, ghastly red wound that gaped across the top of his head.

"Dinah!" he called to her. "You go outside. I'll be with you in a moment."

But she had seen.

"It's Charlie! I knew! I knew!" she cried out, and ran to the bunk.

Clark followed her, dizzy with horror. The memory of the man in all his strength and courage

122

filled his mind and walked beside him. When he came to the bunk, she already with wonderful strength had turned Charlie Bird on his side, and her face was pressed close to his heart.

He caught his breath and waited. Presently one of her hands began to lift and fall with a slow, irregular, faltering rhythm, and suddenly he understood. She was counting the pulsation of his heart. Charlie Bird still kept some feeble remnant of life in him.

She got to her knees. Dauntlessly she examined the wound in the head.

Then she said briefly: "A glancing scalp wound. That's all. The curs thought they had brained him, but he'll live to make them wish that they'd struck harder when they had the chance!"

XV

"After Them!"

They brought water and cleansed the wound. Dinah raced to the house and, coming back with sticking plaster and brandy, they closed the gaping lips of the wound and poured a stiff dram down Cayenne's throat. Still he did not move.

They worked then to resuscitate him by moving his arms and legs as though he were a half-drowned body, and in this manner they kept on till their own arms were weary.

Suddenly, Cayenne Charlie sat upright.

"Hullo!" he said. "Is it time to turn out?"

Then his sleepy eyes grew bright with understanding of the girl and Alfred Clark, who stood before him. He gave one wandering glance to the confusion of the room about him. He started to his feet.

That move was too sudden even for his uncanny strength, and he staggered, until Alfred Clark caught him by the shoulder and held him fast. The man was iron. Half stunned as he still was, the shoulder muscles writhed and played like steel coils under the grasp of Clark.

"Lie down again!" commanded the girl.

"I'm all right," he insisted. "Don't bother me.

Lemme think . . . lemme think it out. . . ." He rubbed a hand across his forehead.

"D'you know who it was, Charlie?"

"That whanged me?"

"Yes."

"No, I dunno. They told me that Buddie Vincent wanted to see me outside. I thought that Buddie had changed his mind and wanted to fight it out, so I went to see him. And as I stepped though the door, somebody dropped me from behind. I heard the swish of the arm in the air behind me, but I dodged too late. I'm not a dead one, though . . . I'm not a dead one . . . I'm coming back. Where's that brandy that I had a taste of?"

They gave him the bottle at once and hurriedly he poured down a huge shot of it.

"That's better," Cayenne Charlie said. He freed himself from the sustaining grasp of Alfred Clark and stood alone, easily, well-balanced. "They've cleared out, have they?"

"Yes."

"By their whisperin' together all evenin' long, I guessed that that was what they were up to. My boys . . . are they gone, too?"

"Yes. All gone. There are only three people on the place, so far as we know."

"Which way did they make their drive?"

"Their drive?"

"If they're gone, of course they've taken the cattle with them! Don't you see? As long as they thought they had the ranch in their hands, they were willing to let things go along peacefully. But when they saw that there was to be a change and the ranch was not for them, then they made up their minds pretty quick. Harry and Vincent, they're the leaders. But which way did they make the cattle drive?"

He was keen, alert, active, apparently suffering almost no reaction from the blow which had stunned him so completely.

"How long ago did this happen?" asked the girl.

"About half past ten. What time is it now?"

"Nearly one."

He groaned, snapping his fingers with impatience. "That gives them a long start. We'll have to move."

Cayenne Charlie himself ran from the bunkhouse, with only one stagger on the way. They followed him outside, and there found him turning slowly to survey the ragged circle of the horizon. On Mount Fortune the thickness of the rain mist was abating, but the Clark River seemed to be running higher than ever.

"Now tell me quick," said Cayenne Charlie. "Where's their nearest market?"

"Straight down through the south pass," said the girl. "They'd drive the cattle back toward Deaconville. That's what they've done! Why didn't I think of that?"

"How far is it?"

"Thirty miles."

"They'd never get them there before you

caught up with them. What other place?" persisted Charlie.

"Nothing except to the north. That's farther, too, unless they take them to the north pass and hide in the canyons there."

"Is that your rustler country?"

"Yes."

"How far away?"

"Twenty miles."

"Then that's where they've run the herd . . . or started them on the way."

"How could they get cattle across the river?" asked Dinah.

Charlie groaned as he looked down to the white stream. "It wasn't so high, then. They could have made the drive through the water at that time, I think. But how could we possibly get across now?"

"Do you mean that you'd want to follow them up now, Charlie?" asked Clark in his mild, grave voice.

"That's what I mean, of course."

"But you see, man, that though there are three of us one is a woman, and I'm no good with a gun. And what is even a Cayenne Charlie against that whole pack?"

"If I couldn't beat them, I might block them," said Charlie. "We'll get horses, and I'll try the river."

They had saddles on three of the best horses in no time at all, and going down to the river they found the proof of what Charlie had presupposed;

for where the current spanned out over broad shallows, the bank was worn and cut by the sharp hoofs of hundreds and hundreds of cattle which had been thrust down this shoot into the stream.

Charlie Bird rode in until his horse was knee deep, but it was instantly apparent, from the way the current boiled around the legs of the horse, that he could not swim across here.

"Higher up?" he shouted, above the roar of the river. "Is there a better crossing higher up the stream?"

"It's like this clear to the foot of Mount Fortune," answered Dinah. "It's no good, Charlie. There's no way of getting across."

He turned his head with an impatient word and then stared again at the stream. A tree went by. It must have been torn from a bank on the mountain itself, for no trees grew on the plain. It struck a riffle, and shot half its length high into the air, then dropped from sight in the swirling mass.

That stream was traveling like the wind. Its force was incalculable. Yet Cayenne Charlie rode down the verge of the stream with an impatient eye fixed upon the chances. Already a thought of some sort had come to him. He took the rope that was uselessly coiled at the bow of Clark's saddle and carefully fastened an end of it to his own lariat.

They came to a place where the current narrowed. The water shot by quietly, as dark and smooth as steel, but just around the bed roared a cataract. They could see the leaping spray of it dancing like pale jewels in the light of the moon.

"We're all going to cross," said Cayenne Charlie suddenly. "You two can tell me the lay of the land. You may be able to do some bluffing, too, if the pinch comes."

"We haven't any wings, Charlie, to get across this water," said the girl.

"I'll lend you a pair then," he said and, turning the horse away from the river, he took it doubling back at frantic speed.

On the verge of the bank they could see it hang, but he spurred deep, and the tormented animal leaped wildly forward. A scream was tingling in the ears of Clark. He hardly knew whether it was his own or from the lips of the girl, as he saw the rider strike the water, disappear, and then as he came to the surface cast the noose of his rope toward one of the rocks that fringed the northern shore.

The cast failed, and instantly, despite the struggling of the horse, the river whirled Cayenne Charlie around the turn toward the rapids. Dinah was riding her own horse into the verge of the water, shrieking something unintelligible.

The rope had been gathered rapidly back into the hands of Cayenne, and now, even while the horse was spinning with him on the brink of the falls, out he shot the noose again. It soared. The wind struck it and knocked the noose crooked. But it fell fair and true over the head of a big rock.

The next moment the line was taut. It vibrated

out of sight in the moonlight. It seemed certain to Clark that it had parted under the terrible strain, but no, it was holding true, and by hauling mightily on it, Charlie was drawing himself and the horse in toward the farther shore. In another moment the force of the current gripped them. They reached the shallows and clambered out onto the safety of the firm land. So in a moment, clad with the glistening wet as with silver armor, horse and man were passing up the shore to the narrows again.

The maneuver was simple now. A rock tied to the end of the line enabled Charlie to throw it across. It was made fast at either end to a strong security, and Dinah was instantly in the water.

It looked, once, as though she would be pulled from the saddle by the grip of the rope, and the pull of the stream against the horse. But they worked through, and Alfred Clark went after them.

It was, as a matter of fact, less terrible than he had imagined. And he came safely through to the farther slope. There he found Cayenne Charlie laughing, his teeth glittering in the moonshine.

"We're winning! We're winning!" he said. "We couldn't have such a good start without making a good ending. Now which way for the pass, and let's ride like the wind!"

Like the wind on wings they rode, in fact. The ground leaped away behind them in great pulsations as the horses galloped on. They spared horseflesh not a whit on this night, but made grand speed across the level, and then through the hills which rose first gently, and then with steeper sides as they got in toward the northern pass. But always the girl rode in front, showing the way.

Once, when a very steep pitch slowed the horses to a walk, and bunched them closely together, she said: "If the herd is still in the pass, we can get up there to the side and from the gap between those two hilltops we can start a double fire. They could see that down in Los Altas. And that's the signal we've arranged. When they see that, the sheriff will certainly come humming . . . if only he could get here before they're through the pass! But are they?"

They had that question answered two minutes later, for as their horses strained over the top of the rise, they saw beneath them the dark throat of the pass, filled, lined, and glittering with the moon-brightened horns of thousands of head of cattle. The whole ranch had been swept clean, and the stock poured out here. The head of the band was already halfway through the narrow gully.

XVI

"Galloping Riders"

Now Cayenne Charlie did not stop to ask for advice. He did not hesitate. He sent his horse down the slope like a falling stone and Clark, with a groan of fear, nerved himself and started to gallop after. He found Dinah at his side, screaming wildly at him: "Let him go! We can't help Charlie in the fight. We can only help by getting the fires going up there in the gap!"

He saw the point at once. The signal, once sent, might bring help in time. But if all three of them were swallowed up in the gorge, then the traitor 'punchers could surround them and take them at their ease. So he swerved his horse to the side and rode with the girl straight back into the gap between the two hills.

They could hear the noise of the guns behind them as they went. No doubt the 'punchers had seen the wild man coming and opened fire. Yes, plainly they could see the man who rode at the head of the herd dismount, take his reins over one arm, kneel, and level his rifle. Once and again that rifle spoke, as Cayenne Charlie rushed in. His own revolver leaped in the moonlight and answered. And the thief rolled prostrate on the ground!

Clark and the girl were at the top of the rise now. Straight before them, they could see the distant lights of Los Altas down the grade. And behind, and to the side, but infinitely closer, was the herd jammed in the throat of the pass, frightened, milling, beginning to bellow like thunder through which the cracking of the guns continued. They could see Cayenne Charlie still. He had ensconced himself in a nest of rocks in the very throat of the pass!

So much Clark saw, then he fell frantically to work in the brush, trying to get dry wood for the two fires which must be built at once. Could it be done?

Dinah had a small axe with which she was soon busy. For his own part, he was tearing frantically with his bleeding, naked hands. He would have willingly worn them to the bone, in this great cause.

He got a heap of tinder together. He unwrapped his matches from their oiled silk. Somehow, he felt as though the salvation of his soul depended on his getting his flame going before the girl. He saw a match glimmer in her hands. He groaned and struck his own. It went out. So did another and another. But at last he had a flame. For what?

For a few miserable, damp scraps of bark peeled off the inside of a thick rind of a dead stump. He tried the flame under these scraps. They hissed with moisture! They sent up a pitiful little white smoke.

No, yonder was a red core of burning, like a fierce eye. It gained; it grew. It spread. The match singed his fingers and dropped, but still the new flame continued.

With trembling hands, with a prayer, he fed it with twigs. He fanned it. He knelt over it as over an altar. Yes, the fire was rising. He placed a small bush above it. The whole of the flames were choked in thick white smoke. Then right above the smoke appeared a glimmering red hand. The whole bush took fire with a rush and a roar, and a similar sound made him turn and see that the girl had accomplished the same purpose.

"Stay here! Keep the fires!" cried Alfred Clark.

"And where are you going?" asked Dinah.

He turned and stared desperately down into the valley. It seemed like a pit of death to him. He could see the guns of the 'punchers flickering in the moonlight, and where the shadow lay, the flash of the explosions. They were forming a circle around the rocks in which Cayenne Charlie lay on guard, fighting back with a shot now and again.

But what would happen when some of them got higher up the slope? To be sure, they must work carefully, for in addition to his own revolver, Cayenne had the rifle of the fallen man.

"I'm going down!" cried Alfred Clark. "If I've lived like a worm all my life, I'm going to die like a man, at least!"

He heard the tingling cry of her protest behind him. But he spurred his horse frantically forward.

He felt the hissing cold of the wind in his teeth as he went down that steep descent.

Then a man stood up from behind a bush and began to shoot at him with a rifle, calmly, deliberately. He snatched out his revolver and fired blindly in return. The rifleman disappeared! No, he was up again, but that revolver shot must have whirred near, for now he knelt protected by shadow.

Past that danger went Alfred Clark. He was in the heart of the pass. He skirted hundreds of frightened cattle. They were running aimlessly, or turning in great confused wheels, and the reëchoed, redoubled thundering of their bellowing stunned his ears. It was as though he already were dead, and riding through the madness and the uproar of an inferno.

There was the gleaming little nest of rocks before him. Wasps hummed past his face. Bullets? Yes, of course. But he seemed to wear a charmed life.

He gained the rocks. He flung himself from the horse and ran inside, while that good animal, with tossing reins, fled on up the pass. Then Clark was kneeling, shuddering inside the circle, and Cayenne Charlie was laughing, and roughly clapping him on the back. Laughing in mockery? No, not at all!

"This'll break their hearts for 'em! They've got two mysteries to deal with now. A dead man come back at them, and you on the warpath, at last. They'll never rush two of us, old-timer! Keep close to the rocks. How much ammunition have you? Twenty rounds? Better than twenty million dollars to me, just now! Ah, that was a grand thing, that charge down the slope. I didn't know you could ride like that. But we have them licked, licked, licked! The curs are holding a council over there . . . some of them!"

The firing had ceased suddenly after the arrival of Clark at the little natural fort. There was utter silence within the fort, also. And then Clark, with a leap of his heart, saw a man skulking close to their rocks.

"Look!" he said to his companion.

The rifle of Cayenne Charlie was instantly up, but he hesitated at the very moment when Clark held his breath.

"Friend," said Cayenne genially, "d'you know that we've got you covered and in hand?"

The other rose suddenly: "Don't shoot!" he called. "I'm with you, boys!"

He came running forward toward them. He leaped over the rim of the rocks, and dropped down again, a rifle in either hand. It was big Thomas. A wild, piercing yell of rage broke out from those who had watched.

"I never liked the dirty business," said Thomas. "I never liked it, and when I saw you come chargin' down, Clark, I swore I'd be a man, too. Thank heaven they didn't get you, Cayenne. That was the stroke that turned me sick of 'em!"

But Cayenne Charlie was wringing his hand. "One honest man!" he said.

"No, there's other honest men among 'em. Only Harry and Vincent have 'em buffaloed. That's all. But they'll never bust the herd through this pass. Not with three rifles to stop 'em."

"They won't try!" said Charlie.

It seemed he was a bad prophet. Instantly, thereafter, a perfect hurricane of lead whipped around the rocks. It was kept up for a full ten minutes. Then silence followed. It lasted minutes. It lasted an hour. Then the noise of galloping riders came into the farther end of the pass.

"They're up from Los Altas," said Thomas. "And that's the beginning of a new day for Clark Valley!"

He had been right. It was the beginning of a new day for Clark Valley. A new era for Alfred Clark started, also.

For Dinah and her husband built him a house exactly to his taste in a pleasant corner of meadow grass beside a creek, with a hill and a grove to cheer him. There he installed his books. There he brought his Boston terrier. There he settled quietly to a dreamy, serene life. He could not leave. They would not let him. And every morning they insisted that he ride on a tour of inspection. He was still the manager. Try as he would, they would not let him give up either title or salary.

"You're a prospector," said Dinah. "You've found a man!"

The Bells of San Carlos

"The Bells of San Carlos" was Faust's title for this story. It appeared under the Max Brand byline in *Argosy* (4/30/38).

It is not such a great step from the magical to the mystical and it is a step Faust took more than once in his Western stories. It is indeed an easy one for a poet to take and Faust regarded himself his life-long as above all a poet. *"Laudato sie, Misignore, cum tucte le tue creature, spetialmente messor lo frate sole, lo quale iorno et allumini noi per loi,"* sang Saint Francis of Assisi. "Praised be Thou, my Lord, through all Thy creatures, but especially honoréd Brother Sun, who makes the day and who through the day illumines us." Faust and his family spoke Italian and his granddaughter, Adriana, Judy's only child, lives today in Florence, the city Faust so loved. Brother Pascual, the friar in the serial Faust titled "The Valley of the Dead" and Don Moore at *Argosy* retitled "Montana Rides Again" (4/28/34–6/2/34), and Fray Luis in this story are two of the most formidable members of the clergy to be found in Faust's Western fiction. Their presence in a story offered Faust the opportunity to embrace, as only a poet might, that seeming paradox of life where, if what is cherished becomes lost and is surrendered without regret, only then can it ever really be found.

Fray Luis was so used to his friar's robe tugging at his knees and awash about his feet that he felt naked in cotton trousers and kept looking down at them and at the thinness of his legs. As for the *huaraches* on his feet, he was used to sandals just about like them, so they made no difference; but he could not grow accustomed to the new lightness of his step and to the absence of that windy whispering which for thirty years had been about his ankles.

He could endure perfectly well the cheap shirt with its tails worn outside his trousers, but he was ashamed to let even the buzzards see his ragged straw hat — the true peon's hat with some hand-made cigarettes tied to the brim. All through the Monotilla Mountains, he had walked with his shame, and though he knew that a man about to die should fix his thoughts on higher things than clothes, still his mind dwelt more on that straw hat than on the purpose which already had brought him a thousand miles from safety. However, when he came within sight of the valley, his heart stopped; his whole world rocked and staggered before his eyes, for the tower of the convent church and the white walls around it no longer stood in the middle of the flat.

It had been many years since he and all the brotherhood had been driven from San Carlos de Piedras. He knew that an accidental fire, six months before, had ruined the old buildings, but even though they might be empty skeletons, he had expected to see them rising high above the ground.

Instead, it was a mere stumbling heap, and it seemed to Fray Luis that all the prayers of centuries and all the sweet songs of the bells from the tower had collapsed and gone from heaven as the monastery had from earth. He felt that this could not be true, but he was such a simple man that the visual loss was like a death of the spirit also. He almost doubted that this could be San Carlos after all, but the mountains looked down on the valley with the same bald heads, the same furrowed faces.

So Fray Luis dropped on his knees, prayed for the mercy of God upon the dead and for the preservation of all the masses, all the music, all the incense-smoke which had lifted upward in their name, and then he rose, strengthened and comforted, and started forth across the level land.

He felt that he was walking in mortal peril. There had been a time when he knew every man, woman, and child in the valley, when he could call every burro by name. In those gentle days no eye looked upon him except with love. Even the dogs which rushed out savagely at a passer-by

142

would silence their tongues when they knew it was Fray Luis.

Now the hearts of men had changed. The new regime had found new creatures to abide by the new law, and there was death abroad in the land for men of the Church. His disguise had taken him safely enough through the mountains, but in San Carlos Valley every eye was apt to know him. That was why the brotherhood had wept when he departed on his mission. Now, as he walked deeper into the valley, he was trying to imagine how death would come.

It was evening. He had lingered during the last march so as to arrive at just this hour of the day, and now the night gathered over him as he came near to San Carlos. The very smell of the cookery meant home to Fray Luis. For nowhere else in the world is the savor of roast kid like that in San Carlos, and the pungent sweet-sour fragrance of beans never is breathed, really, except in San Carlos. The stomach of Fray Luis grew as empty as a church bell without its clapper, and he almost forgot his terrors until a clamor of dogs came rushing out upon him from the village.

It seemed to the poor friar that they must have scented him and were dashing to put their teeth in his flesh, until a thin ghost of a creature whipped past him through the dark night and he realized that it was a coyote with the town curs in pursuit. The whole clamor rushed off through the darkness, and Fray Luis went straight on to the ruins.

When he reached them, he had lamplight from the neighboring houses and starlight from heaven to see by, but his tears filled his eyes with darkness and he had to sit for a long time at the base of a pillar before he could look about him. At last Fray Luis raised his head very slowly.

He could not believe that the huge old beams actually had rotted in the flame but, when he had dried his eyes, he discovered that the church and the monastery were indeed gone. It was hard to guess where one wall had stood, but as he crept about through the wreckage, the plan of the old building returned to his mind, and he found himself looking up to where once the flat head of the bell-tower had leaned against the stars.

The crypt entrance had lain about twenty paces beyond. He made those paces, marked the place, and then began to clear away the ruin.

It was hard work, slow work. He had brought with him a short, heavy iron crowbar to help his hands, but the big flat adobe bricks were almost as tough as fire-baked clay, and they stuck together in ponderous clots which he barely could lift and roll. All that night he worked, until just at dawn, he reached a stone pavement. Wearily he cleared a larger space, until at last he realized that he had been mistaken.

His dizzy brain had remembered steps, and now he had found them, but they were steps that led up into the sacristy, not down into the crypt. No, no, the crypt lay far off on the other side of the entire building.

By this time it was clear daylight, so that Fray Luis dared not attempt to steal off through the town. Instead, he curled himself up among the ruins and fell into a deep sleep, exhausted.

By mid-morning the intense heat had aroused him. All the blood of his body had gathered in his poor head; but in the ruins there was no shade, and he was afraid to show his face. So, through that sweltering day, he endured an agony stronger than anything he had known before, for he had drunk up all his water during the night, and this fire-hot sunshine sucked the moisture swiftly out of his body. The torment was worse even than that march of his through the mountain snows, when one January he had carried medicine and good news to the little village of San José. He had felt for years that this had been the supreme test of his endurance, but this day was worse, burning him like coals in a brazier.

At last the day turned red; the evening rolled down like purple smoke from the Monotilla Mountains; and the stars shone once more. Thirst was swelling his tongue, but he dared not get a drink until the last noises had ceased in the town. Therefore he forced his trembling hands to labor again, after he had marked, as well as he could, the probable position of the crypt entrance.

It was nearly morning before the last dog fight and serenade had ended. Then Fray Luis crawled out from the ruin and got to the well. The very smell of the water made him impatient. He could almost have eaten the wet earth around the well where careless village girls had spilled gallons from their water jugs.

Slowly, slowly, he turned the handle that wound the rope and lifted the bucket, slowly so that the bucket rose with no more noise than the exquisite and tempting music of water adrip. Now it was in his grasp with the image of a star shattering and forming and wavering in the water.

Fray Luis drank with such joy that, when he had to pause to take a breath, his conscience smote him; never before had he taken such joy in the pleasures of the flesh. He looked up to heaven, therefore, to ask forgiveness of God, and then drank again, filled his canteen, and went back to the ruins.

In fact, the water seemed to weigh upon him more than sin. He was weak, and his hands stumbled and fumbled at their work all the rest of the night and, when the morning sounds told him to stop, he had not mined down through the heaped adobe bricks of the pavement.

That second day in the open face of the furnace he endured with only the strength of patience. Forty-eight hours without food drank up the old man's strength, and he looked into the northwest for that rare mercy of rain which came to San Carlos hardly more than twice a year.

Once, when he was praying for rain in the open plaza under the eyes of the people, thunderheads actually had rolled out from the northwestern mountains, and within an hour rain had fallen on the valley. It was because of that miracle that he had been chosen by the brotherhood to return to the ruins of the convent in search of the treasure. Today he whispered his prayer, and still the sky remained white-hot. Fray Luis was the humblest man in the world, and he was sure that the good saint would not favor one mortal with two signs.

He rose from a stupor-like sleep, late in the day, with a sense upon his lips and in his dry throat of words just uttered and still fresh in his ear. And as he opened his eyes he saw a shadow draw back from the hollow in which he lay.

He was sure that his praying aloud in his sleep had brought curious eyes upon him. By degrees, his heart trembling and his breath gone, old Luis stood up half his height and peered about him, but he saw no living thing among the tumbled rubbage of bricks; so he took another sip of luke-warm water from the canteen and sat down again, giving thanks.

Thereafter, out of another drowsy trance, he aroused to find the mercy of the night already in the skies, and still there was life left in him for his work. But he realized that all his power soon would be gone, and so he resumed his work even before the village sounds had been lost in sleep. He moved with the greatest care, breaking up the adobe clutterings and getting deeper and deeper, until the crowbar fell from his hands and made a sound in its fall like the far-off ghost of a chime of the bell of San Carlos.

The disaster kept him trembling for half an hour, but no one approached, and he went on with his labor until he could have sworn he was well beneath the pavement level. Then his hand touched a stone edge as high as his knee. He was below the floor of the church.

He had been so lucky that he had struck exactly above the crypt entrance, and now he was working on the steps. This discovery gave him fresh strength. The old man looked up at the stars and felt, suddenly, that he was not alone in his work, and now good fortune overtook him in a great sweep, for a moment later his crowbar struck through the adobe at his feet. He enlarged that hole eagerly. Some of the adobe fell inward. And the whole latter half of the steps into the crypt was clear. He arrived at the last stage of his mission. He lighted the candle which he had carried with him all that distance from the sea. It was crooked, but it lighted readily and, as he stood on the lower pavement, the vaults grew out of nothing and walked back in ordered ranges of stubby little columns.

Looking down, he found that he actually was standing on the flat gravestone of the good and great Fray Tonio, and it seemed to poor Luis that the sad, patient voice of the dead man rose out of the ground, once more reproaching him for the badness of his Latin. Fray Luis dropped to his knees and kissed the stone.

When he stood up again, he had to use both hand and candlelight to fumble his way forward into that corner where the treasure of San Carlos was hidden. Before he touched the sunken stone in the wall corner, he looked up to pray and knocked his head against the low curve of the vault. He pushed resolutely against the stone, and it tipped promptly, revealing a dark little niche with a bright eye gleaming out of the shadow.

Fray Luis fell on his knees again and gave thanks to God and San Carlos; then he pulled out the little silver box and opened it. The very answer to his prayer was inside. He lifted delicately the edges of the holy silk folded inside the box and saw the yellow glint of the two finger bones. Fray Luis leaned a moment against the wall, sick with joy. Then he closed the open niche, took the bones in their silken wrapping, and placed the parcel gently inside the leather wallet where he had carried the food for his journey.

He had risen to his feet and turned with the candle before he heard even a whisper of sound. It was the small, dry rattling made by a rolling bit of adobe on the stone steps, but his candlelight shone on the faces of three savage men. The shadow of unkemptness was on their chins. The hunger of years sucked in their cheeks and polished their cheekbones, and greed brightened their eyes in the candlelight.

"Ah, Domingo!" whispered Fray Luis, for he recognized one of the three, but that recognition brought him little ease. For Domingo was an unholy gambler and user of the knife.

"Talk to the old wolf," said another of the men. "Talk to him, Domingo, and tell him."

The third fellow darted into the corner and ran back carrying the little silver reliquary in his hands.

"Here's a part of it!" he said. "Look, José!"

"It's only the first drop from the cup," said José. "Talk to him, Domingo!"

Domingo already had Fray Luis by the shirt collar. His knuckles, edged and hard as stone, bit into the windpipe of the friar. "Listen, Fray Luis," said Domingo, "we know that you friars lived here like fat gophers in a hole for four hundred years and, when you were kicked out, you hadn't a chance to take your hoard along with you. Now you've grown thin, and they've sent you here to take a load of their treasure out to them. Instead of that, you're going to open the walls for us and show us the hidden room that's stacked with the silver bars and the vases full of gold coins and the boxes of jewels that you stole, you dogs, from the hands of dead women for four hundred years."

The enormity of these words left the old man calm. He said, "San Carlos be my witness, there is not a jewel; there is no gold; the only silver is this reliquary; and the only hidden place is this turnstone in the wall."

He walked to it, pressed it, and showed them the crevice. Their hands instantly were in the hollow and came out empty.

"And you came," said Domingo, taking a new grip of his collar, "for this little silver box, only?"

"See how he keeps his face!" said José. "They learn to lie in Latin; it's no wonder they lie in

150

Spanish better than other men. Make him talk, Domingo."

"Fray Luis," said Domingo, "be a sensible old man. If you don't show us the stuff now, you will later on, and it's better to talk while your skin is still on. Come, come! You're more an old woman than a man, and though you shake your head at us now and look up to heaven, there's not a saint of them all that will come down to this cellar to help you now. Will you talk?"

"I tell you, in the name of heaven, the sacred truth," said Fray Luis, "that there is no gold, no treasure of silver, no jewels. . . ."

He saw Domingo take his quirt by the lash and swing up the loaded handle, and for an instant Fray Luis recoiled but, when he realized how his flesh was shrinking, he made himself sway forward to meet the blow. He had made up his mind with a sudden effulgence of the spirit that should have made a brightness through the crypt. In his swimming vision there were pictures of saints overwhelmed with rocks, stuck full of bleeding arrows, boiled in caldrons of steaming oil, but always with upward eyes upon a glory that enabled them to forget their pain. So the old man looked up, but this blow seemed to cleave through flesh and brainpan. The breath went out of him and darkness entered.

Afterward he heard a voice saying, "You've killed him, you fool. If you've killed him, we'll stretch your neck for you. There never were any more wits in your hands, Domingo, than in the hoofs of a cow! He's dead! He hardly bleeds at all."

"Bah," said Domingo confidently. "All the blood was dried out of him years ago. You see his eyes are opening?"

Fray Luis was rousing to a terrible pain. Still the fire ate inward through his brain, and the terror ran into the pit of his belly with a dreadful nausea. He sat up. One eye was closed entirely. Something trickled down his face; the salty taste of blood entered his mouth. He remembered his Uncle Miguel taking his slender arm between finger and thumb until the bone ached. "This little one will do for the church," he had said.

And ever since, the fear of the world had lurked for Luis behind a hill. Now it rushed out upon him with the face of a dragon.

"Take him away from the town and we'll make him talk," said Domingo, "but don't let him squeal in here, because if the people come and find him, they might be rough with us. They love the old fool because one day it happened to rain while he was praying."

So they put a dirty cloth into the mouth of Fray Luis, stuffing it in so that he scarcely could breathe, and they lifted him by the hair of the head. He could be sure, therefore, that his prayers were silent when they carried him through the night and put him on the back of a mule, behind José.

And all the jolting way, while the pain tortured his head and the fear worked on his heart with cold fingers, he begged San Carlos that he might be able to hold his peace about the treasure valued more than all the gold and jewels in the world — the blessed relics of the saint that were in his pocket. Or was it better that they should fall into the hands of thieves than to be lost with his body? No, for San Carlos, when he wills, can lead good men with a brighter ray than any star may cast, and at his choice he would have the holy relics again in cherishing hands.

They reached a little shanty with a shed behind it and dismounted at the open door, dragging Fray Luis forward until they were stopped by a strange picture. The rising moon slanted into the cabin a dimness of light by which the friar partly saw and partly guessed at a dreadful figure.

There was a staggering little wooden table with a brandy bottle on it, and a big hand grasping the bottle, and an arm clad in a blue flannel shirt that was open at a breast black with hair, and then a red face loose in the jowls and hard in the nose and the brow. By the insolent glare of the eyes, the friar guessed this to be a gringo. All Americans, as Fray Luis knew, serve the devil in sundry ways, but in this terrible man he could see the complete servant of the fiend.

"What drunken gringo . . . ?" began José.

"Sew up your mouth and be still!" gasped Domingo. "Mother of heaven, it is *Señor* Charles himself!"

"*Mister* Charles, you swine," said the gringo. "And what do you mean by keeping hog-swizzle like this inside a good brandy bottle?"

"*Señor* Charles," said José, "forgive the heat which corrupts good brandy as fast as flies blow a carcass."

An amazement as vague and all-pervasive as the moonshine invaded Fray Luis; for here were three armed and desperate men who shrank before that single figure by the brandy bottle.

Señor Charles said in his heavy, thick voice, "What are you doing with a man so old?"

A faint thrill of hope sprang in the heart of the friar, though from this hairy monster, ugly as a tarantula inside its trap door, he expected no real mercy.

"Old, *Señor* Charles, but evil," said Domingo. "With the *señor's* permission. . . ."

He lighted a lantern that hung beside the door and, holding it high, showed the thin face, the blinking eyes, and the tonsured head of the man of the Church.

"Ah, hell! Is that all it is?" said the gringo. "Take it away and do your dirty work out of my sight and my hearing. That's all. Vamoose!"

So they took Fray Luis into the cattle shed and tied him to the center post. They stood about him.

"Will you talk?" asked José.

"There is no gold . . . ," began Fray Luis. Domingo grinned, spat on the floor, and slashed Fray Luis across the face with the lash of the whip. The old man took breath, stunned with pain so that the scream in his throat would not come out.

"Gag him before he yells," said José. "There's no use in annoying the gringo dog. No one can tell what he will think when he's drunk, but we all have heard what he can do."

The dirty rag was pushed between the teeth of the poor friar. He began to choke, so that his eyes ached. And Domingo laid on the lash with a frenzy of pleasure. He kept stepping back and forth to give greater play to the quirt. He twisted his entire head and body with every blow, so that the friar saw only in glimpses the white teeth as Domingo grinned at his work. And in his expert grasp, the lash whistled in the air and struck the flesh like handclaps.

Fray Luis tried to pray, but even in his mind there was nothing but screaming.

"He's strangling," said José, at last. He dusted ashes from the end of a cigarette with the little finger of the hand that held it. The little finger had a nail as long as the nail of a Chinese gentleman.

"Take the gag out before he chokes."

They took out the gag. The tongue of Fray Luis ached from pressing against it. He thought in fact that he would die at once of the stifling and the agony. The whip had cut him like a knife in a dozen places and still more than the pain was the horrid sense that human hands were striking him, beating down his heart, making a dog of him.

At last he could draw a clean breath and, when it came out from his lips again, he listened with all his might, but made sure that he had not screamed. At this, he knew San Carlos stood unseen beside him, and at a stroke half his agony left him. He felt that if only he could see out of both eyes, he would be able to look death in the face.

"Now, will you talk, old fool?" asked José.

Fray Luis said nothing. His thoughts were high above the roof of that shed. José faced Domingo. "We'll have to kill the pig, then," said José, after a moment. "Fray Luis, will you talk?"

Domingo took out a long six-shooter and played with it.

"Yes, yes, I will talk!" groaned the friar.

"Out with it, then," said José.

Fray Luis held up shaking hands. He said in bad Latin, "I confess to almighty God, to blessed Mary ever a virgin, to blessed Michael the archangel, to blessed John the Baptist, to the holy apostles Peter and Paul, to all the saints, especially to San Carlos, and to you, brethren, that I have sinned exceedingly in thought, word, and deed."

He struck his breast three times and added, "Through my fault, through my fault, through my most grievous fault. Therefore, I beseech you to pray to the Lord God for me. . . ."

A voice said, "May Almighty God have mercy upon you, forgive you your sins, and bring you to life everlasting. Amen. But what damned bad Latin you pray in, brother!"

Fray Luis, looking toward the door of the shed, saw outlined in the early dawn the hulking shoulders and the great head of the gringo. He walked into the lantern light that filled the little place.

"*Señor* Charles . . . ," said José.

"Be silent," said the renegade white. The brandy bottle, which he carried in his left hand, he lifted to his lips and took a swallow. Then he drew a gun. "I told you to take him out of my sight. But I could hear the whipstrokes, José, and they disturbed me. What is this fellow?"

"A sneaking rat of a friar who was prowling around the ruins," said José, "and when we make him talk, we'll all be rich. There'll be mule-loads of gold and bar silver, *Señor* Mister, and. . . ."

"He won't talk, eh?" said *Señor* Charles.

He walked to the friar and leaned above him. With a forefinger as hard as a wooden peg, he pushed back the head of Fray Luis and looked down into his face with reddened eyes.

"You came back to San Carlos like a brave old fool, did you?" asked the gringo. "And now you won't talk?"

He raised his voice to thunder. "You won't talk?" he shouted.

Fray Luis closed his eyes to shut out the frightful vision. The monster obscure in the moonlight had been dreadful enough, but standing now at his full height, his face swollen with greedy evil, his mouth twisted to one side so that his teeth looked out, he was to the friar the incarnation of the master fiend himself. Fray Luis tried to pray but the divine name which rose in his throat was altered by the movement of his lips.

"Mercy, *Señor* Charles . . . ," he heard himself whispering.

In that moment he felt that he had lost his grasp of that heaven to which, through the sweet pain of martyrdom, he was about to ascend.

"Mercy be damned," said the fiend who stood above him. "Why should there be mercy for a scrawny old woman like you with calluses on your knees instead of on your hands? You were sneaking around the ruins of the church, were you? Well, then, what have you found?"

Fray Luis opened his eyes and looked up, envisioning the face of sweet San Carlos, but all he saw was the lowering gringo, more terrible than ever. Fear ran like water though the veins of Fray Luis and tears came into his eyes. "I am unworthy, and therefore I am abandoned!" groaned the friar.

"Do you hear, you fool?" growled the gringo. "What brought you back to the church, and what did you find there?"

He stooped down.

"Hush!" said Domingo to the other two. "What a man is this *Señor* Charles. He does with his voice what we could not do with a whip. The old rat is about to talk!"

It seemed to Fray Luis that he was compelled to obey the gringo. He took from its wrappings the soft little swathing about the finger bones, the blessed relics of the saint, and held them forth. Pure as old ivory, time-polished, they lay in the palm of his hand. The blunt fingers of the gringo seized instantly upon them; Domingo and the other two uttered a vague outcry that was to the friar like the laughter of all the devils in hell.

"What is it? Is it a key?" called José.

"This . . . this is the treasure, eh?" snarled *Señor* Charles.

"Ah, *señor*," sobbed Fray Luis, "it is one of the keys to heaven!"

"By the living saints!" said the gringo. "I think it is, for you!"

He jerked his big body about and waved a hand. "Get out, the three of you!"

"*Señor* Charles!" screamed Domingo. "But give us the key! It is we who found. . . ."

"Out! Out!" roared *Señor* Charles.

"*Amigos* . . . brothers . . . help me!" yelled Domingo, and snatched out a heavy gun, a blue-gray flash of steel.

He did not raise his own revolver much higher than his hip when he fired. Fray Luis heard the big half-inch slug strike the body like a fist. Domingo lurched back against the wall, the wind knocked out of him in a grunt. Then he slipped down in a pile. His head was between his knees. He seemed to be making a sort of collapsed Oriental salaam to some superior power.

The gringo faced the other two as they backed toward the door. The drink kept his body wavering, and the legs sagging at the knees, but his head and his hand were steady.

"Give me a little room, José," said the gringo. "Elbow room. Room to breathe. Get over there beyond the edge of the sky. And don't come inside the horizon with me again or I'll be crowded."

He walked with his wobbling knees to the door after them; hoofbeats began; an angry voice screamed an insult out of the distance; then the gringo came back and cut the rope that tied Luis to the pillar. The old man tried to stand but the effort set his knees to shuddering. He was much amazed when the gringo picked him up and carried him to the hut.

"When did you eat last?" asked the gringo. "There's no more belly on you than there is on a starved sheep."

"I ate on the holy Sabbath," said Fray Luis.

"And in between?" asked the American.

"I have had good water from the well of San Carlos. God and the saint be praised for it," said Fray Luis. "But now, let me die!"

"Why should you die, brother?" asked *Señor* Charles, leaning the red and swollen horror of his face closer to the old man.

"Because I have given up with my own hand the salvation of thousands, of tens of thousands," said Fray Luis, "and God will not have mercy on my soul!"

He began to weep. It seemed to him that the tears were the last blood in his body.

"As for the key to heaven," said the gringo, "you see that it is once more in your hand."

It was true! The miraculous relics were again in his grasp.

"The Lord giveth and the Lord taketh away," whispered the friar. "The Lord giveth. . . ."

He fell into a meditation, as wordless as the music of the wind. Food appeared. He ate and was satisfied, and he fell asleep and awakened so far cured that he even could see out of his damaged eye. The gringo loaded him onto a mule and with him rode across the flats of San Carlos Valley into the northern mountains.

"I think you can go on safely from here," said the gringo, "but if you are afraid, I'll stay with you the rest of the day."

Fray Luis smiled. "Dear son and brother," he said, "I have no longer any fear; holy San Carlos himself is my companion. But how shall I thank you for the life of my body, *Señor* Mister Charles?"

He took the hand of the friar, and Luis felt something very strange in that grasp, so that he looked and noticed that two fingers of *Señor* Charles's right hand were missing. Shot away in some battle, perhaps?

While he was reflecting on this, he discovered that the gringo had disappeared to a sound of hoofbeats down the valley.

Fray Luis rode softly on, still with his mind fixed far off. For he had not yet been able to arrange his thoughts properly and, though he felt by the whip welts on his old body that a miracle had saved him, once he told the story to the brotherhood, he would hardly know how to make the giant appear. So he drew on into the highlands

161

where excellent bunch grass grew and fat sheep wandered, grazing behind their bell-goats.

As he rode, he touched from time to time the sacred relics in his pocket. They were safe, but only safe, he knew, because blessed San Carlos had been with him. But his memory shrank from the death of Domingo — for whom he would pray — and from the face of the gringo, half-bloated like the jowls of a swine and half-hard like the beak of a vulture. He turned his mind then to smaller things, since the holy saints often reveal themselves in the slightest events whose significance is appreciated only by the most understanding minds.

And it was in this manner that he came to think of the name of the gringo, from whose right hand two fingers were missing. "*Señor* Mister Charles . . ." and all at once a mighty light burst upon the brain of the old friar, for the name and the missing fingers joined to make the miracle complete.

He slipped down from the mule and fell upon his knees, overweighted by the divine conclusion which was forced upon him. May not the most glorious deliverers take the strangest forms? And did not this miracle carry its sign and authentication upon its very forehead?

He knew only a few words of English, but now the name "Charles" rang back and forth in his brain, for surely it was the equivalent of "Carlos" in Spanish. The dreadful and mighty revelation rushed upon Fray Luis and pressed him down to his knees; he had been in the presence of a fleshly incarnation of the blessed saint himself! Not shining with an effulgence too bright for the human eye to endure, but darkened and dimmed by the flesh and the brandy bottle, and striking his foes down not with a silent death but through the more obvious mouth of a revolver. A single detail now remembered bolted strongly home the conviction of Fray Luis; for he recalled that the *Señor* Mister Charles had not sighted the gun. Blindly he had fired it, knowing that the sacred bullet would find its own way.

Tears of joy began to fall down the face of the old man, but though his eyes were blinded he had a bright inward vision of all the brotherhood, as they would sit enraptured when he told them his story, and when he showed them the sacred finger bones and told of the living hand from which they had come.

While he still was blinded by joy, he did not notice that a sheep dog ran barking through the flock, scattering the sheep and their bellwethers here and there. When Fray Luis therefore heard a sound of bells, it seemed to him that the chimes of San Carlos were sending the ghosts of their voices after him, music softly echoing among the hills and valleys of time, repeated with infinite, small tongue, and every separate tremor of sound that touched his ears was to him another blessing heaped upon him by the infinite largesse of heaven, so that he seemed to be kneeling in a shower of gold.

Between One and Three

"Between One and Three" was Faust's title for what Frank Blackwell called "Mountain Madness" by George Owen Baxter in *Western Story Magazine* (8/26/22). Who was George Owen Baxter? D. C. Hubbard provided a brief and wholly fictitious portrait of him in the issue dated 4/28/28 along with a pen and ink likeness that showed Baxter to be far more handsome than Max Brand or David Manning (the latter, another Faust pseudonym, was featured in a fictitious profile in the issue dated 6/16/28). Baxter's father had been seriously injured in a stampede when George was in college. While waiting to catch a train back to the home ranch in southern California, Baxter had "started to write a story about the world he loved and knew most about." In departing, he left a note to a friend scribbled on an envelope: " 'Buck, please send to *Western Story Magazine*, New York. Cowboy Kid.' " (At college, Baxter was called "Cowboy Kid" by practically everyone.) He was in the family ranchhouse when the mail arrived. "Baxter says that no thrill — if men will admit they ever have thrills — was quite the same as the one he felt when he opened an envelope addressed to him from New York. The words that accompanied the inclosed check are as clear to him today as if it were yesterday he had received it. 'We liked your story. Won't you please send us more?' "

And what of Frederick Faust? In this story he faced that human dilemma whether a memory is something that we remember or something that we try to forget.

I

"Coffee for Camden"

"He's a stranger to these parts," said Oliver. "That's plain or he'd not be taking that old trail on the top of the hill, when there's this good road in the hollow."

The girl did not at once reply, but screened her eyes with her hand from the stinging mist of rain which the driving wind picked up and whipped almost on a horizontal line into their faces. In this fashion she was able to peer more easily, and through the storm she could see the shadowy forms of the rider moving slowly along the crest of the hill above them. Behind the thin layer of rain clouds there was a full moon in the heavens, and even in the rain the night was not dark. Moreover, since the storm was blowing from him to them, they had come up extraordinarily close, and still he showed no signs of being conscious of their presence.

Silhouetted in this fashion, they saw a big man, his slicker flaring sidewise and his sombrero rolled up by the wind; his horse was a typical cow pony, lump-headed, ewe-necked, and as diminutive as a goat, under the great range saddle. Still it loped along tirelessly and drifted just ahead of the swift-stepping roadsters that drew the buckboard of Hal Vernon. The dance had broken up very early. It had been rather a reception to a popular girl returning to the community than a real dance, although the schoolhouse had been used for it. At any rate it had broken up at midnight, and now Nelly Camden was on the way to her home in the rig of Oliver Cutting.

"Do you suppose," asked the girl, "that I ought to offer him a bed for the night in the bunkhouse? He's a long ride from town, if that's what he's aiming for."

"You let him be," said Oliver without enthusiasm. "This is a queer night for a man to be out snooping around the country. Maybe he wouldn't appreciate invitations any too much; maybe he'd rather be by himself and think that no one has seen him!"

In spite of this ominous prediction, the girl watched the wanderer with the greatest interest, shivering at the thought of his journey, until the buckboard rounded the side of the hill, and they came into view of the splotchy black shadows of the buildings of the Camden Ranch. At the same instant a light gleamed from the house.

"It's one o'clock sharp, then," said the girl.

"How's that?" asked Oliver. "What has that to do with the light?"

"Why, that's the time my father wakes up every night. He keeps the light going from one to three."

"That's a queer habit and a queer hour," said

168

Oliver Cutting. "But then your father ain't like other men, Nelly."

"You never liked him, Oliver," the girl answered with dignity. "That's because he doesn't talk a great deal to any one. He is different from most people."

"One to three!" exclaimed Oliver Cutting. "Why, that's the worst time of the night . . . the dog watch, you might say! Here . . . the rain is letting up!"

The wind had shifted; the rain ceased; and the moon pressed down and lighted the wheeling clouds. By that greater light they saw that the stranger had halted his horse on the brow of the hill and was looking steadily toward the black house and the lighted window. At this moment he seemed to become aware of the buckboard in the road below him and turning his horse he cantered up to the side of the rig, as Oliver trotted his horses on again.

Nelly could see the bald, white face of the pinto forging ahead, thrusting in and out a little with each stride.

"What house is that down yonder?" asked the rider.

"William Camden's house. Why?"

"William Camden!"

His spur gleamed, as he sent the pinto into a sharper canter and forged away through the night. He left the girl silent with interest and Oliver Cutting muttering to himself.

"That's politeness . . . I guess not!" he said

gloomily. "That's a gent that must have been dragged up in a barn . . . he got no raising!"

The figure of the rider dipped out of view beyond a hilltop.

"What's your father do," asked Cutting curiously, "at this time of the morning?"

"He reads," the girl said. "He's a great reader. Sometimes on Sunday he sits all day up there on the bridge and reads."

"What's the bridge?"

"That's the high porch which you see. Dad's windows open onto it."

"I never thought of that, but I suppose that it is."

"There the light goes out! He isn't keeping it going until three tonight, I see."

"He hasn't put the light out. He's only closing the shutters."

"I remember now. It's the only house in the mountains around here that uses shutters."

They reached the building, and Nelly insisted that he come in and put up the horses, so that the latter could have a little rest in the dry shed, and the driver could drink a cup of coffee in the interim. So they put up the team and scurried for the house through the rattling fury of the clearing-up shower behind which a starry sky would unroll.

In the kitchen the girl started a fire, and while the flame was gathering in the stove, and the wood was igniting with a cheery crackle, she put the coffee and water into the pot and then placed it on the stove. The drops on the outside of the pot began to turn to steam at once; before long a subtle and aromatic fragrance of coffee began to creep through the room and brought a placid look to the eyes of Oliver Cutting. His voice in the darkness had been rather gruff, like a man well along in his thirties, but he showed in the lamplight to be a full ten years younger than the sound of his voice suggested. He was a big-boned youth, with lean, rather handsome features. Plainly he worshipped the girl, for his eyes never left her, as she moved deftly around the kitchen.

"Suppose," he suggested, "that we take a cup of coffee up to your father? He ought to like it . . . a plumb cold, windy night like this!"

The suggestion brought a quick dissent from Nelly. No one ever bothered her father during the night, she said, particularly during the period when he was awake.

"Because it makes him terrible nervous," she explained to her guest. "Mother always told me that. They always had separate rooms. Seems that he wants to be alone from one to three with his books."

But Oliver Cutting shook his head. This was entirely too fanciful to suit him. A man who could refuse hot coffee on such a night as this was simply not human. And so convinced was he that Nelly gave way.

"Because," she said, "I've never tried, and so you may be right."

They went up the stairs together; Nelly took

the coffee and Oliver Cutting carried the light. For his part Oliver was rejoiced at an opportunity to appear in what he felt sure would be a favorable light before the stern master of the Camden Ranch and the father of Nelly. A draft was stirring in the hall, and it tossed the flame in the throat of the lamp chimney, and by that leaping light Cutting paused and with a faint chuckle faced the girl.

"Say, this is like last week when the posse sneaked up on the Graven house . . . and bagged nothing!"

"Do you mean when they were trying to locate the counterfeiters?"

"Yes, that was it."

They stood before the door, and Cutting, with another smile over his shoulder at the girl, raised his hand and rapped heavily three times, a solemn rap with a slight interval between each blow of the knuckles. The results were surprising. There came a strange strangling gasp from the interior of the room, a very faint and muffled sound, and at the same instant the light was extinguished, and the door was no longer outlined by the thin penciling of yellow light. The floor quivered with the impact of some one leaping violently to one side or the other. Then, instead of footfalls approaching to open the door, there was utter silence.

Outside the door the two young people gaped at each other in amazement.

"Dad," cried the girl, "it's only I!"

There was a moment of delay, and then a hoarse voice asked from the far side of the room: "Is there no one with you?"

"Only Oliver Cutting."

"Ah!"

At length the footfalls crossed the room, and they heard the grate of double bolts being drawn; then silently the door was drawn slowly open upon well-oiled hinges. It continued to sway gradually back, but to the surprise of Cutting it did not reveal the form of the rancher. The light from his lamp shone steadily into the black void of the room and struck on the shutters of the opposite window.

"What happened?" cried Nelly hastily.

"The wind blew my lamp out, that's all," he said.

He spoke from the side of the doorway. He had simply started the door to swinging, and then he had slipped to the side. No one entering could have looked for him here. It was simply the weight of the door which had caused it to open after the bolts were drawn. Now the rancher stepped into the gap and fixed upon Oliver a stern and searching gaze.

The face of William Camden was almost unbelievably altered. He was known throughout the countryside as a stern and forbidding man, but his manners were much milder than his appearance. People, it might be said, had always waited for an outburst which would reveal the real and violent nature of the man; but that revelation had never come, and to Cutting the momentary glimpse of the pale, set face and the piercing eyes was like the sight of an expected ghost. It reduced him to silence.

"We brought up some coffee for you, Dad," the girl said, "because it's so cold, and Oliver thought. . . ."

"I never drink coffee this time of night. You ought to know that," responded her father.

"But . . . ," she began to protest.

"There are no 'buts' about it. That's my rule. Don't forget it again. Good night to you both!"

And so saying he reached for the door. He did not reach for it with his right hand, although this was the nearer, but he half turned his body without withdrawing his eyes from the face of Cutting and, taking the edge of the door with his left hand, he swung it shut. It struck against the jamb with a surprising weight that made the floor quiver again. "Well," said Oliver Cutting, as they turned back down the hall, "well . . . I dunno what to say, Nelly. He sure was angry, wasn't he? And what about?"

"Angry because we interrupted him, I suppose," she said. "Perhaps he had the chimney off the lamp, trimming the wick, and the start you gave him with the knock at the door let the light go out and. . . ."

She paused. Even in her own ear the explanation was a feeble and unsatisfactory one.

"I guess that must be it," said Oliver Cutting in agreement.

Glad that he was so easily persuaded, she looked askance at him and encountered exactly the same sort of a side glance directed at her. She knew at once that he believed what she had said no more than she did.

"But what *could* have been the matter?" she asked impulsively in the kitchen, when they had returned.

"No matter what may be," said Cutting with undue solemnity, "I sure ain't going to ask any special questions, and I ain't going to repeat what I've seen and heard tonight!"

II

"A Daughter's Doubts"

It was only after he had left that the import of his strange solemnity came home to her. Oliver Cutting not long before had decided to use some of his spare time by becoming a special deputy to the sheriff to assist him in the labor of running down the counterfeiters who had been traced as far as these mountains, but the clues to whom disappeared in this district. The very week before there had been a false alarm about a hot, new trail that started the sheriff and his band into the hills, where they had thrown their net around a deserted house and finally closed upon it, only to discover that there was nothing whatever inside of it except the ashes of fires started by tramps who had taken advantage of that shelter.

But Oliver Cutting had returned with exciting tales of the expedition, and what they hoped eventually to accomplish. No doubt, then, it was in the capacity of an officer of the law that he had taken it upon himself to speak as solemnly about her father. In a single word he suspected that William Camden, her own father, was the long-sought criminal, or the head of the band, and that the regular midnight work of the rancher was no less than the work of making illegal paper money to be "pushed" elsewhere and by others!

Nelly Camden uttered a moan of terror and dismay at this thought, and the moan was echoed by the sound of the wind outside in the night. And then she began to look back over her knowledge of her father. It was like seeing a stranger. All of her life she had been attributing to him emotions of kindness, tenderness, of which he had never given a sign, now that she came to think of it. His manner to everyone, including herself, had been as cold as chilled steel. Was it because he was covering the secret life of a criminal?

She could remember now that whenever there was a great need for money, it was always forthcoming. When other ranchers in the vicinity suffered in seasons of poor grass and falling prices, William Camden had always a sufficient supply of cash to float him through the crisis. Perhaps it was because he had piled up savings in the interim of good seasons, but she could not help reverting to the suspicion which Oliver Cutting had obliquely cast at him. That was an easy source from which to draw to meet an emergency. And, as the wretched gloom of this suspicion grew on her, she tore her mind away from it and went back to the one impassioned recollection of her father. It was at the death of her mother, an event which had occurred in her childhood, and which was in her eyes entirely obscured by the memory of her father's wild grief. Sometimes that picture of the big man on his knees by the deathbed flashed back on her in odd places in the middle of the day, and always with a blinding light that filled her mind. Of the mother, indeed, she remembered practically nothing; but the grief of her stern father on that occasion had built up by inference the picture of a lovely saint. The portrait which she had showed a beautiful face, and for the rest it was pleasant and easy to guess. From William Camden himself she had never been able to draw a single scrap of knowledge. Quiet as he was about most things, on the subject of his dead wife his lips were absolutely sealed. That he had feeling, she could not doubt. But often she felt that upon that point only there was emotion in his heart, and all the rest of his nature was a desert so far as gentleness went. Never a caress of a pleasant word fell upon her ear from the end of one day to the next.

Was it not because he was constantly defying the law and silently living in steady danger? She let her thoughts go to his room, the bleak, empty chamber, with only the single row of well-worn books above the mantelpiece, the fireplace in which no fire was ever lighted, and the rugless floor, the plain wooden table. There was a built-in cupboard at one end, however, which she had never seen opened. What might the contents of that cupboard be?

It was not that she gave herself over to constant brooding and instantly believed the worst about William Camden. For while she half accepted the suspicions of Oliver Cutting, yet she fought against the self-acceptance of them with all of her might. Her determination, first and last, was that she would do her best to prove an ally of her father in the time of crisis. That time, she felt, had come to him. For with one man dubious about the honesty of the rancher, others would soon fall into the same attitude.

But suppose that the light of the lamp from the hall had penetrated more fully into the room and showed the work at which her father had been engaged at the table? Would they have found small plates, ink, paper, and all the utensils which Oliver Cutting had told her were the tools of the counterfeiter? She saw a strange picture of them, a picture made up of a thousand indistinct parts. They were scattered before William Camden on the table, with the light of the lamp shining over them and he at work upon them, striking off the impressions of money which only an expert's eye could distinguish from the honest greenback. Then, in a swift revolt, she told herself that there was too great a soul in her father for a thief, no matter what direction that thievery took.

It was in such a conflict of the emotions that she tired herself that night and finally fell into a short sleep which was broken by the jangle of the alarm clock calling her to a gray and cheerless dawn. She rose at once.

Her father kept up one rather strange custom for that part of the country. He did not eat his breakfast with the hired hands. The Chinese cook ministered to the men's needs in the long dining hall which adjoined the bunkhouse. But in a separate kitchen his own daughter cooked the family breakfast, just as her mother had cooked it in the years before.

This morning she expected that it would be difficult to meet him with a smile and sit cheerfully opposite him. But she found that he was not the least altered. It was the same square-jawed, deeply seamed face, with the mop of uncombable gray hair above it. He ate in silence, as always, nor did he refer to the evening before and the interruption, but when his second cup of coffee was finished he simply asked if anyone had come to apply for work since he had sent to town the day before to have an experienced hand sent out to him.

"No one will be coming out in this sort of weather, I guess," she said. "Look how it's blowing!"

Just then the wind carried icy gusts of rain, sometimes frozen to hail, and at all times cold and stinging the skin. These gusts crashed in volleys against the windowpanes and left a coating of water that made all outside misty and blurred. To this scene she pointed as she spoke, but William Camden turned an imperturbable face toward the storm.

"That's nothing," he said. "When a man wants something, weather ain't going to turn him back. And when you find a man that weather will turn back you can put down your money, Nell, that he ain't any good. I said for some good men to be sent out here, and I'd pick the best of 'em; and I said for 'em to ride their own hosses out here. If nobody shows up, it means that I don't want them that would have come if the day had been fair."

It was an extraordinary long speech for him. He now rose from the table and stood close to the window, a broad, strong man, wearing his revolver unusually low, for the simple reason that his hands hung far down at the end of long arms. Standing up he was not more than an average height; sitting down, his shoulders were level with the shoulders of a man six feet and three inches in height.

Nelly Camden sipped her coffee and watched him sadly, curiously. Often before she had felt that there could really be no tie between them, he was so constantly aloof. Now that she suspected him of crimes which would put him in grim peril, he seemed suddenly nearer and dearer to her, for reasons which she could not understand.

Someone tapped at the kitchen door.

"Who can it be?" she murmured as she rose to answer the knock.

"A man come out to ask for a job," answered her father at once.

At that instant a freshening gust caught the house and shook it, as a teacher shakes a naughty boy. The very stove rattled in the kitchen. Surely, she thought, only a man who had no mercy on his horse would ride out the trail from town, eight miles uphill and down on such a morning! It would mean starting before dawn to arrive at such an hour in the morning.

She opened the door. Before her stood a very tall man, with a very wet, brown face.

"I've heard some talk about a job out this way, ma'am," he said. "Can I talk to the boss about it?"

And, while he waited for her answer, he raised to his lips a cigarette which, by some miracle, he kept lighted in spite of the downpour. He sheltered it deftly, under palm and fingers, and then blew forth a thin mist of smoke which the wind wrenched into a myriad odd forms and then caused to vanish. Her father had been right. There were men who would face even such weather as this and think nothing at all of it! "Come in," she said.

He stepped past her and threw back his slicker from his shoulders and stood there, dripping on the kitchen floor. Once inside the room, for some reason he seemed much larger than he had been outside. As she turned from closing the door, she saw that the back of his neck was red-black, as that skin only becomes through a whole lifetime of exposure.

"This way," she said and pointed through the door.

He went forward with a long stride, but she noted and was surprised by the lightness with which his feet struck the floor. Also there was none of the wobbling clumsiness to the gait that there usually is in a cowpuncher bred to the ways of the saddle and used to walking a mile to saddle a horse and ride a furlong.

"Are you Mr. Camden?" she heard his strong voice asking in the next room. "I'm Joe Noyes. I've heard tell you want help out here."

Here she glanced out the back window from the kitchen and saw huddled against the wall of the bunkhouse, only partially shielded from the wind and the rain, a miserable, bunched-up cow pony, with a bald, white mark across his face.

III

"Block the Door"

She knew instantly and with a perfect surety that this was the horse which had passed her and Oliver the night before, and this was the tall rider who had asked the question of them and then spurred away into the night before Oliver could open a conversation with him. It struck her cold, though she could not tell why. But she wanted to get to her father at once and warn him that there was an impending danger — that she felt it in her soul, the presage of evil to come.

In the meantime she heard them talking, blunt-mannered men, equally.

"Where you been working?"

"Any place I could get a job."

Are you going to stay on steady?"

"If I like the place, I might stay a season."

"No more'n that?"

"One round of calves being born and cows being sold . . . ain't that long enough for a man to stay?"

She knew that the 'punchers often thought in this manner, but she had never before overheard one speaking his mind to an employer. Usually they kept their grumblings to themselves. Now she changed her position in the hope that through the kitchen door she could catch the eye of her father and dissuade him from hiring the new man.

Moving in this fashion, she brought them into view. Standing over her father the height of the stranger was more apparent than before. But whether his rangy, sinewy strength and activity, or the more solid bulk of her father, were the more formidable, she could not decide. The contrast made them both seem like fine fighters, the bulldog type and the wolf type. Victory might incline according to the conditions under which they fought. At close quarters she could not conceive her father being overcome.

She roused herself with a start as she became aware that she was making such comparisons. What earthly purpose was served in wondering what the outcome of a mortal combat between the two would be? Of course there could never be any real trouble and yet, no sooner had she convinced herself through reason that all was well, than telltale instinct rose hot in her and declared that there was danger ahead.

"You come out with me," her father was saying. "I try out all my hands before I hire 'em."

The other shook his head.

"I don't do tricks," he said. "Not to please no man."

Her father hesitated. Plainly he was of two minds whether to send this independent spirit on his way or to test him farther. At length he said, "You better come along. I ain't going to ask you to show off, but I got to make sure that the gent that works for me can do two or three things pretty well . . . you see? First he's got to be able to handle a rope, and then he's got to sit a saddle pretty well, because my saddle stock ain't pets, and finally I like to see 'em mean with a gun, because the coyotes are plumb nauseating the way they herd on my range."

"All right," said the other after a moment of serious thought which he employed in rolling a cigarette and staring boldly at William Camden, "I'll go along."

"Have you had breakfast?"

"No."

A shadowy smile flitted for an instant across the stern lips of her father. It was plain to be seen that he was pleased for having discerned this truth.

"Go out to the cook and tell him you're ready to chow."

Joe Noyes nodded and then turned his back and slunk across the kitchen, with that singular long light step which she had noticed before. In spite of herself she could not help shrinking a little from his path and, as she did so, he turned his head suddenly toward her and his eyes met hers with a baleful flash.

It was only a glint, nothing that could be described, and yet it left her weak and, the moment the door had closed on him, sent her swiftly to her father.

"Dad," she said, "you mustn't keep him!"

Camden busied himself in the filling of his pipe without deigning to reply. So she hurried on with her account of how she and Oliver Cutting had passed the solitary horseman on the trail home after midnight, and how they had seen him halt his horse and inquire about the house in the hollow, and how, after he had heard the name of the owner of the house, he had spurred away through the storm without staying to thank them for the information he had received. Where had he gone that night? If he wanted shelter, why had he not gone directly to the ranch house on a night when no one with a heart could have refused him food and a bed? Why, last of all, had he chosen to ride all this distance out to their ranch the following morning, when there was a shortage of men through the countryside, and he could have secured employment on some place much nearer to the town, at equal or better wages than Camden would pay?

She poured out these questions tersely, one after another, and her father listened with a profound interest, so it seemed to her, but at the end of her speech he simply replied: "A gent that will ride ten miles on a morning like this, without breakfast and with nothing but cigarettes to keep him going, is the sort of a man that I want. Besides, Nell, don't you think that he talked rather queer talk for a man that really wanted a place that bad?"

It was a longer answer than he usually made. It almost approached an argument, and she found that it was hard to find a ready response to make to him. But when the tall stranger came back to the house after he had finished his breakfast in a surprisingly short time, she decided that she must find out more about him by watching his trial. Accordingly she waited until the two had sauntered off together and, when they disappeared in their wet raincoats around the edge of the first long shed, she herself, wrapped from head to feet in a long slicker, followed to make her observations at close range.

It was not hard to spy on them. The wind was beating from the far side of the shed, and therefore all the noise of her approach was muffled. Crouched inside the sliding door of the barn, she looked out and saw them at work.

The test for roping came first. A wild young steer was loosed into a round corral. He had been taken up for feeding and care because of a deep, barbed-wire cut, and on such fare he had grown as vicious as any spoiled pet. Now, enraged by being loosed into the cold storm, the steer plunged here and there, shaking his long horns and bellowing. Joe Noyes presently followed and climbed onto the top rail of the fence and sat there, the dangling rope coiled in one hand. The steer made a rush at him, but he sat secure, though his whole body quivered, as the big beast crashed into the fence just below him.

The steer, shaking his bruised head, turned and trotted in the opposite direction. Would the rope be tossed now? No, instead of throwing the rope,

Joe Noyes swung over the fence and dropped lightly into the enclosure. He walked straight after the steer and had almost reached the center of the ring before the latter realized that the man was at his mercy.

The moment that knowledge came to him, however, he whirled with incredible agility, considering his bulk, and darted for Noyes, while Nell hardly restrained a cry of warning and horror. She looked to her father on the opposite side of the fence; now even that imperturbable warrior had clenched his hands, though he would not draw his revolver to protect the man in the corral.

The latter, however, seemed undismayed. He stood at ease, his left hand resting on his hip, the rope idle at his side, until the rushing steer was two paces away and the head with the wide-branching horns went down. Then like a flash he leaped to one side. It was a slinking, panther-like bound, such as she would have expected from him, having seen him walk across the floor of the kitchen. Even that leap did not carry him entirely clear, and he had to twist his body to make the sharp horn slide safely past his ribs.

The steer with a roar of rage braced himself to come to a stop and wheel again at the victim, but now Joe Noyes was prepared to act. The rope came to snaky life in his hand. Then the noose shot forward, close to the ground. It fell, and then it flicked up again from the muddy surface and two legs of the steer on the left side were whipped together.

Down went the giant, spurting afar the water from several little surface pools. Noyes, with a twist or two, worked the rope loose. Then he stepped close and raked his long spur across the hip of the steer. The latter sprang bellowing to its feet, but now all the fight was gone from it. A blow of the rope along its flank sent it scurrying through the gate which the rancher now swung open. Noyes approached his would-be employer, coiling his rope.

"I've sure messed up this rope," was all he said.

The wind blew the words to her in fragments of sound which she had to piece together. But now, looking at him with new eyes, she discovered what she had failed to notice in her previous excitement, that he had not taken off his slicker to fight the steer. Her admiration turned to wonder. And she saw the pipe in William Camden's mouth tilt up to a sharp angle, a sure sign that he was greatly moved by what he had seen.

"That's enough rope work," he said. "I guess you're handy enough with a rope to suit me. And now about riding, Noyes . . . d'you mind stepping into yonder barn and saddling that old brown hoss in there?"

The tall man nodded, disappeared into the designated shed, and presently a storm of wild noises issued from the interior, squealing, tremendous kicks that set the side of the shed quivering, and the snarling voice of a furious man. Then all the noise stopped abruptly.

After a moment old Brownie, celebrated in

seven counties for his prowess under the saddle and his skill in tossing the most expert riders into the air, came trotting peacefully out of the door of the shed, throwing his head and with his ears glued wrathfully back to his neck, but making not the slightest effort to buck the rider out of the saddle.

Noyes rode the horse up to the rancher who was now frankly astonished.

"Plumb sorry, Camden," said the 'puncher. "I guess I can't do any demonstrating on this old hoss. He changes his mind about showing off, or maybe I got the wrong hoss after all?"

His face was not nearly so innocent as his voice and his words. His eyes were gleaming; a faint smile was twitching at the corners of his lips. Suddenly she saw in him something more than the mysteriously sinister stranger. For now under the mask he was simply a mischievous boy looking for trouble, and he was delighted beyond words because he had found it. And in that instant of revelation she saw for the first time that he was some half dozen years, at least, younger than she had hitherto thought him. For, whereas she had been putting him down as thirty-one or thirty-two, she now perceived that he could not be more than twenty-five at the most, though a hard life had made him seem much more mature.

The grin disappeared on the 'puncher's face, as the rancher admitted that Brownie was in fact the trail horse, and Camden even went so far as to say that Noyes was the first to ride the old warrior into subjection.

"And now about the shooting, Noyes. Do you want to go in out of the rain for that?"

"When it comes to shooting," said Noyes, the words clipped off short at his lips by a fierce gust of the wind, so that they were blown strangely to the ears of the girl, "a gent can't pick his weather. I'll try my chances now. What's the target?"

"Why, you might try that post across yonder. That one with the white knot near the top and the two nails sticking up."

"That's a pretty long shot and a pretty small target," said the new cowpuncher gloomily. "Howsomever I'll try it!"

Nelly herself craned her head so that, through the crack behind which she stooped, she could make out the post with the two nails sticking up above. Then she saw the long revolver come into the hand of Noyes.

"Take your time," said Camden. "I'd rather have accuracy than speed any day."

Noyes raised the gun, steadied it for a long moment, while Nelly saw the barrel beaded by the falling of the rain. Then it exploded, but no hole was torn through the post by the big slug.

"Missed, confound it!" cried Noyes. "But this time I'll get it!"

The gun went off again. Again the post escaped, but now Nelly saw that both of the nails had disappeared from the top of the post.

"Lemme have another try," cried the cowpuncher, apparently very angry.

"Two tries is enough, and more than a gent usually gets at a coyote," said Camden, smiling. "But I guess you're good enough with a rope and a hoss to make up for it . . . if you know cows."

"I know 'em pretty fair. Matter of fact, I ain't anything to talk about with a gun, partner."

His failure seemed to have softened him. He was almost apologetic. And now he turned Brownie away, rode him back to the barn from which he had been taken, and rejoined the stolid form of the rancher.

"We'll cut back for the house and talk about wages," said her father, and they started straight for the shed where Nelly was hidden. She had barely time to understand that they intended to take a short cut through her shed, and then she hid herself. The next moment they were in the shed, walking past the long line of stalls, when suddenly she heard her father cry out: "We've got him, sheriff! Block the door!"

IV

"Conspirators"

Peering over the top of the haymow in which she was buried, she saw that the words had a magic effect upon the tall man. He sprung to one side, crouching, so that in an instant he was sprawling against the side of the barn. His revolver was out of its holster, and another gun, hitherto concealed, had come into his left hand. So swiftly had he moved that his hat had blown off and a quantity of long blond hair tumbled about his face or stood on end, waving in the draft. One weapon was directed squarely at her father, and the other pointed toward the far end of the shed. As for William Camden, he stood with both his arms thrust stiffly above his head.

The scream had not yet passed her lips when she heard her father say quietly: "I thought so, but I had to make sure. Sorry I had to put you through this, Noyes."

Noyes slowly uncoiled his length and stood up by the wall of the shed, his face colorless, or rather a dirty gray like ashes which have been wet by the rain. His gun was still pointed at her father.

"Camden," he said, "you came within a wink

of death that time. You mean to say that's your idea of a joke?"

"What's wrong with it?" asked her father calmly, now lowering his arms. "What have you to fear from a sheriff?"

"Nothing," answered the tall man sullenly, "but I ain't going to be cornered . . . not even by them that got the law behind 'em. Is that straight, Camden? As for you and your job, to the devil with both! I'm on my way to some place where they got less sense of humor and more sense of another kind!"

Plainly he was in a raging fury. Only the fact that Camden was a middle-aged man, she could see, was protecting him from attack. But to her surprise, as her father stepped back, he was smiling faintly and nodding toward the younger man, as though he approved of him hugely.

"You've played fool by trying to draw the wool over my eyes, Noyes," he said.

Noyes started violently.

"What d'you mean by that? What d'you think that you know about me?"

"I know," said the rancher, "that when you pretended to miss that post, you knocked off a nail at each shot."

Noyes fell back a step and jammed his revolver into the holster. Then, with a movement at once so easy and so swift that she could not follow it, he stowed the other revolver somewhere on his person inside his coat.

"When a man has to pretend to be a worse shot

than he is," said Camden, "there's usually a serious reason for it. That was why I played the little trick on you."

"Well," said Noyes, "nothing come of it. We'll balance that breakfast against that trick and call it quits. So long!"

"Wait a minute!"

The rancher stepped up to his tall cowpuncher and touched his shoulder.

"I never ask questions," he said, "when I think that they might be hard to answer. You understand?"

The tall man halted and stared down at him.

"Look here," he said, "what are you driving at?"

"Nothing," said the rancher.

Joe Noyes slowly rolled a cigarette and, as he worked his fingers, he stared deliberately into the face of Camden until the girl wondered how her father could endure the strain of that test. But endure it he did, and finally Noyes nodded and lighted his smoke.

"We won't worry about the wages," he said. "Where do I start in working?"

So amazed was Nelly by the sudden pacification that she did not hear the rejoinder of her father and, when the two had gone out of the shed, she slipped away and circled back to the house as quickly as she could.

It was not half an hour later that she confronted her father.

"How did the test come out?" she asked as quietly as she could. "I hope you don't like him

". . . I hope you don't intend to keep him, Dad."

"Hm," replied William Camden.

"Dad," she cried, "there's something in a woman's intuition. He's going to be dangerous to you, and. . . ."

She stopped, for she was recalling again the boyish and mischievous face which had suddenly peered out at her when he was on the back of Brownie. Was she not wrong after all?

"He suits me. He ain't a ladies' man, but I ain't no lady," replied William Camden, and so the matter was closed.

So it was closed for Camden, but not for Nelly. All that day what she had seen and heard haunted her, and she was glad when the weather cleared shortly after noon, and Oliver Cutting rode up to the ranch house. She was so glad, indeed, that she had the door open and was smiling at him, while he was still in the act of throwing his reins. That smile made Oliver crimson to the hair. He fairly leaped from the saddle and came to her with his eyes on fire.

Nelly bit her lip in her vexation. It was not the first time that she had been taught that she must not be too cordial. She had hardly rounded out of the period of childhood before a smile and a touch of kindliness on her part was apt to bring forth a proposal of marriage from the nearest man. Now she carefully donned a manner of perfect indifference, which had the effect on Oliver of a violently used curb on a horse with a tender mouth.

At least she knew him well enough to break in at once upon her desire. She took him through the house and out to the small pasture near the corrals. He followed, much mystified.

"Look yonder," she said. "D'you see that bald-faced pinto yonder near the fence?"

"The one that just kicked at the bay mare? Yes."

"D'you recognize it, Oliver?"

"Never saw it before."

"But you did . . . last night."

"You mean the man we passed in the rain? How the deuce can that be, Nell?"

"It's a fact. He came riding out from town this morning and asked for a place. He'd heard in town that we needed another hand, and he was so anxious to get the place that he came out without his breakfast. Two other men came out later in the day, but Joe Noyes . . . that's his name . . . had the job long before them."

Here Oliver faced squarely toward her.

"What's all this driving at?" he asked quickly.

"It's driving at this," she answered him. "I don't like the looks of our new man. He may be all right, but he looks like sudden death to me if anybody should have trouble with him."

Oliver started and then laughed.

"That might worry me if your father wasn't the sort of a gent that he is," he declared. "But a man that could get the upper hand of William Camden . . . why, Nell, anybody will tell you that it can't be done. Too many have tried it in the old days, and it always failed to work out."

"In the old days . . . yes! I know he has a terrible reputation because of the fights that he had when he was a young man. But he's no longer young, Oliver. He still practices with his guns, and he still keeps in training, as he calls it, but in spite of that he isn't as quick or as strong as he once was, and. . . ."

"That's nonsense, Nell, really. You're letting your scare run away with you. Just the reputation of your father is enough to stop the worst of 'em."

"Oliver," said the girl with great solemnity, "I give you my word of honor that no kind of a reputation will ever stop this Joe Noyes, if he makes up his mind to do a thing."

"As bad as that?" asked Oliver Cutting.

"Oliver, am I apt to be scary?"

"No," he admitted a little more soberly, "you aren't. But go on about him. Tell me the rest."

"I can't tell you everything. What I found out was that he was a wonderful shot, a fine rider, and a good hand with a rope."

"Humph!" grinned Oliver, not impressed.

"I tell you," she said fervently, "that he's so very good with a gun that my father is keeping him simply for that reason . . . because he says that Joe Noyes is so hard a man that he wants to have him on the ranch."

"It isn't the first hard man your father has hired. They're all a tough lot. He seems to like to have them come that way."

"I know that. But the others are simply . . .

well, simply children compared with this Noyes. Oliver, he gives me a queer, scared feeling, partly as though he were being hunted and watching for somebody to come on his trail, and partly as though he were *hunting!* You see?"

"I sort of follow your drift. If that's the case, I'm ready to do anything I can, Nell, but I don't just see what you think I can do."

"You can find out about him."

"What?"

"Aren't you a policeman, or something like that now? Weren't you telling me the other day that you could look up the records of most of the men who had committed crimes?"

"Yes, there's a whole stack of photographs and records in the sheriff's office. He's right up to date, Sheriff Crosby is!"

"Now wait till you see Joe Noyes, then look up the record."

"I could do that."

"I know he's stepped on the toes of the law at some time and some place."

She recounted briefly the scene which she had witnessed between her father and the new hand in the barn, and the shooting at the post which she had witnessed previously. Before she had finished, Oliver Cutting was on his toes with excitement.

"And yet," concluded the girl, "there's something about him that's attractive. I'm almost sorry, now, that I've told you about him. He gives you just a glimpse now and then that makes you think he's simply a boy that's got into trouble and ought to be taken care of."

Oliver Cutting raised his hand to stop.

"That's enough of that line of talk," he said. "I've heard the sheriff talk. He says that every one of the really big criminals has that same sort of an attraction, a kind of irresponsibility that makes other folks want to look after them and take care of them. You let me get on the trail of this new hand!"

V

"A Knock at Her Door"

She felt immensely comforted and secure after Oliver cantered his horse away that evening, having seen Joe Noyes come in from work to the bunkhouse.

"I can remember that face of his among a thousand," he declared, "if the camera gets anything of his expression. I'll drop down to the sheriff's office this evening and run through the pictures and see what I can see."

With the feeling that they were greatly secured from all possible danger from Joe Noyes, since work was under way to discover what his past might have been, Nell was singing when she turned from the window as Oliver dropped out of view over the first hill along the road.

In the meantime sounds of uproar rose from the bunkhouse, the long, low building, with the bunk room at one end and the dining hall and kitchen at the other, fairly bulging with noise of shouting and laughter and a thin, raw edge of music piercing through the tumult. It was a most unusual sound at a most unusual time. Before dinner the 'punchers were a gloomy, depressed lot, very apt to dwell upon grievances and the troubles of the day. Only liquor, she felt, could explain this hubbub.

To make sure she went out to the kitchen, and there she found Wong, the Chinese cook, humming in a quaint fashion as he moved about his work among the big pots and kettles. He even smiled at her when she came in, and as a rule Wong had nothing but scowls for those who intruded upon his own domain. Opening the door to the dining room she discovered the cause of the disturbance, by looking the whole length of the dining room and so into the bunkhouse beyond. For from this the uproar issued, and now through the open door of the bunkhouse she made out Joe Noyes seated upon a stool, with a mouth organ at his lips, his cheeks puffed with the loudest possible blowing, and beating out the time with the thumping of his heel against the floor. Around him pirouetted half a dozen cowpunchers, laughing and shouting and singing. There was no liquor in sight, but at this moment Noyes ceased his efforts, threw back his head, and broke into the heartiest laughter.

Nell closed the door and went slowly back toward the house. It was another and a most interesting side light upon the character of the new hand. Dangerous she had that morning seen him demonstrated to be. But this was a sure proof of the thoughtless and boyish light-heartedness which she had guessed at before.

What could she make of such a man as this? And might it not well be that in raking up the coals of his past, she might be doing him an unnecessary wrong? If her father were satisfied with the new hand, she certainly might safely accept his judgment.

That evening at the supper table she studied her father as she had never studied him before. It seemed to the girl that he had actually changed during the past twenty-four hours, and yet she knew that it was simply because she was looking at him with a new and more critical eye. She had never before deliberately sat down to analyze the lines which marked his face, the full, rather staring eye, the straight line of the mouth, habitually compressed, and the lifted brows. She had always felt him too forbidding to be looked upon closely. Altogether he gave the effect of a man terribly worn. He was forty-eight years old, she knew, but at first glance he seemed at least a dozen years older. To be sure a natural and gigantic strength had not yet deserted him, and he was still shrouded by a terrible reputation which made every man in the neighboring mountains look up to him in time of battle; but that great strength was barely resisting the ravages of time. In a short period he might begin to crumble.

These thoughts crowded upon her so insistently that she felt a breathless expectation growing upon her during the meal. He was even more than usually silent tonight, and after she had cleared away the dishes, instead of going at once to his room or else sitting in the big library reading, he simply drew up a chair beside the window, like one who looks out upon the scene beyond — though the windowpane now presented, with the reflection of the lamplight in it, an impenetrable wall of glossy black.

And seeing him seated before that window, through which he could not look, a great pity for him welled in the breast of Nell. She remembered that he had no friends. So far as kindly companionship was concerned, that window was typical of the blank wall of the world to him. He sat there for a long time, unmoving, with his head thrown back.

When she finally came in from the kitchen, her work finished for the day, she thought that he must have fallen asleep, something which he had never done before his hour of retirement. But when she tiptoed around to a view of his profile, she saw a knotted and twisted face, as though he fought silently against some internal agony.

The sight of that pain awed and frightened her. Yet she dared to presume more than she ever had before in her life. She came up behind him and rested her arms upon the back of his chair.

"Dad," she said, "you're in trouble. What am I good for if I'm not good to help you when you need help?"

She expected either silence or a curt dismissal, with a hint that he could manage his affairs without her assistance. But to her speechless amazement he answered in a strangely broken voice: "Aye, Nell, in great danger . . . great danger!"

That almost groaning tone reverberated

through her very heart. It was the accent of a man whose strength is worn away, and who is about to sink and give up the struggle. It paralyzed her, so that she could neither speak nor move. It was very much as a worshiper might have felt when addressing a statue, if the statue actually responded in intelligible words.

While it brought her father closer to her in a rush of affection, it also dazed and bewildered her. And now his hand rose and clasped hers, where it hung just above his shoulder. He turned his head and pressed that soft hand against his wrinkled forehead, pressed it almost fiercely, and then started up suddenly from his chair, as though bitterly ashamed of this weakness. He threw a good night to her, as he left the room, without turning, and she heard his steps go up the stairs slowly, the boards creaking solemnly under his great weight.

When she was able to move, she flew after him and overtook him when his hand was on the knob of his door.

"Oh, Dad," she pleaded, panting, "if there's danger, we have friends who will come to our help!"

He turned to her with a black scowl.

"Look here," he said, "there'll be no running about telling folks what I may have said to you. Danger? I said that there was danger, but it's nothing to be talked about, and it's nothing that all the men in the world could help. Mind that, and don't let me catch you chattering about it to that young fool, Cutting."

He turned his back partly upon her, and then for the second time that evening he startled her. He faced her again with a sudden movement and took her in his arms. She felt the ruins of that glorious strength holding her. In the dim hall light his features were softened, so that she could imagine him as a young man, such a man as even that pretty mother of hers might conceivably have married.

"Ah, Nell," he said, "it ain't what we work for that we get. All I've worked for ain't mine . . . it don't count, the ranch or nothing that's on it. All that I have is you. Good night, dear!"

He kissed her forehead and was striding into his room and slamming the door in her face before words came to her. Then she pressed close to that door and with her face against it wept silently. If only she could tell him what she suspected . . . what she almost knew to be true . . . about those criminal labors which occupied him in the middle of every night! If only she could entreat him to share the secret with her and let her bury the implements for once and forever!

But she remembered with what a blank indifference he had received her hints which she dropped during the course of the day about the industry of the new sheriff and his labors to run down the counterfeiters. If he could assume such a mask of carelessness in the face of her hints, she dared not speak of what she suspected.

Presently she went back to her own room. She

was possessed with that same joyous sorrow with which men go from the witnessing of a tragedy upon the stage. The glimpse of the harrowing sadness of her father had been so unexpectedly combined with the first true show of tenderness toward her, that her spirit was drawn in two ways, like a warm sun shining on a day of cold winds.

Afterward she lay in her bed, with a great, kind resolve growing in her to find a way to serve that grim-faced man and make his happiness. In the midst of that resolution sleep poured over her.

She wakened as suddenly as though a voice had called loudly at her ear. Lying with prickling skin and with a horrible feeling that a moment before something had been moving in the room, she dared not move for a time. Indeed she was incapable of it. But at length she cast off the torpor and, reaching to the bedside table, she found and lighted a match. She cupped her hands and directed a glow of light toward the window and then toward the door.

Both were exactly as she had left them. She then, with the last flame of the match, examined the clock. It was exactly two. Her mind flashed back to the same hour of the night before when the stove had been roaring in the kitchen and the coffeepot was smoking fragrantly upon it. That memory restored her calm. She explained the terror in which she had wakened as the effect of some hideous nightmare which she had forgotten.

Sleep was once more spreading pleasantly over

her when she heard a loud knock down the hall, repeated at regular intervals. Once more her mind darted back to the evening before, when Oliver Cutting had knocked in exactly the same manner and with practically the same rhythm at her father's door. For a moment, in the dismay with which this reflection filled her — for, of course, Oliver could not be in the house again — she lay still in the bed. Then she sprang up, threw a bathrobe around her, and slipped out into the hall.

At the same instant the door of her father's room was thrown open with a crash. She heard his voice shout: "Come now! If there's a dozen of you, finish it now!"

Then she saw William Camden rush out into the passage, with a lantern swinging in one hand and a revolver in the other. He was fully dressed, but his hair was wildly tousled and showed that he had lain down during the first part of the night.

He glared up and down the hall, with an expression so terrific that she feared he had lost his reason. Then he whirled in the opposite direction and ran down the hall with a lightness and speed of which she would not have believed him capable, saving when in a frenzy. He darted down the stairs, and she heard the outer door slam.

In a sudden burst of insight into the working of his mind, she knew that he was going to find Joe Noyes, convinced that the disturbance must in some way have been caused by the new hand. She went to her window and, looking out, could see the lantern swinging toward the bunkhouse, the light gleaming silver on the shallow surface pools which the rain of yesterday had left. Beside the lantern ran a great blotchy shadow.

Her father disappeared into the bunkhouse. The light stirred and grew bright in each of the three windows, as he went the length of the quarters of the hired hands. Then it returned at once. With a great breath of relief she saw him coming back at a slow and regular step, as though his fury had left him as quickly as it had in the first place seized upon him. But she felt that it would be far better if she did not face him while he was in this dangerous mood. She went back to her bed and lay there shivering and listening to his heavy footfall come slowly up the stairs and down the hall until it paused at her room, and there was a heavy knock against her door.

VI

"Bolts and Books"

Unreasoning fear choked her, and she was not able to speak until the knock had been repeated. Then she called to him to enter. The door was flung wide. She stared eagerly toward his face and she made out that the convulsed fury was no longer there, knitting his brows and making his eyes glare. It was still a stern and desperate face that she looked into, but at least the touch of madness was not there.

"Have you heard anything in here?" he asked.

"Nothing," replied the girl.

He raised the lantern and let the light fall full upon her.

"D'you mostly sleep in your bath robe like that?" he asked sarcastically.

She had quite forgotten it as she had slipped into bed again, when she saw him coming back from the bunkhouse.

"You didn't hear me call out a while back?" he asked.

"I . . . yes," she admitted wretchedly.

"Some joker," said her father, "some scoundrel of a practical joker rapped at my door and waked me up!"

"Do you think," she asked, "do you think it could be Noyes?"

He started and looked at her more keenly.

"You're bright for a girl," he said slowly. "You look fast and sharp, Nell. No, it wasn't Noyes. I went out to the bunkhouse and seen him lying there sound asleep . . . and his boots was off and dry! It wasn't Noyes!"

He passed a hand across his forehead and groaned: "I wish it had been! I wish it had been him!"

"But why?" she asked.

"Why? To have it over with, Nell. To get this cursed soul-killing business over with and ended. If it had been Joe Noyes, I could have ended him, or him me and. . . ."

He stopped, glowered at her, as though angered at having spoken too much, and went to the window.

"Nothing in here?" he asked. "Nothing bothered you a while back before you heard me?"

"Nothing," she answered.

He leaned over the window sill and then exclaimed. Instantly she was out of the bed, and leaning beside him she made out a small smudge of fresh mud on the sill, such as might have been made by dragging the sole of a muddy shoe across the wood.

"This is the way he came in," said her father through his teeth. "He's flesh and blood, anyway . . . flesh and blood, God be praised!"

He said this with such a profound sigh of relief

212

that she stared at him, amazed.

"Yonder he climbed up onto the roof of the kitchen. Then he sneaked along and came up the drain pipe, right to the window. . . ."

"But not even a sailor could climb like that, Dad!"

Here he whirled upon her with a gasp and flung the light of the lantern into her face.

"Who's been talking to you about sailors?" he asked.

His lips were trembling, and she saw that his whole body shook with his emotion.

"Nobody's been talking to me," she managed to say.

He glanced at her for another moment and then turned and strode for the door and passed through; presently she heard the door to his own room slam.

Nell sat down on the side of her bed and felt the color come back into her face by the slowest of slow degrees, while she reviewed in detail the strange scenes of that night. What madness was filling the air around their house? What was this talk of gratitude because ghosts were not walking the halls and rapping at doors?

What was the meaning of that start and that abrupt anger when she mentioned the sea? But there was no clue by which she could decipher such mysteries as these. She went back to her bed and lay there for a moment wondering how she could have been so happy two days before, when the very atmosphere which she breathed was already laden with the miseries which were now beginning to break over the home of William Camden.

She could only attempt one feasible explanation of part of it, and that was that her father was being hounded to his grave by the fear of detention in his work as a counterfeiter. This, to be sure, had nothing to do with his singular start and exclamation when she spoke of sailors, and it also had no apparent connection with other parts of his conduct.

To get at a truer explanation, however, she made that night what amounted to a desperate determination, and this was not only to invade the privacy of her father; but the very next morning, when he had ridden out to work, to enter his room and there attempt to open the doors to the sunken cupboard, the contents of which she had never seen.

That morning, when it dawned, found her tired from two short and broken nights of sleep, but William Camden was unchanged. Her own eyes were circled with purple; her color was gone; and her brows was beginning to be crossed with a perpendicular wrinkle between the eyes. It made the unaltered appearance of her father the more remarkable to her.

But then she realized that all of his nights, as far back as she could remember, had been both short and broken. Sleep and rest apparently came to him only in small bits, here and there. And he was used to the interruptions which had worn her out in the space of two days. She watched him ride away to his work that morning, and no sooner was he well out of sight than she stole up to his room to carry out the plan which she had formed the night before. But for the first time she noted two or three unusual things about the room.

In particular she remembered what Oliver Cutting had said about the door being so exceedingly heavy that it would swing open by itself, in spite of a contrary draft. And today for the first time she examined that door particularly. She had long before noted that the door was difficult to handle, comparatively speaking, but she had always attributed this to some stiffness about the hinges. But now looking curiously along the outer edge she saw, where the paint had flaked away, a glint of raw metal.

She examined it more carefully and scratched it with her thumb nail. It appeared to be a slab of fine steel set into the middle of the door, with a thin sheathing of wood upon either side! No wonder, therefore, that when one knocked upon this door, it gave forth the hollow and the booming sound, such as had echoed down the hall on the previous night. But why should that steel be here?

Filled with a new surmise she ran across the room and tried the shutters. There was no question about them. Ordinarily her father handled them, and she did not touch them. But now she found them to be, as she expected, of solid slats of metal! Both the door and the windows to the room were armored so that the slug of a revolver could not penetrate them.

With what a chill feeling of dread, therefore, did she look about her on the once familiar furniture in the room, where it seemed to her that everything was altered. There was no doubt in her tormented mind now. Those armored apertures were to secure the counterfeiter at his work, and in the cupboard, which was sunk into the wall, were the implements with which he worked.

Sternly she went about opening those doors. Oliver Cutting had shown her how to pry up from the bottom of a door and so force doors outward. She did not even need this resource but, working with the bunch of old keys which she had assembled, she finally found one which worked in the lock and turned the bolt.

The doors opened, and with that opening a musty old odor drifted out to her. Then her heart sank. For in the entire cupboard there was only one article, and that was an iron-bound chest of the most solid workmanship, exactly such a thing, she told herself, as a counterfeiter would keep his tools in.

She tried the lid. To her surprise it gave easily and rose under her hand. But when she peered down into the depths she was delighted and surprised to find only a stack of old books covered with that fine sifting of dust which seems to be able to breathe through the smallest apertures in old houses. She raised the upper book. The cover almost fell apart in her hands. She glanced at the contents and found it to be a book on navigation.

Beneath it were more books. She put the *Practical Book of Navigation* back and took out instead a large scroll of paper, very much the dimensions of a diploma. But it unrolled into a large sheet on which was drawn with great care the plans for a sailing ship, *The Lady Nancy.*

She waited to see no more. All of her suspicions in a breath were banished to a mist. Hastily she restored all as she had found it, lowered the lid of the chest, which she now discovered to be marked in faded paint with crossed anchors, and then closed and locked the doors of the cupboard. She turned to see her father standing with folded arms at the entrance to the room.

VII

"Joe Graham"

Silent as he generally was, she had known him to explode into fits of wild and shouting anger, and she expected some such outburst now. She was the more terrified when he crossed the room to her with a quick, uneven step and gripped her wrist. The force of that grip ground the flesh and bruised it against the bones of the wrist. Yet she was so utterly terrified that she felt no pain at that moment. His face was livid — first furious red had rushed up to his temples and then subsided to a smoky purple.

For a moment he could not speak, but at length he forced out the husky words: "What did you find, Nell? It took my daughter to go trailing me like a snake . . . it took my own flesh and blood to put a curse on me! What did you find?"

"Nothing!" she cried. "Oh, Dad, if. . . ."

He cast her arm from him with such violence that it turned her half around.

"You lie!" he snarled at her. "You've spied, and you've . . . but tell me what the name was? Tell me what the name was that you found inside the books? Speak to me!"

"I found no name," she stammered.

"What? Still lying?"

She shrank from him. Fear and rage had combined in his face. It was like madness, and it froze her cold when he stepped nearer to her.

"Only one name," she breathed. "Only . . . *The Lady Nancy*!"

"*The Lady Nancy*!"

He threw up both his hands, as though calling on God to witness his agony or this mockery, and his voice was half sob, half laughter.

"*The Lady Nancy*! You found that?"

He was closer to her again.

"And what else, Nell? What else?"

"Nothing, on my word of honor!"

His excitement was partly abated.

"Nothing?"

"Oh, Dad, try to control yourself . . . you. . . ."

He struck a hand across his face, and the blow seemed to sober him.

"I'm as calm as a lamb," he told her, but the effort to control his voice had only changed it to a ghastly caricature of good-natured speech. "I'm quiet, Nell. I'm speaking gentle and thoughtful to you. I . . . I was only joking before."

She shuddered.

"Don't shrink from me, Nell. Is my own little girl afraid of me?"

Much as his rage had terrified her, his own terror now and his attempts to pacify her were even more awful.

"I'm not afraid," she said slowly. "What it's all about I don't pretend to understand. I won't try to understand . . . not if you don't want me here. Why, I came up . . . it was because . . . but it doesn't make any difference. Only people have begun to notice that you have the light on here at night."

"From one to three? They started in noticing that?"

"Yes."

"Who? Who's noticed it?"

"Oliver Cutting."

"Curse him, is *he* bothering me? Is *he* hounding me? Have I got so old and so low that a yaller hound like that can make me think twice? But he'd better watch his way after this! If he can only. . . ."

"No, no, he means you no harm! As a matter of fact he's trying to hunt down the counterfeiters who. . . ."

"Counterfeiters?"

Suddenly her father broke into uproarious laughter, but it was of a kind that brought no answering smile to her lips.

"Is that all?" he thundered. "Is that why he's been hanging around here?"

"Yes," she said, hugely relieved that he took the accusation so lightly, but wondering vaguely what else could be burdening his soul.

"And maybe that's why *you* came up here, Nell?"

"I . . . Dad, forgive me! Yes, that's why!"

He cast himself into a chair and sat with his head supported in both of his hands for a moment, trembling violently.

"Thank God," he gasped at last. "Go downstairs, Nell. I want to be alone!"

She turned sadly toward the door. If such a charge as counterfeiting could be considered a light one, what was the heinous crime with which he connected his fears of discovery? She had not reached the door when he overtook her hastily and laid his hand on her shoulder.

"Nell!" he whispered.

"Yes, Dad?"

"You've a good memory?"

"I hope so."

"Use that memory now to make you remember that you have to forget. You understand?"

"Yes."

"Don't speak it so easy or so light. Turn your eyes inside and look at your heart. Swear to yourself that you'll forget. *The Lady Nancy* . . . that's a small thing to remember. Make it a small thing to forget. You hear me, Nell?"

"Yes, Dad, I hear you."

She turned back to him and attempted to put her arms around him.

"Oh," she whispered tremulously, "if you knew how I ache to be a help to you . . . if you could only tell me. . . ."

But he stepped back from her.

"I know you. Out of them smiling ways and them bright eyes comes trouble. Your mother had 'em, and trouble came out of her because I thought she was a blessing, and she turned out

221

to be . . . Nell, go downstairs! No, go on outdoors and take a walk. I want to be alone in the house for a while!"

She could only obey him and, going slowly, miserably down the stairs, she told herself that the time had come when she must no longer attempt to understand either her father or any of the strange events in which she was becoming entangled. It was better to go blindly ahead; knowledge might be the worst of all.

She put on a hat and walked out onto the path which led across the field and toward the road from town. For every twenty steps she took she stopped at least once, and so it was half an hour before she reached the side of the road to town and turned and looked sadly back to her father's house.

She was surprised to see that smoke was issuing in a thin stream from the kitchen chimney; and it was a thin smoke which darted up a considerable distance, as if a very quick and hot fire were burning below it. Yet there had been no fire at all in the stove when she left.

How could she account for that? Just then she saw a burning fragment blown up, flutter, and then fall, a transparent film of cinder. It was paper which was being burned in the house, and the explanation dawned suddenly upon her. Her father was tearing to pieces and burning up the books, all the contents of the iron-bound chest which she had seen in the cupboard of his room.

At that instant she heard the swift drumming

of approaching hoofbeats, and she turned with a guilty start to see Oliver Cutting near at hand. Would he look toward the house? Would he wonder who tended the fire there at this time of the mid-morning? Would he ask embarrassing questions, after the manner of the formidable Sheriff Crosby himself?

Half of her fears were removed when Oliver swung out of the saddle and came toward her, the very picture of good health and good cheer. It would be impossible to keep a mystery in mind when Oliver Cutting was there. He was like the noonday compared with the mists of night. He was alight with excitement now. She remembered! Joe Noyes, about whom she had nearly forgotten.

"What have you found out?" she asked. "What is he?"

"A murderer!" cried Oliver.

She merely stared at him, then she turned up her eyes.

"God help us . . . a murderer!"

"I ran across him almost at once," said Oliver Cutting. "Just as if something were guiding my hand, I dug into a pile of photographs that the sheriff hadn't pasted into his albums yet. And the first thing I got was the picture of Joe Noyes. That's the face that I saw, though the name was different."

"What was it?"

"Joe Graham. Of course, a man like him can't go about with his real name; nobody would have him around, I suppose. They'd be afraid to."

"But . . . when are you going to arrest him?"

"Never until he does something new. He's saved from what he did before."

"What!"

"Yes, pardoned. The governor pardoned him, the governor of Montana. I didn't get the whole story. The sheriff only knew a part of it, and he said that he would look the whole thing up. By the way he remembered it, this Noyes or Graham, whatever his right name is, had a fight with his best friend when they were out on a prospecting trip. And the other man, Tompson, was shot and hurt bad. Noyes fixed him up and brought him to the nearest shack . . . there's that much to be said for him. Then he went on with the prospecting trip, and when he came back Tompson's two older brothers were waiting for him. All three started shooting the minute that they caught sight of each other, and both of the Tompsons went down, and one of them died afterward from the wounds."

He stopped and drew a breath.

"That's the sort of a man that Joe Noyes is!"

To his amazement the girl was poking at a clod with the small toe of her shoe. She was much more thoughtful than shocked.

"But that sounds to me like a fair fight, Oliver," she said.

"Fair fight? Maybe it was! But fair or not, it means that he shot down three men. That might not be so bad if he were an ordinary sort of a man, but just remember his face, Nell."

She called to mind that alert, wild face, that long and slinking stride.

"I know," she said, "there's something terrible about him! But how did he get his pardon?"

"That's the missing link in the sheriff's story. All he knows is that Graham or Noyes, whichever you want to call him, jumped out of the country and disappeared toward the East. Pretty soon he came back, gave himself up, got tried, was convicted of manslaughter, and then was pardoned by the governor. It all worked through so smooth that it looked certain that the job had been fixed up before, and that Noyes knew that he was going to be pardoned if he was convicted. Must have been some pulling of the wires here and there! Politics, you know."

"Why," she surprised him again by asking, "why might not the governor have been persuaded that he really didn't deserve a prison term? Haven't a thousand other men been killed in gunfights, and haven't the winners gone free?"

"You're certainly a cool one, Nell!" declared Oliver, his eyes wide. "You're your father's daughter, right enough. Why, Nell, I think you almost like this man-killer!"

"Like him? At least I wouldn't call him a man-killer. He seems like a fighting man, I know, but. . . ."

She paused and glanced over her shoulder toward the house. A bit of burning paper was soaring high above the roof. She watched it go out and fall.

"What is he here for?" she asked. "What can he be doing here, Oliver?"

"I dunno," said Oliver a little stiffly. "You seem to think that there ain't any harm in him. I'll leave you to guess what he's here for."

VIII

"Another Light on Noyes"

Now, of all times, she surely needed the help and the counsel of Oliver Cutting. He was, perhaps, justly irritated by her attitude, and yet she could not persuade herself to change and conciliate him. In two minutes matters had progressed from bad to worse, until poor Oliver in a temper threw himself into the saddle and departed the way he had come.

As for Nell Camden, she went back toward the house, but when she was almost at the door she remembered her father's command not to enter for the time being, and she veered toward the pasture, where Joe Noyes this morning had been directed, she knew, to break two newly purchased horses of the famous Burnsides stock of roans. A Burnsides roan was supposed to represent the highest explosive that existed in the line of horse-flesh. More than one luckless cowpuncher had cursed the day when that breed invaded the ranges.

Yet ranch owners persisted in buying them and prizing them. They wore out men, but men rarely wore out the Burnsides horses. Neither did the savage winters or the white-hot summers of the range break their spirits. As long as there was life left in them, they could find forage where other horses simply stared at the snow and perished. It was said of them that they could smell grass through two feet of snow, and when they smelled it they could dig like a moose to get at it. These qualities of durability, which brought them through the longest day of roundup work ready to kick the hat off the head of their rider, made them invaluable to the ranch owner, and though the cowpunchers groaned at the thought of backing such mounts as these, yet the hardier class of 'puncher was proud to be seen on the back of a Burnsides. It was a sign of his prowess. It was like the golden spurs which proclaim the knight.

She came in view of the pasture, then, with a feeling of considerable interest. And there she found the two horses and the man. The other cowpunchers, no doubt, would have given a month's pay to see this battle, but they were in distant quarters of the ranch today. Only Wong stood by the fence, with his arms folded and his long, thin-stemmed pipe in his teeth. At one side of the little pasture stood one of the roans, down-headed, with sweat still trickling down its heaving sides and the saddle mark outlined with drying foam. One battle had already been fought, and it needed only a single glance at the exhausted horse to tell who had won the fight.

The other roan was a youngster, not more than three years old, and much daintier of limb than any other Burnsides horse that Nell had ever seen.

The saddle had been cinched on his back, and he was bridled, but the cowpuncher, so it seemed, was not yet ready to take the stirrups.

Instead he stood before the head of the horse, a cigarette in his lips, wobbling up and down, as he talked to the roan. That talk seemed almost intelligible to the young horse. At least one of its ears would prick and then the other. Sometimes it snorted; sometimes it crouched, shuddering violently in every limb, as though about to leap away at a racing gait. But again it straightened; and finally with both ears pricked, with its head thrust out a little toward the man, it faced Joe Noyes, and listened to his talk.

Nell, amazed, looked from the horse to the man and from the man to the horse. She had heard of such methods as this, but she had never seen them used. Before she had recovered from her first astonishment, Joe Noyes, alias Graham, stepped to the side, raised his foot, and gently inserted it in the stirrup.

The roan whirled with a squeal of doubt and anger. Once more the cowpuncher stood at its head and talked. Then he tried the stirrup again, only to be countered with the same swerve. This time the girl waited for an explosion of curses from Joe Noyes, but to her astonishment his patience did not seem at all strained.

Once more he stepped to the head of the horse; once more he talked softly to the animal, and again he tried the stirrup, failed, and repeated. It must have been the tenth or the eleventh trial before he could put his weight in the stirrup, and then he pressed down on it very slowly.

The roan stood for an instant and then plunged sidewise. Nell looked to see Noyes crash to the ground, but only the very toe of his boot must have been in the stirrup, and he was lightly on his feet after the young horse and ready to begin the game again.

It went on for an hour steadily. And before that hour was over it seemed to Nell that the young colt had taken on a personality. She herself would have been infuriated by a tithe of the resistance which the big man endured without a murmur. But as the minutes went on the fear of the roan did not seem so entirely stupid and vicious. Instead, her heart began to warm toward the poor, ignorant, timid creature, only dangerous because of its great strength. And when, at the end of the hour, Joe Noyes was permitted to climb into the saddle and gently guide the horse around the corral she felt like cheering.

Then, without using his victory of the day to make the horse carry him any distance or to show off before others, the rider dismounted at once and removed the saddle. He started toward the fence, and the young roan rushed away to its companion which had been conquered earlier by the use of brute force. For a moment it nosed the other horse, and then it whirled and came back to Noyes and followed him daintily toward the fence.

Here the Chinaman removed the pipe from his

mouth and nodded toward the victor.

"Good!" he said. "Velly good, Joe!"

She was surprised to hear a word one way or the other from the taciturn cook, but when she looked more closely at his ugly mask of a face she could see that his eyes were twinkling. She herself had come to look more closely into the character of the new cowpuncher, and what she had seen was a new story entirely. Now Noyes saw her and with a smile took off his hat.

She met him, as he swung over the fence, carrying the heavy range saddle as though it had been a feather. Even the more solid bulk of her father did not possess, she felt, a much greater sheer strength than there was in the long limbs of the cowpuncher.

"That was a fine thing to do," she said as she came up to him. "Oh, I know you could have beaten the poor horse into submission in five minutes, the way you did the other, but the time you put in won't be wasted . . . not a minute of it!"

He shrugged his shoulders with the greatest apparent indifference, both to her praise and to the work which he had just finished.

"The first gent that comes along in a hurry," he said, "will spoil that hoss plenty. I dunno but what a gent is wrong to use kindness on a range hoss that he don't own. Because, when you talk smooth to a hoss one day and beat 'em up the next, it drives 'em crazy. Hosses, they tell me, and women. . . ."

He stopped abruptly, as though realizing that his tongue had carried him astray. Then he grinned down at her.

"I know what you mean," she answered, equally amused. "Horses and women have to be treated the same way. You must be gentle or beat them . . . but you mustn't mix treatments. Is that it?"

"I'll leave my ideas on that there subject all roped and tied," he declared. "They don't need air."

She walked back with him toward the shed to which he was carrying the saddle. He was bubbling with good humor, and they both laughed most of the way, but suddenly she stopped when they reached the door. She was recalling the dark news she had heard of him so short a time before that morning.

When she looked up again she found that he had faced toward her and was staring fixedly down into her eyes, not with the savagely penetrating glance which she had seen him use more than once before, but with a mild and melancholy air. When she told him she must go back to the house, he answered nothing, and when she was a dozen paces away she looked over her shoulder and saw that he was still standing there with the saddle draped over his forearm and his gaze bent upon the ground.

Plainly he had sensed the suspicion which had rushed over her mind, and plainly he was hurt by it. And this after all was the most amazing thing which she had learned about him: that a destroyer of men should be so sensitive as this to the whims of a girl who was a stranger to him.

All the rest of that day perplexing surmises tangled in her mind. What was the truth of Joe Noyes and his battles with men? What was his errand here, or had he any errand at all? When she remembered what Oliver Cutting had told her, she thrilled with horror; but when she remembered the scent of the Burnsides roan and Noyes in the pasture, her mind changed again.

At least she shifted the burden of worry by telling her father all of the evil she had heard about Noyes and none of the good. But the gray-haired man listened and shrugged his heavy shoulders and said nothing. It was at the supper table that she had told him, and it was not until the end of the meal that he expressed himself.

"Seems like that Cutting boy has some sense after all . . . a pile more'n I laid to his credit. I'll fire Joe Noyes in the morning. I don't mind bad ones, but I don't like them that kill their own partners!"

After he had said it her heart smote her. For suppose after all that she had done Joe Noyes a great injustice? The last two nights were now beginning to tell on even the iron nerve of her father. He had seemed much as usual that morning but, as the darkness fell around the house, his manner changed, and his face altered, as though body and spirit began to fail him when he faced the prospect of another trial by night. It was only this weakness which spoke in her father's decision to discharge Noyes, she told herself. She had urged him when he was at the breaking point, and therefore Noyes must go. But had she not possibly done the big fellow a serious injustice?

She determined that her eyes would not close that night until the dawn came, so sternly would she force herself to watch. Therefore she sat down in her room by the window and rested her elbows on the sill, while the hours wore on toward midnight. But still the moonlight slept peacefully over the roof and the land beyond, and her fears grew less and less. At length she determined to lie down without undressing, but keeping a vigilant watch all the while. And thirty seconds after she was stretched upon the bed her eyes were sealed in a profound slumber.

IX

"A Bundle of Papers"

She was wakened, as she had been wakened the night before, by a terrible cold sense of fear which lay heavily upon her; she opened her eyes, suddenly alert, but weak of body. Once again she dared not move for a time, and then she raised herself cautiously in bed and peered anxiously into the darkness.

It seemed to her in her excitement that dim forms rushed toward her in the shadows of the room, but all vanished before they reached her. At length, recovering a little from the nightmare dread which was in her blood, she lighted a match from the tray on the table near the head of the bed and, as she had done on the previous occasion, looked at the face of the clock. It was exactly a quarter past two o'clock. And the nearness to the hour at which she had wakened the night before was another shock.

The match was burning down toward her finger tips, and it was now that she heard again the same sound which had paralyzed her with fear once before — the loud and resonant beat of a hand knocking at the door of her father's room, a rap three times repeated in a slow and solemn cadence.

Presently the deep silence returned upon the house. She lay for another moment, incapable of stirring. Then she forced herself to stand up. She found and gripped in her hand the light .32 caliber revolver which she had been taught to use with some skill. With this she stole to the door and peered down the hall, just in time to hear the door of her father's room close softly. At this she raced down the hall until she was opposite it. It was framed with a thin streaking of light. That seemed to show that all was well. She pressed her ear to the crack and listened, but the only sound which she could make out was the muffled hammering of her heart, a sound loud enough to drown all other sounds.

After that she raised her hand to knock at the door. The silence was more terrible than noise. If the three knocks could make her father rush frantically out of his room one night, why did they bring not a whisper from him the next? Yet she paused and stopped herself twice on the verge of knocking. It was only after she had gone through an agony of indecision and suffering that her hand fell lightly against the door. It brought a sudden roar of anger from the rancher.

"Nell, go back to your bed and go to sleep! What d'you want at this time of the night?"

She shrank away without an answer, and in her own room she sat down shuddering by the window. What was wrong? Never before had he spoken to her in this manner. Never before had she heard such a wealth of grief and anguish of spirit in his voice. What had happened tonight in the silence that had not happened the night before when he dashed from the bedroom?

She looked out the window. The moon was white on all things smooth. The rocks gleamed in the fields. The watering trough was filled with heavy liquid silver. Then, lying in the eaves of the roof beneath her, she saw a bright white rectangle which she had never seen there before. She stared at it, astonished, and now the wind stirred and lifted it — a sheaf of paper!

But how could it have come there? If it had been dropped from one of the windows, it must have been from her own window. And yet there had been no such bunch of paper in her room the night before. Neither could it have blown there. The answer was simple: someone had climbed upon the roof and left this behind him, no doubt inadvertently.

She resolved to have it — not that she expected that it would reveal anything of importance, but simply because she could not remain there in her room doing nothing, while that ghastly, pregnant silence brooded over the house. Any sort of action was better than inertia. She slipped through the window and on hands and knees lowered herself until she was at the eaves. There she reached to the bundle of paper, scooped it up and, in terror lest he who had lost it should return and see her in the act of making the theft, she scurried up the steep angle of the roof again and reached her room in safety, though with a heart whose terrible beating nearly stifled her.

Now she locked the door, closed the window, and lighted the lamp. Then she withdrew to a place where nothing could look in upon her through the window, saw to it that her revolver was loaded and deposited in her lap, and at last made ready to examine the papers.

As far as she could see the document consisted simply of several sheets of ordinary typewriter paper of a stiff, fine quality, and written upon not with a machine, but in a small and crowded handwriting.

The first page was evidently blown away. The second began with a sentence which stopped her heart for a long instant and then froze her whole body with fear: ". . . and therefore I have waited to tell you the story of *The Lady Nancy* and what happened on her that night, until I made sure that you had been freed from all danger."

She dropped the letter into her lap.

The Lady Nancy! That was the name of the ship which she had seen drawn out at large on the scroll of paper in her father's secret chest. Perhaps that very drawing had been among the things which the strange old man had consigned to the fire. *The Lady Nancy* and what happened to her that night!

She could not for a time pursue her reading. It seemed to her that something was stealing up the hall — that it had paused to listen at her door — that it was about to burst in upon her.

So vividly did her imagination work that she

raised the revolver and leveled it with set teeth at the door, ready to fight for her life, if the owner of that letter should come in. But the ticking sound which might have been the stealthy creak of flooring under a soft tread continued again, and she presently recognized it for what it was, the action of the wind, slightly shaking the entire house.

By this time she was afraid even to look at the black face of the mirror, narrow from the extreme angle from which she looked upon it. How could she tell at what instant an armed hand might not shatter the pane and a fierce face be thrust inside? And would she in that crisis have the courage to level her revolver at the intruder and shoot to kill? She told herself tremulously that she would, and then she turned again to the document which, she felt sure, would prove the key to the secrets of her father's strange life.

X

"The Buried Past"

"And therefore I have waited to tell you the story of *The Lady Nancy* and what happened that night, until I made sure that you had been freed from all danger," she read again. And the story went on: "For I again repeat that there is no debt of gratitude owing to me, even now that my efforts have, it seems, saved you from prison. In the first place the sentence which consigned you to prison was an outrage, and I feel convinced that the governor was influenced rather by the facts of the case than by any so-called political 'pull.' Manslaughter, they called it, but only because the jury was packed with fellow townsmen of the dead man. But how they could call it manslaughter when two men simultaneously attacked you, I cannot understand. It makes me feel that the West is not the land of fair play which it has been represented."

Once more the girl dropped the paper and stared before her. There was no shadow of a doubt now, putting together the story of Oliver Cutting with this letter, that Joe Noyes was the man to whom the letter was addressed, and therefore that it was he who had climbed upon the roof — that it was he who had entered the house by her window the preceding night — that it was he who was threatening her father.

She continued the reading.

"So, in short, you may consider that by helping to give you justice, I am only in a small measure repaying you for a great service which you have already done me. But there is something more than payment and repayment, I hope and have always hoped. There is such a thing as friendship between men which does not make debtor and creditor. And such is the relation between us, as I hope, my dear Joe!

"I told you, when you were here, that there was one great service which you could perform for me in the West, and that that service consisted in finding William Campbell for me, that I might run him down to the ground. I am now about to tell you why it is that I cherish such a steady hatred against a man whom I have not seen for over twenty years. When you know everything, I am assured that you will feel an interest only second to mine in seeing that retribution overtakes him."

"William Campbell?" murmured the girl to herself. "And William Camden? Has one of those names anything to do with the other?"

She continued her reading of the letter.

"In the first place you must forget everything that you know about me . . . forget my education, such as it is, and my work and place in the world. Consider the John Minder whom you know as transformed from a white-headed, bent, prematurely aged invalid to a robust youngster of twenty-five, brown as a berry, wild as the wind, and sole owner at that early age of the good sloop, *Witch*, which sailed from the port of Connington with a little fleet of other sloops and fished in all weathers.

"Think back to such a picture as that, my dear Joe, if you can. Rub out your mental image of me as I am. Think of a fellow not as tall or as heavy as yourself, but still a strapping lad. Instead of these shaking nerves of mine, try to summon up a picture of a man as cool as the next one and ready for fight or fun as the occasion served. In short, Joe, figure for yourself a youngster filled to the brim with strength, good spirits, and an optimistic mind, with a good deal accomplished along his chosen lines of endeavor and a good deal more, apparently, opening before him in the immediate future.

"Follow him to the docks, while he stands at the helm of the sloop, and the wake is white behind him. Then from the dock go with him up the main street of the town, and beyond the cluster of houses in the village to a little house on a hill beyond it. There you could have seen a pretty girl come running out, more than twenty years ago, to welcome me. Pretty? Aye, Joe, that is no justice to her.

"But call up to your mind's eye a picture of the girl you will marry some day and then imagine her lovelier than your imaginings . . . and there you'll have a picture of my Nancy.

"Consider how happy I was in how many ways! Youth, strength, health, a booming fortune among the fishermen, good luck for my companion, and the prettiest girl on the coast for my wife-to-be!

"All that lacked was for the marriage ceremony to take place, and for that I was waiting only until my new sloop should be built. I was selling the old *Witch* for a good round sum, and in her place I was buying a neater, roomier, faster craft which I had ordered according to my own plans, and which I was going to take out for a sort of honeymoon sail in the June weather, before there was ever the scale of a fish aboard her, and before that queer smell, which can't be got out, was soaking into her timbers.

"Well, Joe, consider that the great day was only twenty-four hours off. My suit for the wedding is hanging pressed and cleaned in the closet in my cottage. I've bought the ring. All is prepared. And the evening before I have gone down to the boat and stand aboard her with my lady on the one side, pretty Nancy running here and laughing there, and on the other side there is my best friend, big William Campbell, the strongest man in the village, the hero of the fishermen, you might say, who has been known to bring his ship through The Narrows in a storm?

"But you don't know The Narrows, so of course that would mean nothing to you. But I want you to call up to your mind the picture of a wide-shouldered, deep-chested, long-armed man, without much of a neck to support his head, with great hands and feet and an eye that looked straight into a man. That was William Campbell, and he was my best friend.

"But now I have the stage set for the story.

"I went back to my room that night, with my heart full of the face of Nancy and the deep voice and the good wishes of William Campbell. I fell asleep and dropped into happy dreams. I was wakened late in the night by Bill Campbell leaning over me.

" 'John,' says he, 'it's a good night for a spin down the bay. What d'you say to taking *The Nancy* out and stretching her rigging before to-morrow?'

"I sat up in bed. Outside the wind was humming and growling. It was a wicked black night. But I wouldn't have Bill think that I was backing down. In a minute more I was in my clothes, and we started down the hill with the wind blowing us sidewise every third step.

"Down at the water level it wasn't near so windy. The most of the gale was blowing as high as the top of the hill, but still there was a good stiffish breeze at the water level. We got *The Nancy* started down the bay, and she ran before the wind like a queen. I listened to the water sing beside her, and the wind boil in the ropes, and it seemed to me that just the having of a boat like that was enough good fortune for one man, to say nothing of the real Nancy who was asleep somewhere up yonder among the lights on the hill.

"I was thinking these things when all at once a noosed rope dropped over my shoulders. I was jerked down, and in a minute I was tied hand and foot. I struggled, but what with the surprise of the attack and the strength of Bill, there was no chance for me.

"He had me trussed safely, and then he jerked me up and sat me down facing the bows, while he stood behind me at the helm. We'd fallen right into the eye of the wind while that work was going on. All at once the wind stopped blowing. In the quiet I heard the clock in the village church striking one — a faint, far-away sound. I had to shake myself to realize that I was not safely back in my bed, but really out there on the deck of *The Lady Nancy* with the wild clouds blowing over the top of the mast.

"Then I said: 'Bill, what in the name of God is into you? What sort of a joke is this? You've mashed my face against the deck. You've split my lip, and I'll have an eye as big as a potato. I'll be a sight. We'll have to postpone the wedding, and I'll never forgive you.'

"And Bill said — ah, Joe, I can hear his big voice roaring — 'The wedding is off and over with, as far as you're concerned, Johnnie! You get the idea of it right out of your mind!'

"I sat stunned, trying to think, but not able to make head or tail of what was happening to me.

" 'Bill,' I said, 'what's wrong with you?'

" 'Nancy!' he said.

"It came crashing home in me. Heaven knows it's a strange thing that we can see more looking back than we can when we're facing things. I'd never seen it before to notice, but now I remembered all at once a queer, hungry way that Bill had of looking at her, as though her face were a printed page that had good news for him in it, and how Nancy always used to fight shy of having Bill around us. She never had liked him, so she used to say. She was afraid of him. As a matter of fact most people were a little afraid of big Bill Campbell, and one roar out of him, when he was in one of his ugly moods, would empty a whole dock. And now I could see, looking back, as I say, that for years Bill Campbell had been loving my Nancy with all the strength of that dark heart of his. And all at once I felt sick and done for.

"Because I knew that I didn't have the strength to stand up to Campbell. There was something terrible about him, do you see? It was more than just physical strength. He seemed to take my mind in the palm of his hand and hold me helpless. It was the same way on the deck of that ship. I felt paralyzed. And then I began to wonder what would happen.

"But he didn't say another word for a long time. The wind had caught us again, and the mast was creaking, and we shot down the bay like a bullet.

"When he tacked and came about, the boom fairly whizzed over the deck, he brought her about so fast, and on that tack it seemed to me that he was making pretty dangerously near to The Narrows. But at that moment The Narrows meant nothing to me; my brain was in a whirl.

" 'Bill,' I said at last, 'what are you planning . . . what's in your head?'

" 'Nancy,' he said.

" 'That isn't an answer,' I said.

" 'I've got to have her,' he said.

"Well, that was an answer indeed. It curdled my blood, and by the quiet way he spoke I knew that he meant what he said. He meant to have my Nancy!

"I tried to be equally quiet: 'Bill,' I said, 'you know that can't be. You can't betray me like a. . . .'

"A string of curses hung on my tongue, but I kept them back. I was a mighty religious man in those days.

" 'Don't talk about betraying and that sort of rot,' said Campbell to me. 'Talk sense . . . you need to now!'

"And there was a snarl in his voice when he said this.

" 'Johnnie,' he said after a minute more, 'I'll tell you why you can't have her. You haven't the nerve for her. And I have, and she belongs to a brave man.'

"Once more I came within an ace of cursing him.

" 'It's because you haven't the nerve, Johnnie,' he said, 'that you're going to weaken . . . you're going to knuckle under!'

"And then he told me what he intended to do.

Either he would run the boat into The Narrows and let her go to smash on the rocks, or else I must swear to him, swear on the Bible he had brought with him, to give up all my claims on her.

"I tried to laugh at him and tell him that if I went down, he would be going down with me, but he did not answer, and every minute I could see the white of The Narrows ahead of us and hear the roaring of the tide going out through the great rocks.

"I threw myself back along the deck and closed my eyes and tried to tell myself that I was going to die, but that I would never surrender. But all the time that infernal roaring of the water grew louder and louder, and — Joe, you see that I am exposing all the black weakness of my heart to you — I could not help opening my eyes and sitting up.

"Now we were driving straight down toward the passage, and in a few more moments we would be in the foam and the crash of it. I fought the horror away, and I swore that I would not give in. And then I turned and, as the moon looked through the clouds for an instant, I got a glance at the face of Campbell, and it was as hard as brown stone.

"Then the roar of The Narrows filled our ears, and I saw that it was too late, one way or another. We were bound to go into it. He could not tack in time — the drag of the current would suck us into the jaws of the passage!

"I gave way then — I shudder with the shame of it, Joe, but let the confession help to clear my soul — I gave way and took the Bible which he offered me. Then I screamed out the oaths which he prescribed, that I would give up Nancy and leave the town without telling her where I had gone; I agreed to do all that if only he would bring me safely back to the shore.

"I can hear the shout now, with which he heard me and jumped to his work. He had out a knife and slashed the ropes that tied me. Then I was up and, while he held the helm, I worked at the ropes.

"Well, Joe, I can't go through all the horror of that passage, and how he fought the currents like a demon, and how at last he brought the good boat through, and how we tacked back under a changing wind until at last we floated into the smooth clear water under the lee of the town, and when we got there, I heard the church bell chime in the church tower, where the old watchman was tugging at the rope, one, two, and three. It seemed two ages that we had been afloat, but it was only two hours.

"And so it happened, Joe, that I left the town, as I had sworn to do, without sending a word to Nancy. And when I came back a month later I found that she was the wife of Bill Campbell.

"How he had persuaded her, I can't say, but at least she was his wife. As for me, I was a ruined man. I dared not show my face among the fishermen after jilting pretty Nancy. So I had to sell out, and Bill Campbell was the man who bought *The Lady Nancy*.

"I sold out, Joe, but afterward I found Bill and put my curse on him. I told him that I would take my time, but that sooner or later, between the hours of one and three in the morning, I would find him and torture him, as he had tortured me, and kill his body as he had killed my heart!

"It daunted even Bill Campbell to hear me speak. A fortnight later I heard that he had left the village with his wife, and I never heard of him again.

"He left me a prematurely aged man. I changed my name and my way of life, and in everything I did I have prospered, as you know. It seemed as though the devil wanted to repay me in cash for that terrible time in The Narrows when I had sold my soul through fear to him.

"But now you have the whole story, Joe, and you know why I have asked you to hunt through the West until you find him, and when you find him. . . ."

Here the girl lowered the paper and fell back in her chair with a gasp. And then the paper slipped from her loosened fingers and rattled to the floor.

XI

"The Order"

What she saw in the flash of that moment was the face of her mother and the wistful look which had never died out of it, so far as she could dimly remember. And in this paper was the explanation of that look.

She saw more: the reason for the strange aging of her father and that habit of his of wakening between one and three in the morning. It was the fear of vengeance, which had kept him from sleep every night. No wonder he had grown savage and mournful under that unceasing strain.

A revolver exploded, the echoes crowding back in the house and running loudly up and down the hall. Nell Camden was up like a flash, with all of her fear forgotten. As she raced, she knew that there had been two shots, and that the sounds of them had merged together.

In spite of that silence in the room of her father, then, she had been right; tall Joe Noyes had been inside, and the older man had been looking death in the face all of this time. She darted down the hall; she threw open the door, for strangely enough they had not locked it; and there she confronted such a picture as she could never have dreamed of.

Directly before her and facing toward the far end of the room, was big Joe Noyes. He was saying, as she rushed in: "Are you ready?"

And from the far end of the room came the voice of her father, saying: "Yes!"

He sat upon the bed, his left arm thrown out to support him, a revolver clutched in his right hand, and a crimson stream, from a wound in his shoulder or upper breast, pouring over his bosom in a rapidly spreading stain. He had been badly hurt in the first discharge of guns in that murderous duel across the length of the room, but he was awaiting, indomitable of spirit, the second trial. Then Nell Camden threw herself between them and seized the gun in the hand of big Noyes.

He shoved the gun readily into the holster.

"I'm through with this rotten business," he said. "I owed a good deal, but I never owed a murder!"

She only waited for that assurance and then she turned and fled to her father. He was sinking fast, but his courage was unfaltering.

"Get out of the way!" he said. "Luck was against me on the first throw, but I'll get him on the second. Stand out of the way, Nell. Are you going to shame me?"

But she forced him back and, when he struggled to push her away, Noyes appeared suddenly at her side and took the weapon from the fingers of the older man. They forced him back upon the bed. He was already weakening, and now they cut away his shirt and exposed the wound.

"He's dead," sobbed Nell. "It . . . it's through the heart!"

"It ain't within a mile of the heart," said Noyes coolly.

"You'll hang for it," cried the girl. "I'll see you hung for cowardly murder!"

"And I'll keep him from dying in spite of what you say!" he replied. "Gimme those bandages."

He seemed to work with lightning speed and precision, and Nell, realizing that here was a skill which made her own seem like futile circumstances, stood by. Presently, as the whirl which was close to a faint cleared from her eyes, she heard her father commanding Noyes, with many tremendous curses, to start for his horse before the cowpunchers, alarmed by the sound of the shot, should come and capture him.

"Let them come," said Noyes, still furiously at work. "I'll have the bleeding stopped in another minute. But if you live or die, Campbell, I want you to know that I've changed my mind. When I read that letter, I got to hating you as though your heart was all black, but now I just begin to see that there's another side to it. If he didn't have the courage to see the boat through The Narrows, he didn't deserve her. And if he ain't man enough to work out his *own* vengeance, he'll never have it!"

There was a crashing of many feet up the stairs and down the hall. The cowpunchers began spilling into the room, red-hot on the trail of a disturbance, but there Nell, with her arms stretched out, stopped them.

"There was just an accident," she informed them.

"An accident with a gun . . . after midnight?" they growled at her.

"An accident," she insisted. "Get back to your beds!"

Slowly they retired, throwing over their shoulders baffled glances in the direction of Noyes. When they were gone, she heard her father muttering: "There's some sense in a few women, Noyes. You can pick 'em few and far between, and Nell is one that has a little. Eh?"

The tall cowpuncher in place of answering turned his head and directed one blazing look at the girl, a look so full of admiration and wonder and another thing which she dared not analyze, but it took her breath.

The bandaging was done. Her father lay back on the bed and demanded a pipe which she filled and lighted for him. With this between his teeth, smoke boiling from his mouth when he spoke, he seemed like one who has been pleasantly entertained rather than a man who had narrowly escaped from death.

"Campbell," said Noyes, "I'm going to tell you now that I'm sorry, and that I'll start right in trying to wipe out the fool things that I have been doing in this house leading up to tonight."

"You shut up apologizing," said the older man.

"All these twenty-odd years I been figuring that I had to look at death sooner or later, to make up for what I made him go through that night on *The Lady Nancy* between one and three. And now that you've come along, why I feel that there's a weight off of my mind, son. You've done your duty. I don't hold a grudge and . . . Nell, close that door and come here. I've got to tell you a story, and you might as well hear it now. No, don't stop me! Why, Noyes has done it up so plumb comfortable that I don't even feel it. Nell, I'm going to tell you. . . ."

"But you don't have to," she said, "because I know it already. And whatever the details may be, I agree with Joe Noyes, or Graham, whichever is his right name" — here there was a start from the cowpuncher — "that a man who hasn't the grit to die for the woman he loves, why he simply doesn't deserve her!"

There was a sort of groan from William Campbell.

"My guns," he said, "and here I've gone all my life never daring to tell my girl the truth of what happened, or my wife before her. But," he added after a moment, "maybe it was a truth that needed an ordeal before it could be seen!"

He stopped and looked sharply at the others. They did not seem to have heard his last words, so busy were they staring into one another's eyes.

The Gift

"Ronicky Doone, Champion Of Lost Causes," a seven-part serial by David Manning, concluded in *Western Story Magazine* (12/10/21). The first of eight parts of the next Faust serial, "Ronicky Doone And The Crosslett Treasure," continuing this saga, did not begin until the issue dated 1/7/22. "The Gift" by Max Brand in *Western Story Magazine* (12/24/21) was the only Faust story to appear in the Christmas issue for that year.

Happy Jack is a most engaging character. Much, I suppose, after the fashion that Thomas Mann remained fascinated for years by his early creation of Felix Krull and had to return to him again years later, Happy Jack must have stayed with Faust since this character is surely only an earlier version of Happy Jack Aberdeen who appears in the six-part serial, "Happy Jack," published in *Western Story Magazine* (4/26/30–5/31/30) and subsequently in book form as *Happy Jack* (Dodd, Mead, 1936). The themes of "The Gift" unite what Henrik Ibsen considered a "life-sustaining illusion" with the notion of coming home again and so provide a fitting close — in the Homeric sense of καιρός — to this odyssey of the human spirit that began with "Cayenne Charlie."

I

"The Warning"

There was not a breath of wind. The storm which had howled across the mountains for well nigh a fortnight was now gone. It left the summits and all the higher valleys moon-white with snow. And over this snow the moon itself, rising early, cast the dark pointed shadows of the pines. The silence was as profound as the arch of the sky, as pure as the shining stars; it was a hallowed quiet, well fitted for this night above all nights, Christmas Eve.

Over the white summit the rider came like a stain, and the shape of his galloping horse, struggling misshapen over crusted snows beside him, made a bitter contrast with the still shadows of the pines. The rider brought an element of labor and effort into a place where there should have been only the white, sleeping mountains and the dark, sleeping trees.

But he saw no beauty in what lay around him; and because he saw no beauty, all beauty ceased to exist. The peaks and their forested sides became of less importance. The whole focus of interest was on that lonely, frightened horseman.

About his fear there was no doubt. When he

reached a hilltop, he invariably looked back and sighed with relief when he saw, perhaps, an empty upslope behind. Yet his sense of security was ever short-lived, and the next instant he would be spurring wildly down the grade beyond, as though danger dogged him in the very shadow of his horse.

He came headlong as a landslide into the great hush of Bender Valley, coursing through the trees almost regardless of the windings of the trail, then sheering straight off to the left, where there was no trail at all, only the solidity of the forest. The panting of his horse, the grunt of pain as the poor beast slipped and recovered in the snow, became more audible in the quiet of this wood. Trees are almost like mirrors. They reflect the souls of those who come among them. To Shorty Dugan these pines seemed stealing close to him, listening and watching and keeping the tidings of that which they had seen.

Still he spurred. And under the goad the pinto lunged ahead with shrinking quarters, as though into a collar, without really increasing his speed. That collar was utter exhaustion. He went no faster, because it was impossible for the outworn mustang to swing his legs faster or drive them more strongly through the snow.

He stumbled into a little clearing. It was so small that the trees seemed to lean out toward it from all sides. Shorty Dugan flung himself out of the saddle and landed in the snow, sprawling and slipping, for long riding had numbed his legs. The horse, relieved from the burden, dropped his head, spread his trembling legs, and puffed great clouds of frosty breath into the moonshine. Shorty flung the beast a curse over his shoulder as he regained his footing; it was Shorty's habit to curse the nearest living object whenever a mishap overtook him.

Then he stumbled on toward the cabin. It was very small. The shadow from the eastern treetops cut across it. One half of the cabin was lost in blackness. The other half was dead-white in the moonshine and, against this whiteness like a jewel on a dead face, a yellow lamplight glimmered in a single window.

In spite of his haste, Shorty checked his rush. He stole to the side of the shack, peered through, under a shading hand, at the interior of the lighted room, and then, nodding in satisfaction, hurried back toward the front door. No sooner had he opened it and sprung into the darkness within — for his agility redoubled as the blood ran warm again through his muscles — than the door was slammed shut again and he himself was tripped and pitched to his face, falling right into the yellow shaft of light that came through the open door of the room in which he had seen the lamp.

He yelled as he dropped, whirled in falling, and tugged at his gun, but he found himself lying on his back, looking up along the barrel of a long Colt and into a quiet, thin, shadowy face behind it.

"Don't!" he gasped. "Don't! I'm Shorty! Don't shoot!"

The other touched him scornfully with a toe and slipped his gun back into its holster.

"Get up!" he commanded.

Shorty obediently clambered back to his feet.

"Don't you know me?" he kept whimpering. "Don't you know I'm all right? Don't you know me?"

"I don't know nobody," said the man of the cabin. "I don't know nobody that comes tearing into my house without knocking or nothing."

"I seen you sitting all quiet in your chair in the other room a minute ago and I thought . . . and . . . I'm Shorty. You know me?"

This disjointed and frightened speech made the tall man smile.

"I don't know you," he said in a grave tone, which had in it a certain hardness of contempt. "I ain't seen you for three months. Maybe you ain't what you used to be!"

"Wait till you hear what I got to tell you!" exclaimed Shorty. "Maybe you think I been bought off, or something. Is that it?"

"Go inside where I can get a look at you," ordered the host.

Shorty obeyed, and he was followed into the cozy little living room by the other. They were opposed types. Shorty lived up to his name. He had the short, bowed legs which generally connote strength. A barrel chest, short, thick neck, bulldog face, and fighting features made him, so far as was physically possible, different from the lithe man of the cabin. The other was above six feet in height and looked still taller. He had gray eyes, almost colorless and very steady; and his thin features were of a cruelly predatory cast. His contempt and reserve now had a biting edge.

"In the old days," he said, "as chief I would've horsewhipped a gent that come blundering in like this." He added, as though aware that he had gone too far: "Not that that's really my way. Only, I don't like to be busted in on like this. Lucky for you I waited to make out who you were."

Shorty changed color. "You might of knowed by the way I come smashing in that I was a friend!"

"Never mind what I knowed. You said you had a message for me?"

"A big one, too!" said Shorty, swelling suddenly with importance. "Happy Jack's coming! Happy Jack himself!"

"Never heard of him. Who's he?"

"Who's he?" gasped Shorty. "You don't know Happy? Why . . . why. . . ."

He blundered hopelessly, as a man will when confronted with the necessity of defining some great abstraction. Suppose one were to be asked to define lightning!

"You remember young Jackson," began Shorty, feeling his way toward an explanation, "the gent you had us bunco out of the claim? The gent that Murphy drilled?"

"Well?"

"Happy Jack's his friend. He found out that you were behind the killing, and he's started on your trail!"

"And you come a hundred and fifty . . . two hundred miles to tell me that? To tell me that some gent I never heard of is out for me? Say, Shorty, are you plumb crazy? Do you know me?"

This biting contempt stung Shorty. The blood gathered dark in his tanned face.

"Listen, chief," he said, "you know these parts, but you don't know things in the south. Was Murphy a good man with a gun?"

"Was he a good man?" answered the other, frowning. "Yes, and he still is! One of the very best. I trained him myself. How come you say 'was?' "

"He'll never pull a gat again," answered Shorty, reveling in this chance of overwhelming the other. "He'll never pull a gun again, Sandy Crisp!"

With a profound relish he watched the gray eyes of Crisp contract and glitter beneath the colorless, bushy brows.

"Happy Jack met him. There was a fair gun play. Jack beat him a mile. Jack shot him down. He smashed Murphy's shoulder to smithereens. Murphy'll never pull a gun again!"

Sandy moistened his colorless lips.

"Go on," he said almost gently.

"He found out from Murphy, Happy did," went on Shorty, "that you was behind the buncoing and the killing of young Jackson, the tenderfoot. Seems Jackson used to be a friend of his. Happy was on the trail of them that done for him. When he found out that Murphy was only a tool of yours, he left Murphy and started north. Then I come like a whirlwind. I've changed hosses twice, and the plug I got outside is plumb spent. Chief, climb on your hoss and run!"

There was more curiosity than fear in the manner of the chief.

"You think I'd better not wait for him? Not even with you here to help me? Or will he come with a band?"

"He's a lone rider, chief. But you ain't going to have me here with you. No, sir! I'm gone again, *pronto!* I know how good you are. I've seem you work half a dozen times. I ain't any slouch myself when it comes to a pinch. But stay here and wait for Happy?" He laughed without mirth in his voice. "Nope, I ain't tired of life!"

"He's as bad an actor as all that, eh."

"Go south," said Shorty. "Go south and ask about him."

"What's he done?"

"Plenty. And he's so good that he don't have to shoot to kill. He fights for the love of fighting. That's all. And he's so fast and so sure with a gat that he just nicks a gent and drops him."

"I've heard about that kind!" The chief curled his lip as he spoke.

"I've seen him do it!" said Shorty, with an ire of almost religious awe. "I've seen him do it."

His voice was hardly more than a whisper.

"He could of killed Murphy ten times. He didn't."

"You saw the fight and didn't try to help Murphy?"

"I saw the fight and buckled the flap of my holster, so that devil wouldn't pay no attention to me!"

"Hm!" muttered the other. "This gent hypnotizes folks, maybe. Old?"

"Young."

"How's he look?"

"Fine looking. Clean as a whistle. Blue eyes. Tall as you and big, heavy shoulders and a tapering build."

"And you think I wouldn't have no chance against him?"

"I don't think. I know."

"I've never been beat, Shorty!"

"I know. But this gent . . . I don't know how it is . . . but I figure his luck is all before him. He ain't used it up yet. The time ain't come for him to lose! So long, chief. I'm gone!"

"Wait a minute, you fool! Does he know . . . did Murphy tell him . . . where this cabin is?"

"No."

'Then he'll never get me. Nobody knows about it except our boys."

"He'll find it. He'll smell it out."

"How?"

"How does a buzzard find a dead one when its clean out of sight?" asked Shorty.

He waited for no more talk, but flung himself

out of the room, and Sandy Crisp went to the window and pressed his face close to the frosted glass after rubbing out an eyehole. He saw Shorty mount with frantic haste and, glancing over his shoulder, spur his reeling cow pony into the shadow of the trees. There was something ludicrous in his fear of nothingness, and it set Sandy smiling.

The smile was still lingering on his lips when he turned from the window and saw, leaning against the doorjamb, a tall, broad-shouldered youth who was rolling a cigarette. But his blue eyes were not fastened on his work; they were regarding, with a sort of amusement, the features of his host.

II

"Happy Jack Off Guard"

Whatever the thoughts which passed through the agile mind of Sandy Crisp — and judging by the flicker of his glance about the room there were many — the idea of striking at once at the invader was not executed. Instead, he deliberately turned his back on the silent visitor, walked across the room, drew up a chair before the fire on the open hearth, and waved the stranger to another seat.

"Sit down and rest your legs, Happy," he said. "Sit down and make yourself to home. If you're cold inside as well as out, I got some moonshine that ain't half bad."

"Thanks," said the other, lighting his cigarette with a deft left hand, as Sandy noted with a side glance, "I see that kind, these days when liquor's hard to come at, but I don't use the stuff myself. It's hard on the eyes."

Sandy Crisp nodded, grinning.

"I didn't think you'd come in on that old game," he said, "but a gent never can tell. Sometimes the wisest step into the oldest door. Sit down?"

"Sure."

Happy Jack walked slowly across the room. The

moment he came into the yellow of the firelight, Sandy could appreciate how truly big and powerful the stranger was, and the easy grace which told of strong muscles flowing in smooth harmony. He was handsome in a singularly boyish way. His face was brown as a berry, which made his eyes a more startling blue; his whole expression gave an index to mischief, rather than cruelty, in the heart of the man. A single glance at his face was enough to justify his nickname: Happy. In age he might be from twenty-four to twenty-six. This faint, quizzical smile with which he now regarded his host made him seem even younger. Sandy was favoring him with an equally calm regard.

"You don't seem in no special hurry," remarked Happy Jack.

"I'm not," answered Sandy. "I'm trying to place you. I seen you somewhere once."

"Ever been south as far as Tuckertown?"

"Nope."

"Then you've never seen me."

Sandy shook his head.

"I've seen you or a ringer for you," he went on genially. "Well, kid, you've sure got ambitious, ain't you? Stepping right out to make a name for yourself by dropping Sandy Crisp?"

His cold mockery did not disturb the quiet content which brooded ceaselessly in the blue eyes of the stranger. His expression was as mild as that of a child when it sees a new and curious toy for the first time.

"I ain't been thinking about collecting any fame for myself," he answered, smiling, and showing a flashing line of white teeth. "You see, down my way they don't know you, Crisp. You ain't even a name."

"I guess you'll have to tell 'em about me, then," went on Sandy, still sneering to break down the nerve of the younger man.

"I don't advertise much," replied the other.

Sandy Crisp bit his lip. This was not at all to his liking. Such perfect solidity of calm amazed him. His mind reverted to something Shorty had said. The luck of this handsome youth seemed all before him and undrained. Calamity, failure, could not even be dreamed of in connection with those laughing blue eyes. All that could be wondered at was the possibility that fighting rage, the lust for battle, would come into that boyish face. It was inconceivable. A strange hollowness appeared, now, in Sandy Crisp's stomach; a chill struck up along his back. His fingers were growing uncertain. A sense of weakness flowed through him. What could this be?

It was fear! He knew it suddenly and with a devitalizing pang. He, Sandy Crisp, the invincible, the cold-hearted, the dangerous in battle, was afraid! And yet an imp of the perverse drove him on to draw out his young visitor.

"Not fame?" echoed Sandy, sneering now to conceal the whiteness which he felt must be growing about the edges of his mouth. "That ain't what's brought you up here? It was simply because you wanted to get square for the killing of young Jackson, eh? You trying to tell me that you were that fond of the fool?"

"Was he a fool?" answered the other, snapping his cigarette butt into the fire. "Was he a fool?" As he spoke he lifted his head, and Sandy Crisp saw that the boyishness was gone from the face before him. The nostrils were beginning to quiver, the mouth to straighten. "He was fool enough to trust men," said Happy Jack. "That's what Jackson was fool enough to do. He trusted me. He put me up and fed me and took care of me and staked me and sent me on my way without ever expecting to get anything back for it. He took me in because I was hungry. And when I went off and got a stake and come back to pay him what I owed him, I found him dead! You hear? Dead!"

He had changed still more while he spoke. He was rising from his chair as though great forces within now fought for a chance to exercise themselves. And a veritable flame of rage was burning in his eyes.

"Him you call a fool was dead, and you'd done it through your man Murphy. I fixed Murphy, and then I started for you; I've found you, and you're going to pay, Crisp, so that my pal, Jackson, seeing you go down, will know I ain't forgotten what a gent owes to his partner!"

He sprang to the center of the room.

"I've come here and waited, hoping to hear you say you were sorry for the dirty murder you had

Murphy work. But you ain't sorry for nothing. You killed Jackson. You left his wife and his three kids with nothing to keep them except sorrowing for him you killed. Does that worry you? Not a bit! You got no heart, Crisp, and I'm going to kill you with a smile . . . same's I'd kill a snake or a mad dog, because you ain't a human."

The tirade burst out with incredible emphasis, the words driven through drawn lips. And the whole of Happy Jack's big body trembled from head to foot with his passion. He had been a handsome boy a moment before. He was suddenly a madman.

With a great effort Sandy Crisp retained his smile, for he had known men to go blind with rage in the face of that taunting sarcasm.

"You're tolerable sure you'll finish me, eh?"

"Sure of it? Aye! A thousand times sure. I'm waiting, Sandy! I'm waiting for you to start!"

Still, making no move to rise from his chair, partly paralyzed by the chill of fear which was now more and more stiffening his limbs, Sandy Crisp looked up at his antagonist, and always his forehead was creased by the puzzled frown which it had worn from time to time since he first saw the big man from the south.

When would that chill of terror depart from him? When would he be able to rise to his feet?

Suddenly he knew that he was beaten. Another five minutes of delay, and he would be incapable of action. The terrible certainty of Happy Jack, the certainty to which Shorty had paid such a tribute not long before, was unnerving him. If he fought, he must fight now.

"Once more!" shouted Happy Jack. "Will you stand up, or do I have to come for you bare-handed?"

And as he spoke, he laughed suddenly, wildly, as though the thought of that conflict, man to man and hand to hand, were inexpressibly preferable to the sudden fight of guns. But while he laughed, stealing a long stride nearer to Crisp, the latter thrust out his hand.

"Wait! Happy! Wait!" he called. "I been trying to think. Now I got it. I got the name of the gent you're like in the face! Your laugh showed me!"

And he himself fell back into his chair and burst into long-drawn, hysterical laughter, until the tears came into his eyes.

The other stood frowning in wonder and glaring down at Crisp, until the outlaw straightened again with a sudden gesture of friendliness, as if inviting Happy Jack to step into a secret.

"Here you come on a killin' trail," he said, the laughter not quite gone from his voice, "and here I sit up to this minute just choosing the place where I was to plant a bullet in you. But as a matter of fact, Happy, we ain't going to fight. Not a bit of it!"

"What?" exclaimed the younger man.

"Listen," said the other, growing more grave. "D'you know what we're going to do? We're going to be partners, son! We're going to be partners!"

He laughed again, overflowing with joy.

"Me?" Happy Jack sneered. "I'd rather be partners with a coyote. That's what I say!"

"Sure you would, if a coyote could make you rich. But it can't, and I can."

"Crisp," said Happy Jack ominously, "I dunno what the play is that you figure on making. But I wouldn't trust you a split part of a second. If you think you're going to talk me off my guard, you're wild in the head. You can lay to that!"

"What would you say," broke in Crisp, "to being the heir to a ranch worth about a million, more or less? What would you say to shaking hands with me and coming into an estate like that?"

"What," said Happy Jack solemnly, "would Jackson say if he seen me shake hands with you?"

The other seized upon this thread of argument.

"Why, he'd be happy, because he'd know, then, that you'd be able to take care of his widow and his kids. Wouldn't that make him happy?"

Jack rubbed his bony knuckles across his chin.

"Go on, Crisp," he said coldly, "I'll wait till you get through talking. If I could make sure of taking care of them four lives . . . well, here it's Christmas time, and it's sure the right season for making gifts, eh?"

He smiled sourly, as though he had no real hope that through Sandy Crisp he might attain this charitable power.

"Sure," and Sandy Crisp chuckled, still study-

ing with keener and ever keener interest the face
of the man from the south. "And what's more,
you're going to be a gift yourself . . . and you're
going to be a gift this same night. Come to think
of it, this is Christmas Eve, ain't it? The time the
old women and the young fools get soft-
hearted?"

Happy Jack stared closely at him.

"Yes," he said softly, "the time they get that
way." And while he spoke his eyes were as cold
as steel.

"Listen," ran on Crisp with a growing enthusiasm, "when you threw back your head and
laughed a while back, I seen young Johnny Neilan
again, standing on top of the logs in the jam and
going down the river. A minute later, while he
was laughing and waving his hand at the rest of
us boys, and knowing well enough that he had
about thirty seconds to live, the log turned, he
went under, and that was the last ever seen of
Johnny!"

Happy Jack listened quietly, waiting until the
other came to the point of all this talk.

"Well," went on Sandy Crisp, "I'll go back a
little ways farther. Yonder, over in the hills, where
the good range country begins on the far side of
the valley, lives old John Neilan and Mrs. John
Neilan, his wife. They're the hardest, closest-
fisted, meanest pair in the mountains, and they
got enough money to choke a herd of elephants.
They got no charity locked up inside of 'em. They
pay their hired men less, they feed 'em worse,

than folks around here that ain't got half so much coin.

"Twelve years ago they were a pile different, but pretty hard even then. They were so hard, in fact, that they made life miserable for their only child, and that was young Johnny Neilan, junior. Johnny was going on fourteen, a straight-standing, wild-eyed kid. One day he ups and runs off because the old man had been giving him a tongue-lashing for something. He disappears, anyways, and he never was found, and it plumb busted the hearts of the two old folks. If they was hard before, they got like pure flint afterwards.

"Well, nobody got trace of Johnny, till one time I come up to a logging camp in Canada, and among the gents I seen a husky youngster about eighteen that looked pretty much like Johnny Neilan. I couldn't be sure, because kids change so darn much between fourteen and twenty that you could hardly tell your own brother if you was away from him five or six years. Anyway, I laid a trap for the kid and made him confess, after a while, that he was Johnny Neilan. That was the morning of a big jam in the log drive. About ten seconds later, after he'd told me who he was, Johnny had run out onto the jam and was working away. All at once the jam busted. The rest of the boys got off safe. But Johnny was stuck out there by himself. He seen they was no chance to get safe to shore. So he just stood up and waved good-bye, laughing. And the next minute he went under and never come up, just the way I told you a while back. Twenty logs must of smashed him to bits the minute he went under the surface of the water.

"I come back to these parts, and I dropped in on old Neilan and told him what I seen. Can you believe that the old fool just cussed me out and swore it wasn't true? He and his wife had gone on, all those years, wishing to have the boy back, so that he couldn't stop his wishing even when I told him the out-and-out truth. He took it serious enough to go up north, though, and find that logging camp.

"There he found out that none of the boys had knowed Johnny by his right name. And they gave old Neilan a picture of the boy the way he was just before the logs got him. Well, Happy, you know how pictures are. Johnny had sure changed a pile in the four years. He was man-sized. And that picture showed him with a face all covered with four days' growth of hair. Old Neilan took one long look and then took a great big breath of relief. He'd just nacherally made up his mind that that wasn't Johnny. His boy was still alive and would come riding back home some day, and everything would be hunky-dory on to the end of the story. You know the way old folks get? Plumb stubborn and foolish? That's the way he got. Wouldn't listen to no sense. And him and his wife are still sure that young John Neilan, junior'll come back. And they're right! They're going to see him come back!"

He jumped out of his chair, laughing joyously,

and pointed at Happy.

"You're the man!"

"Me?" gasped Happy.

"You!" shouted the outlaw. "In about ten minutes after you get there the old man will remember what the kid and him had the argument about the time his kid left. It was because young Johnny got the key to his old man's safe . . . the old fool keeps a pile of cash in his house . . . and got to tinkering with the lock. Old Neilan caught him and raised the devil. Well, he'll be so plumb tickled to have you back that he'll make you a present of the key. All you got to do, then, is to sneak down late tonight, grab the boodle, and then come out to me. I'll have hosses ready. Man, we'll clean up a good forty thousand if we clean up a cent."

His ecstasy of greed was sharply checked by the shake of Happy's head.

"You think I'm fool enough to try that?"

"Why not? You're sure like Johnny. Maybe not if he was alive and standing beside you now. But he was a big kid, and you're a big man. You got the same color of hair, the same color of eyes, and the same funny way of throwing your head on one side when you laugh. You can step right into his shoes!"

"But suppose they get to talking about old times. . . ."

"Mostly you'll be able to say that you've forgotten a good deal inside of twelve years. And you've only got to stall them off for one evening, or maybe two. Then you can grab the money and kiss 'em all good-bye. One minute they have a Christmas present, the next minute they have it not!"

He fell again into hearty laughter, but stopped short at the shudder of Happy Jack.

"Sandy," said Happy Jack, "d'you think I'm skunk enough to fool that poor old man and his wife?"

"Poor old nothing!" snorted Sandy. "They're the meanest. . . ."

"I've done tolerable bad things in my day," said Happy slowly, "but I wouldn't make money that way."

"Then don't keep the money for yourself," said the elastic-minded Crisp. "Don't keep it at all. Just turn over what you get to Jackson's widow. Ain't you been a lot cut up because her and the three kids didn't have nothing to live on? Well, Happy, you take the coin from them two old skinflints and give it to the widow. That'd sure be a good deed, if you want to fall in with the Christmas idea. Does it sound good to you?"

Happy Jack sighed. For that single instant he was off his guard, staring through the window. Sandy's hand made a furtive motion toward the butt of his gun, but it came away again at once. There was too rich a game in sight to imperil such chances in order to make a kill.

"It don't seem like no good can come out of dirty work like that," muttered Happy Jack at last. "But the last I seen of the widow and the three kids they was sure a mournful lot. Suppose they're hungry tonight, with this cold. . . ."

He stopped short.

"Blast your soul, Sandy," he growled out, "I s'pose I'll try it! But you're going to pay some time for the murder of Jackson. I'll see to that. Now tell me what you know about the Neilan place and the folks on it. Or d'you know nothing at all?"

"I know every inch of it," answered Sandy, ignoring the threat. "Ain't I scouted around that place twenty times getting the lay of the land? I've had my eye on Neilan's safe for ten years, more or less! Now listen hard!"

And, sitting down again in his chair, he began to talk swiftly. Happy Jack listened in gloomy silence.

III

"The Home-Coming"

The dinner table was a shrine of silence in the big dining room at the John Neilan house. It was a silence which Mary Thomas dreaded, always; but on this Christmas Eve it seemed to her that that silence was an accusation leveled at her head. Again and again she stole furtive glances at the stony faces of the old people. But they had no glance or word for her. Neither had they a glance or a word for each other. Their attention was fixed upon their own thoughts, and these were deadly, frozen things.

She was out of place here. Even from the first she had felt that she was out of place, since the very day when the two old folks, a dozen years before, had taken in the newly orphaned child in the hope of filling, to some extent, the vacancy formed by the loss of their son. But she had not filled it. She had only served to make the loss more visible. To be sure, they would not send her again into the world to find her own way; but, on the other hand, they could not prevent letting her see that she was ever a thorn in their sides.

And she, with the keen perception which comes

to those who know grief early in life, had understood from the first and shuddered at her understanding. They never spoke cruel words. But with such silences as these they crushed her spirit time and again. When she first came, and after she learned what was wanting, she had longed many a bitter hour to change her form and face. And if wishes could change flesh, she would certainly have become like the picture of that handsome impudent-eyed boy which ever since his disappearance had remained sacred to the memory. But wishes, alas, can change neither features nor minds.

She remained the same rather pale, pretty, large-eyed girl. If she could only have had some touch of Johnny's manner! If she could at least have been a tomboy! If she could have ridden horses bareback and run and whooped about the house, she might have partly filled the niche.

In this respect she strove to change also. But she could not. She loved horses. But a bucking horse chilled her with fear. And for the rest, she was feminine of the feminine, and rather more demure than the average. The more she fought against herself, the more she became like herself. And she knew that, as she grew older, the rancher and his wife were more and more tormented by her presence.

They insisted on giving her a good education. Sometimes she thought it was because they wished to get her out of the way in this manner. But during vacation times she had to return home. And those vacations were such things of dread that they gave her nights of tearful, wakeful anticipation.

But of all vacation times Christmas was the worst, and of all the Christmas vacation there was nothing to match the horror of Christmas Eve. For on that night, whenever the eyes of the old folks fell on her, they twitched away sharply, as though in pain. She was too gentle of heart to blame them for it. She knew that, since the boy left, their lives had been passed in a long winter of despair. Even his wealth was a torment to the rancher.

He was still saving, but it was merely the effect of habit. Why build a fortune to which no one could fall heir except a girl — a girl who would probably marry and thereby bring the Neilan fortune into the hands of a stranger? There was no other heir. And sometimes Mary Thomas felt that Neilan actually hated her because she could receive the wealth he had created. And yet he still saved his pennies, scrupulously pretending, as he drove a hard bargain or made a niggardly purchase, that it was not for his own sake, but for the sake of Johnny, "when the boy comes home."

How often she had heard that! "When the boy comes home!" She had dreamed of it. She had seen him coming in a thousand guises, repentant, defiant, sneaking, heroic.

The Chinaman, the sole servant in that vast house, barn-like in its silences, padded around the room, serving the plates of chicken as John Neilan carved it. And whenever his misty old eyes fell on the face of the girl they lighted a little, as though he understood and wished to give her the warmth of kindliness which she never received from the old people. But in return she dared not so much as smile with her eyes, for mirth and happiness were sins in the house of the Neilans. What smile was worth seeing save the smile of their lost boy?

Yet, when she looked down to her plate, a faint smile did come about the corners of her mouth. It was always chicken at Christmas time at the ranch. Turkey would be too much like the real festival; and there must be no reality to Christmas until that blessed day when the boy came home. Really, they were a little absurd about it! But when she looked from one to the other of those white heads, those iron-hard faces, all sense of their absurdity left her. Twelve years of constant practice had made them, so to speak, specialists in pain.

"You haven't told us much about the school this time," said Mrs. Neilan at last, by way of breaking in on that solemn quiet. She assumed a faint smile of interest while asking the question, but her eyes looked far off.

Mary sighed.

"The same courses and the same teachers as last year," she said. "There isn't much new to tell about them."

"Just as many parties as ever, I guess?" asked

John Neilan suddenly. "Young Harkins still calling on you?"

"Quite often."

A glance of satisfaction passed between Mr. and Mrs. Neilan, and Mary noted it shrewdly. How well she understood them, and how gross they were not to see that she understood! Their chief interest was merely to see her well married and off their hands. Young Harkins was acceptably well off, and therefore they considered him eligible. She thought back to him with a shrinking of the heart. Perhaps, some day, driven by the constant unhappiness of her life in this home, she would accept the suit of Harkins. But seeing, in vision, the meager form and the dapper ways of that brilliant youth, she could not help sighing again.

"Why don't you ask him out home some vacation time?" asked Mr. Neilan. "Why don't you do that, Mary? You got to make some return, him spending so much time and money toting you around places. Eh?"

How could she tell them that Harkins would be alternately bored and amused by this ranch life and the people of the ranch? She obviously could not say that. But doubtless Jerry Harkins would go to the ends of the earth with her if she so much as hinted that she desired his company.

"I suppose he wants to spend his vacations with his own folks. Besides, he wouldn't be at home with us. He doesn't know ranch life and ranch ways."

"Some gents are that way," observed Neilan. "They ain't got the knack of being at home no matter where they may be. Take Johnny, now. He's different. He used to be at home in every house within thirty miles of us. That was a way he had. Give him a nail to hang up his hat and a box to sit on, and he was all right any place!"

Mary Thomas glanced sharply at Mrs. Neilan and saw that the old lady was trembling; but there was no stopping John Neilan. All year, every year, he was silent on the topic of topics. But on Christmas Eve and Christmas Day his tongue was loosened. But the mother never named her missing boy, perhaps because she did not share the absolute conviction of her spouse that Johnny was still alive, or because she feared that to speak cheerfully, as though confident of his return, might irritate a capricious Providence. She merely nodded to John Neilan with a wan smile and, in a trembling voice, turned the subject of the talk.

And Mary Thomas reached out suddenly, covertly, and pressed the hand of Mrs. Neilan under the cover of the table cloth. Mrs. Neilan started and then stared at the girl as though she feared the latter had gone mad. But, understanding that that pressure of the hand was meant by way of consoling sympathy, she flushed heavily and frowned. Mary Thomas winced back into her chair. It was always this way. They fenced her out of their inner life. In the midst of their household they kept her a stranger.

"Hush!" said John Neilan suddenly.

Outside, borne strongly toward the house on the wind, came the sound of a galloping horse and the singing of a man. There was something indescribably joyous about the song. The rhythm of it matched the swing of the gallop. There was the quick-step of youth in that singing, a great, free, ringing voice that went on smoothly, hardly jarred by the gallop which carried the singer so swiftly toward the house.

"Who is that?" asked Mrs. Neilan. "Who is expected today?"

"Nobody!" answered her husband. He added, pushing back his chair: "Who'd you think it could be?"

The question in his voice, the wild question in his eyes, made Mrs. John Neilan turn white.

"Don't, John!" she whispered! "Don't say that! Don't think that!"

Mary Thomas looked from one to the other. Long as she had lived with them, she could hardly understand a grief so bitterly vital that it turned the chance-heard sound of a galloping horse and a singing traveler into a promise and a hope!

Then — they heard it indistinctly — a heavy footfall ran up the steps.

"The side steps, John!" breathed Mrs. Neilan, swaying forward and steadying herself with her withered hands against the edge of the table.

And Mary remembered, Johnny in the past had always used the side entrance.

"Wait!" gasped Mr. Neilan.

And, commanded by his raised hand, they

dared not draw a breath. And then — the door banged with a jingling of the outer screen! The stranger had boldly entered without knocking. He had entered from the side; he was coming, singing softly. His footfall was swift and heavy. The old flooring trembled beneath the shocks of his heels and set the glasses quivering on the table. No, that vibration was caused by the shaking hands of Mr. and Mrs. Neilan!

Suddenly the mother was strong and the father was weak.

"Listen!" breathed John Neilan. "It's the old song . . . his old song, 'The Bullwacker!' "

Mary Thomas, who had hitherto pitied them for their excitement, was caught up in the contagion.

"Don't, John!" pleaded the old woman.

"I can't stand it!"

He dropped into his chair and covered his face with his hands. What old hands they were, and how much they had labored, and how much they had made his own — all for the sake of that lost child! But Mrs. Neilan rose and went swiftly around the table and went to him. There she stood, with her hand resting on the bowed head, facing the door. All at once Mary knew how pretty the withered old woman had been in her youth. And her eyes, beneath their wrinkled, puckered lids, were now as brilliant and liquid as the eyes of a girl. The door from the library opened into the hall. The singing now boomed out at them, was hushed to a humming sound. Then came a silence, and in the silence Mary saw the knob of the dining room door turn slowly, without sound.

Her heart stopped — then bounded violently.

The door swung open, and there against the darkness of the hall appeared a tall youth of mighty shoulders, handsome in a singularly boyish way, brown as a berry, so that his eyes in contrast were a deep-sea blue.

There he stood smiling, his hat in his hand, a thin powdering of snow across the breast of his coat gleaming in the lamplight like diamond dust. The brain of Mary Thomas swirled with a hundred thoughts. Could this be he? Were those straight-looking eyes the eyes of the mischievous, untrustworthy boy of whom she had heard so many tales? Could it be that he had returned, in fact, on this day of all days?

Suddenly he was frowning.

"Why, mother, don't you know me?"

That word removed all doubt, swept away all hesitancy to credence.

"John!" cried the mother. "It's . . . the boy! Oh, Johnny, my dear!"

What a cry it was! The long winter of grief was over and broken. The green and golden springtime of happiness had come in an instant. She ran across the room with a step as light as the step of a girl. She reached up her arms and caught them around the big fellow in the doorway, and he, as lightly as though she were a child, lifted her bodily from the floor and kissed her.

John Neilan came stumbling blindly toward

them, his hand stretched out to feel his way. And then a great arm, a great brown hand, swept out and gathered in the old man. The three were a weeping, murmuring unit.

What was her place in that room or in that house? Mary rose and slipped from the dining room.

IV

"Mary Thomas's Intuition"

In her own room she went to the window and peered forth. The night was frosty-clear. The stars were out. The trees were doubly black against that pure white of snow which, now and then, puffing up like dust, was whirled past the window, obscuring the landscape.

Truly there was never a more perfect night for a Christmas Eve. There was something wonderfully pure and honest about that great outdoors. It could not have allowed a fraud to come out of it to the house. Fraud? No, the deep-blue eyes gleaming out of that brown face were ample assurance of his honesty. And, indeed, he had come like fate. And the instant his voice was heard, had not the father guessed? Blood spoke to blood. There was something terribly moving about it all. The heaven, full of stars, was splintered with party-colored rays; she was staring up through her tears. Her dear ones could never come to her out of the night. Out of the past she gathered the few memories which had clung in her child-mind — the tender eyes of her mother, the deep voice of her father. That was all she had to take to her heart on Christmas Eve.

A light, faltering tap was heard on the door and then Mrs. Neilan came running in. How changed she was! Joy bubbled up within her and looked out through her eyes. Was this the iron-hard woman she had known and feared? She came to Mary and passed her arm about the girl.

"John saw you leave the room, dear. He wants you to come back. And . . . oh, Mary, isn't it like a miracle? Isn't it like an answer to a prayer? Are there really fools who don't believe in a God . . . even on Christmas Day?"

"You ought to be alone with him," said Mary, "on this first night. And I think I should be alone, too."

Ordinarily the least resistance to suggestions angered Mrs. Neilan. But she was a new woman tonight and, turning the girl toward the lamp, she studied her face and the tear-dimmed eyes.

"I know," she said. "I think, I know. Poor dear! But you must come down. We have happiness enough to spare for the whole world. And why should we care about one night? He's promised that he'll never leave again. Never!"

Mary could not resist. She went down the stairs with Mrs. Neilan, their arms about each other like two friends of one age. That dark stairway had always been a place of dread to Mary, but now she felt as though she were going down into a sunshine presence.

A new place had been laid at the table, and the wanderer sat at it with a plate heaped high. He rose at once and came to them.

"They've told me about you, a little," he said. "I figured maybe you'd think that this was just a family party, and that you were out of it. But, to my way of thinking, you're as much a part of the family as I am. Let's all sit around and be sociable, eh?"

He took her to her chair. He drew it out and seated her. Then he hurried around to his place again and attacked the ample provisions which Mrs. Neilan had heaped before him. And what a time followed! How the father heaped questions — how the mother warded those questions away until her boy should have eaten! And eat he did with tremendous appetite. He talked as he could in the brief interludes.

"Where have I been? Everywhere! North, but mostly south. What have I been doing? Everything! Remember I was a work hater? Well, I've had to swing a pick and a shovel and hammer a drill. I've had to pitch hay and mow it and stack it. I've had to feed on a baler. I've roped and branded and bored fence holes and strung wire. Look there!"

He extended his long arms so that they dominated the whole table — what a huge fellow he was! thought Mary — and, turning his palms uppermost, he exposed to their view hands callused from the heel of the palm to the work-squared tips of the fingers. And as he flexed them, the big wrist cords stood out, mute testimony to lifting of weights and struggling at burdens!

"Poor boy! Poor Johnny!" and his mother sighed.

"Poor nothing!" The wanderer grinned with an irrepressible smile of good humor. "It's been a twelve-year lark. I've had to work, sure enough; but those calluses are the price of freedom. By the way, I figure there's no price too high to pay for that?"

"John!" murmured Mrs. Neilan. "Johnny, dear! Do you mean that?"

"Oh, no fear of me slipping off again," he said, flushing a little. "I've had my fling, right enough. What you see, Dad?"

The old man had taken the right hand of the newcomer and now examined it earnestly.

"The other hand is tolerable pale from glove wearing," he said slowly, "but this one looks as though they ain't been many gloves on it, son!"

Raising his eyes gravely, he added, as he relinquished the hand: "I dunno where you been, but around these parts you may remember that gents that don't wear gloves on their right hands keep 'em bare for one reason; and that was so's they'd be quick and clean on the draw!"

"John!" cried Mrs. Neilan to her husband. "You have no right to accuse Johnny of being a fighting man! And on his first night home!"

"I've done my share of fighting," said the wanderer, his face darkening slightly as he looked down to the sun-browned right hand which was now the center of the conversation. "I don't deny that I've had my troubles, and I guess I have to admit that I ain't been in the habit of running away from fights. But" — and here he raised his head and looked around with a suddenly bright smile — "I can say this much: I've never picked on any gent on the ranges, north or south. I've never forced a fight. I've never hunted trouble. And I've never taken an unfair advantage. If what you're driving at is that maybe some think I'm a gunfighter, well, I got to admit that I've been called that. But I've never used a gun to get a gent that hadn't done me a wrong or wronged a pal of mine. I've never used it to get something that wasn't mine by rights. Does that clear me up?"

And he looked a straight challenge at John Neilan. The latter laughed softly and joyously.

"D'you think I expected you to turn out a softy?" he asked. "D'you think I expected you to turn out a ladies' man? Ain't you John Neilan's son?"

Here the door from the hall opened, and the Chinaman, who had been absent from the dining room for some time, now stood grinning and nodding before them. Mrs. Neilan rose at once with a flush of pleasure.

"Chung has something to show us," she suggested. "Let's see what it is. You first tonight, Johnny!"

The big fellow stepped smilingly ahead, crossed the dark gap of the hallway, and passed on through the open doors of the parlor. It was a flare of light from the huge lamp which hung in chains from the center of the ceiling, and from three or four more big circular burners placed most effectively to cast their light on one corner. And in that corner stood a young fir tree, with gay trimming heaped upon its branches, and all about it on the floor was a jumble of wrapped-up boxes and packages. Some of the paper on those packages was yellow with time; other of it was fresh and crisp. It was a huge pile, spread wide across the floor.

"What in the world!" exclaimed the wanderer.

"It's twelve Christmases all in one!" said the mother, with a trembling voice.

"See what's here, Johnny! Open them for him, Dad. No, give them to him to open!"

"Here's the first one," said the old man, quickly making a selection. "I remember getting it. More'n twelve years ago! Here you are Johnny!"

And he thrust a long, slender, heavy box into the hands of a stranger.

Mary Thomas glanced to the big youth with an expectant smile, but her smile went out. He, too, was attempting to smile, but his face was white and his mouth pinched in at the sides.

"You been remembering me every Christmas since I . . . left?"

"Remembering you? Son, have we remembered anything but you?"

"Open it, dear!" said the mother. "Open it!"

The big hand strayed slowly down the length of the package. Any one could guess from the shape and weight that it was a gun.

But instead of opening it, he repeated slowly: "Every Christmas?"

"Aye, every one!"

"It's been twelve years," said the big man huskily, "and that's a long time to wait. I ain't written to you. I've treated you plumb bad all the way through. And still . . . every year . . . for twelve years . . . you ain't forgot me a single time at Christmas."

"Open up them packages and see!" said John Neilan eagerly. "Ah, Johnny, it's been a sad business, getting presents every year and never knowing if you. . . ."

"I knew," said Mrs. Neilan suddenly. "I always knew he'd come."

But Mary Thomas heard their voices no more distinctly than if they had been ghost whispers. She saw nothing but the face of the wanderer, gray and drawn with pain.

"I didn't know," he muttered, "that fathers and mothers could be like this. I didn't know what Christmas could be!"

"You didn't have much cause to find out from me," said the father. "I treated you pretty bad, son. I was too busy making money and stacking it away to pay much attention to my own boy. But I've learned different in these twelve years. I know now what's worth while in the world. You remember what we had the last trouble about? About the key to the safe?" He laughed in excitement. "The safe is in the cellar in the old place, and here's that key to the lock! Take it, Johnny, and keep it for me, and if you want everything in the safe, go and take it and don't ask no questions. Money? Money's dirt compared to having you back!"

The wanderer accepted the key with a trembling hand and then offered to return it.

"Too much trust is like too much liquor," he said. "You sure you want me to have this? You sure it ain't going to turn my head for me."

"That's only the beginning," declared the father. "What you do with things don't matter. They're yours! Now open the packages, son!"

"Not now," said the stranger slowly. "Not now. Seems to me the way used to be to open up things on Christmas morning. Ain't that right? I . . . I'll open 'em up then, all together!"

But for some reason Mary Thomas knew, as she watched him, that he would never break the string on one of those packages. Instinct told her that, and she wondered at it.

V

"The Fight with Conscience"

In all that followed throughout the evening, Happy Jack was aware of one thing only, and that was the watchful eye of Mary Thomas. Whatever he was doing, she caught him with a glance now and then, and it seemed to the big fellow from the southland that the steady eyes looked through and through him and found out his guilty secret.

In the meantime, fresh tides of life and uproarious noise began to invade the house. From the cheerless bunkhouse, where they were drowsing on this unhappy Christmas Eve, most melancholy of all nights to the wanderers, the cowpunchers of the Neilan outfit were roused and brought to the big house itself — an unprecedented act of hospitality on the part of the rancher, for since the disappearance of Johnny hardly half a dozen strangers had succeeded in getting past the door of the house.

They came haltingly, prepared to find it a false invitation which the Chinaman had extended to them. But they found, instead of a chilling reception, open arms! Mrs. John Neilan with color as high as a girl of eighteen floated here and there among them, making them at home. And Mary

Thomas, with fewer words, was an even more effective worker. The resources of the kitchen were called upon. The big dining table was spread again. From the depths of the cellar heavily cob-webbed bottles of sherry — how long, long ago they had been stored there and for twelve years been untouched! — were brought up. One by one they disappeared. It was like turning a hose on the desert, save that the dry throats of the cow-boys gave some return. They opened in song. They toasted old John Neilan until even his hard eyes began to twinkle. And they gave a tremen-dous rouse for the returned prodigal. And then they all stood up and sang for Mary Thomas and drank to her. It was a very great occasion. It was an evening when no one could remember any-thing that was said. But all were riotously happy.

Gifts were found for all. One robust cow-puncher received a fine revolver, another a watch, another a saddle — and so on until every one had his share. This was wild liberality, but old John Neilan cared not for possessions on such a night as this.

"The old boy's gone mad," one of the 'punch-ers observed.

"Nope, he's just woke up and come to his senses," insisted a second. "This is the way he would of growed to be if the kid hadn't walked off in the old days. Now he's making up for lost time. What d'you think of the kid?"

"Why, I figure he'd be a tolerable good partner, and a tolerable bad one to have for an enemy.

You seen old Chip step on his toe a while back?"

"Nope. What about it?"

"Nothing happened. But just for a second Johnny Neilan give Chip a bad look. And he sure swings an ugly eye, I'll tell a man. Like a bull terrier that just walks up and sinks a tooth into your leg without letting out a growl. Look there! The kid may have wandered around a lot, but I think he's found home, eh?"

This last remark was caused by an earnest, head-to-head conversation which was taking place between Happy Jack and Mary Thomas. Certainly the wanderer evinced a great and growing interest in the girl. As for Mary Thomas, her color had risen. She was talking with animation and laughter, and a rather grim smile of appreciation played around the lips of Happy Jack.

The dinner for the cowboys was now breaking up. They were comparing the gifts which "the Old Man" had brought out for them. They were exchanging yarns and slaps on the back and guffawing hugely at nothing in particular. Someone had brought in an armful of fir boughs and scattered them here and there at random, so that the air breathed with the resinous scent which means Christmas.

"Hey, Chip Flinders!" called one of the two whose comments have just been noticed. "Hey, Chip!"

An oldish fellow with hair dull gray at the temples and a weather-worn face paused near them.

"What's biting you," he asked, without a smile.

"There ain't any cloud in the sky except you, Chip. What's wrong?"

Chip Flinders regarded his questioner without pleasure.

"Don't you see nothing wrong?" he asked at last.

"Nope."

"Have you took a look at Johnny Neilan?"

"A pile of 'em, and he looks like something that's all right to me."

"Does he? Maybe he is. I dunno. But he reminds me powerful of somebody that ain't all right."

"Who?"

"I dunno. That's what I'm figuring on and trying to remember . . . where I seen him before with a gun in each hand and. . . ."

He wandered on, his head down, his face thoughtful.

"Huh!" grunted one of the pair who had asked the questions. "What if the kid has done some fighting. Is that ag'in' him? If fighting is so plumb bad, old Chip himself had ought to watch out. He's done his share in the south, they say."

"Yep, and he bears the marks of it. I've seen him stripped. All chawed up like as if a mountain lion had wrastled with him."

But there was no other blot on the good cheer of the occasion. Only the frown of Chip darkened the affair until the hour of midnight was turned and Christmas Day itself was ushered in with a ringing carol.

After that they broke up quickly and, while the people of the house went to their rooms, the cowpunchers returned to the bunkhouse with broad grins of content, each man with the warmth of sherry in his blood and Christmas in his mind and a gift in his hand. Only Chip Flinders stared gloomily down at the snow over which he was striding.

From the window of the room to which John Neilan had led him, Happy Jack looked down at the procession of the cowpunchers with a frown as dark as the frown of Chip. For he, too, was striving with all his might to remember where he had seen that face with the tufts of gray hair above the temples and the solemn, worn expression. But he could not remember. The harder he concentrated the more his mind went adrift from the past, and when he felt that he had discovery under his mental finger tips, an image from this gay and crowded evening would flit across his eyes and obscure the past.

At length he turned away, as the last of the cowpunchers disappeared through the door of the bunkhouse, and looked about the room. It needed only a glance to make sure that this was the only room where Johnny Neilan had slept in the old days. From the wall a huge, dim enlargement of a photograph looked down at him, showing a youth with faintly smiling lips and a twinkle of mischief in the eyes. Even in the picture of the boy there was a startling resemblance to Happy Jack. No doubt if Johnny Neilan had lived to maturity, he would have been sufficiently different; but in his childhood he possessed the promise of all the features of Happy Jack. It was not strange that the sharp eye of Sandy Crisp had marked the resemblance and taken advantage of it.

Sandy Crisp! What a devil incarnate he was!

Thinking of the outlaw, Happy Jack moved about the room making what discoveries he could. And there were plenty of things to interest him. He found in the bureau drawers heaps of undergarments, and dozens of socks, some worn and neatly darned, some fresh — the equipment of Johnny Neilan, no doubt. In a big closet, large as a little room by itself, he found a great assortment of guns and fishing tackle on one side and articles for riding on the other side — bridles and spurs and saddle blankets. Truly, the boy had been given enough things to amuse himself. What had caused the discontent which eventually drove him from the house?

As though to answer him, at the moment his hand brushed aside the curtain from a little row of bookshelves, and there he found row on row of textbooks. There was a Latin grammar and a tattered "Commentaries." There was a copy of "Classic Myths" and a translation of the "Iliad." And so, on and on, Happy Jack picked up book after book, all unfamiliar to him as strange faces in a strange land. Had poor young Johnny Neilan been forced to struggle through all these?

He opened them. The interiors presented page

after page filled with crude drawings of bucking horses and guns. These had formed the occupation of young Neilan when he was supposed to be imbibing knowledge. And beyond a doubt this was the nightmare that had driven him away from the ranch and north on the endless trail of adventure until he died there on the log jam, laughing and waving his hat. No doubt he had been a wild youth. But perhaps there had been little harm in his wildness. Had he grown up he might have done things as fine and brave as his death scene, and far more useful.

Happy Jack was hard enough. For there are few, unfortunately, who acquire such calluses of labor on their hands without getting similar calluses about the heart. But, sitting in this room, the presence of the dead boy was around him like a ghost, rattling at the fishing tackle in the closet or handling the guns or humming in the wind which now curled around the corner of the house in a steady gale.

A foolish insistence on the study of books had driven young Neilan away from his home. And did not the father deserve the pains which had come to him? He was a hard man. There was no doubt of that. Sandy Crisp had said so with profound conviction. And had not Happy himself watched the painful intentness with which the rancher followed the raising of each glass of his precious sherry? One large and kindly impulse had induced that sacrifice of good liquor, but it seemed that the old fellow sighed at once because of his own generosity. Hard he certainly was, and though the return of his son, as if from the grave, had loosened his spirit, might it not be a kindliness of the moment only and no permanent change? And, indeed, even in that happiness there was a selfish motive. John Neilan had acquired someone to whom he could leave his property. Hence he rejoiced.

In the meantime, he held the key to the safe!

Happy Jack drew out the key and then the plan of the house with which Sandy Crisp had furnished him. He glanced over it to make sure that he had every winding of hall and stairway in mind. Yes, it would be perfectly simple to steal down the back stairs and into the basement and return the same way, then make his exit through the window of his room and over the roof of the verandah to the freedom of the snow beyond. To slip out to the stables with his loot, saddle his horse, and then ride to the rendezvous in the neighboring woods where Crisp waited — that would be a simple thing.

Happy Jack stood up, resolved to act. So doing, his glance fell full on the eye of the boy in the photograph, and Happy shrank back with a curse.

For a moment he wavered, the good and the evil fighting in him for mastery. But it has been said that Happy had elements of hardness in his nature, and he showed it now. On the one hand he was betraying a trust for the first time in his life. On the other hand he was securing a "stake"

— for young Jackson's family even more than himself, it's true — for the first time in his life. He made a rough accounting between right and wrong, as he stood there scowling at the image of the true Johnny Neilan.

To be sure, this was a scoundrelly thing to do. But had not other men done scoundrelly things to him? How many hundreds — aye, thousands — of dollars had he not loaned to "friends?" And how many cents on the dollar had been returned to him?

He had gone through life giving with both hands, not only of money but of his personal services. He had not pried into the right and wrong of the requests which were made of him. Out of a whole heart he had done his best to meet every demand. The result was that he found himself past twenty-five without a cent in the world — with no possessions except his horse and gun.

What was the result of all of this reasoning? Why, simply that the world owed him something for what he had given the world. He wanted both principal and interest back and, if he got it from Neilan, what was wrong? It was only a fair exchange, taking from a man who really had not a need for his money.

It was certainly a tortuous course of reasoning such as has led to many a crime being committed. But when he concluded the silent argument, it must be said in favor of Happy that his forehead was cold and wet with perspiration, so that he growled: "Maybe I'm losing my nerve!"

That decided him. He tightened his belt, looked to his gun, and saw that it came easily from the holster under his touch; then he advanced to the door of his room, opened it an inch or more, and listened.

VI

"Between Nobility and Crime"

There was a hall light burning, a pendent lamp which, with the wick turned low, cast a dim, yellowish haze up and down the corridor, only bright where it fell on the red carpet in a circle around the black shadow of the bowl. The walls advanced and receded in faintly glowing yellow-gray, and every doorway, sunk into the thick, old walls of the house, was a gaping depth of black. Happy Jack peered up and down this gloomy tunnel and then listened to the faint thudding of his heart against his ribs.

He had read in stories and he had heard in tales about the camp fire of men hearing the beating of the heart in moments of fear; but in all the battles which had marked his stormy life he had never known it before. Danger, to him, had been something to be greeted as a friend rather than an enemy, a thing to rush at with extended arms, even if those arms ended in clenched fists. But this new emotion, this fear, was a stranger to him, and he wondered at himself.

He was continually compressing his lips to swallow, but his dry throat refused to obey. And his fingers trembled on the doorknob, in sign of the tremor of the nerves all through his big body. He hardly knew himself in this great, shaken hulk of flesh.

The thought came to him that his crime would be discovered as soon as the morning came. He closed the door to the hall and leaned heavily against it, panting. His thoughts wrestled him to and fro, the perspiration still streaming down his face. If only this money were to be gained by facing some actual danger! But no, there was no one in the house to fight. An old woman and a young one, and a man well past his fighting days. They were the only ones to face him! His enemy was shame, fierce and biting shame. Suppose that fresh-faced, clear-eyed girl, Mary Thomas, should spy him out, should look in on him as, with guilty hands, he opened the door of the safe and took out the greenbacks!

He found himself staring at the wall like one stricken with the sight of a ghost. But this was all perfectly childish. He must go down at once. At once! The world owed the money to him.

Suddenly he was through the door and out in the hall. He advanced now very steadily, finding his progress much easier after he took the first step. The start was the hard part. In the meantime the boards of the flooring creaked terribly under his feet. Strange that they had been so silent when he came upstairs to his bed just a few minutes before. But dread and horror of the thing which he was about to do sharpened his perceptions, and a murmur of board rubbing against board that could hardly have been heard a yard away seemed to Happy Jack loud enough to waken every person in the house.

And had they not been wakened? Was not that the sound of someone sitting up in bed, the springs creaking under the shifted weight? And was not that the thudding of a guarded footfall approaching a door nearby? And was not that the rattle of a lock on which a hand had fallen?

No, it was only a straying draft which had shaken the door, but for a moment he paused, frozen with fear. When he went on again, he was shaking like a leaf — he, Happy Jack, famous through the southland as the hero of the Morgan Run fight! But now he was unnerved — and by a woman!

The creaking of the boards in the upper hall was nothing compared with the noises which accompanied him down the stairs. They literally swayed and reeled beneath him. They groaned from end to end under his descending weight. It seemed as though the dead timber of the house were living and attempting to warn the inhabitants of the dastardly crime about to be committed by this trusted guest, this false son of the family.

Such fancies made play in the brain of Happy Jack, and each one of them was almost a real possibility. He gave each a serious consideration until he felt, before he reached the bottom of the steps, that he should go mad.

But there he was in the great open rooms of

the lower floor. In a far corner, barely visible against the dim square of a window, stood the Christmas tree, like a gaunt ghost holding out arms. Happy Jack caught up a hand against his eyes and shut out the reproachful vision.

He returned down the hall to the rear of the house, opened the door which, on his plan, was jotted down as the entrance to the cellar, and found himself staring down into utter darkness. He took out the little electric lantern with which Sandy Crisp had thoughtfully provided him, and snapped a small torrent of light that tumbled down the damp steps and showed brown-black dirt below.

Then he went down, cursing the squeaking boards with each step, next blessing the muffling dirt under his heel. He found the safe room easily. Certainly Sandy Crisp must have studied the house in the most minute detail, just as he had said.

"Go in blindfold," he had declared, "and I'll give you a plan so good that you can feel your way around and come to the right place."

The safe was kept in a room walled off by itself. The walls were of foundation stones, each one of huge dimensions and solidly mortared together; the great door was adorned with a tremendous padlock, of a device such as Happy had never seen before. Double-fold idiot that he was! Sandy had warned him to get the key to the padlock as well as the key to the safe.

Suddenly he breathed a sigh of relief. He could

not get that key tonight. He would go out and tell Sandy that the deal was off, and that he wanted to have no more to do with it. No, that would send Sandy abroad with a huge tale about the weak nerve of Happy Jack — how he started out to do a robbery and lacked the courage to carry it through.

As a matter of fact, a crime once started was as good as completed, so far as one's own conscience went. So argued unhappy Jack as he stood staring at the padlock. Automatically, not with a hope, he tried the safe key in the padlock. At the first turn something yielded. Astonished, he turned it again, and behold, the lock was sprung!

Happy Jack blinked. But, after all, it was perfectly clear. The rancher had simply ordered a padlock which would duplicate the lock of his safe.

The door now began to swing open without pressure of his hand, and presently Happy sent the shaft of light from his torch straight into the face of a big, squat safe, older than three generations of men. The lock on the door and the lock on the safe had been too implicitly trusted by the old man for, once an expert cracksman got at the safe, with even a "can opener," the safe would be gutted of its money.

To Jack, of course, it was a very simple affair. In half a minute the door of the safe was open, and he was pulling out drawer after drawer. The one was piled with documents, another was crammed with account books, and in the third he found the money. When his fingers closed over it, he waited for the exultant leap of his pulses, but it did not come. He did not pause to count but, glancing at the denominations of a few of the bills and then estimating the thickness of the pile, he figured it to be between thirty and forty thousand dollars that he held.

Why did the rancher keep so much money on the ranch? Was it because, miser-like, he loved to sun himself in the presence of hard cash?

A door slammed heavily. Happy Jack whirled with the speed of guilt, which is swifter by far than the speed of a striking snake, and his gun was in his hand as he whirled. But in a moment he knew that the door had banged somewhere in an upper story of the house. He was safe, unobserved as yet.

He felt a sudden panic, a blind, strange thing, spring on him out of the thin air and cling to him like a writhing, living object. Danger was all about him. It was grinning at him from the shadows. It was lurking beyond the door!

Not stopping to close and relock the door to the safe, Happy sneaked out to the door of the little room and crouched there, shooting flashes of light from side to side and combing the cellar to make sure that no one was watching and waiting.

Then he cursed himself for his stupidity. What was so likely as the light itself to attract attention? He snapped it out and started at a run for the stairway leading to the floor above. As though in key with his emotions, a terrific gale at the same time smashed against the house and howled about the corners, wailing and shaking doors and windows. And in that wild uproar, springing through the darkness, Happy Jack reached the stairs and flew to the top of it.

He was through the door, shut it quickly behind him, and then leaned against it to shut behind the danger which seemed to have snapped at his heels and barely missed him as he darted through to safety. And his heart, all the time, worked like a trip hammer. The violence of its actions shook him.

Ten seconds more, and he would be through the door, outside, and on his way. What should prevent him? He pulled the hat lower on his forehead and looked up and down. The house was quiet. The wind had fallen. Sudden calm was everywhere. And Happy stepped quickly to the front door of the house.

With his hand on the knob he paused, remembering that he had taken off his coat and left it in the room above. But what difference did the coat make?

He began to open the door, and yet he closed it again without stepping out. The coat made every difference, now that he came to think of it. As long as he was committing burglary, he should do it both boldly and smoothly. And to run out like a frightened child in his shirt sleeves — certainly that would bring a smile to the sinister eyes of Sandy Crisp.

On so small a thing the fate of Happy Jack was hanging. One step through the door and he was committed forever to a life of crime. But if he turned back — who could tell? He was not yet entirely across the border line of the law, perhaps.

He went up the stairs more swiftly than he had come down. Now that the matter had been pushed so close to completion, he would brazen it through the last stages with a rush. In his room again, he caught up the coat and shoved his arms into the sleeves, leaving it unbuttoned, for in that manner he was given a freer play at his revolver butt.

Again he hesitated, in the act of stepping from the room. Would it not be better to leave something as a message?

He tore a flyleaf out of a book and leaned over it to scribble a note; but, while he searched for words, a gust of wind from the open window flicked the paper from under his fingers and tossed it to the floor. He scooped it up with an oath and found lying before him, printed on the leaf: "The New Testament."

Happy Jack crunched the paper to a ball, while he drew his breath in a deep intake. That was the book of Christ, and this was Christ's day! His hand, swinging back against the pocket of the coat, struck the package of greenbacks, and he jerked his arm wide again, cursing. Fate was against him.

Well, he would get clear of this house. It was

beginning to weigh on him with a mortal burden, even the necessity of being under its roof. He turned to the door, in time to hear two light knocks upon it.

The sound stopped his heartbeat.

It was utter folly, of course. What had he to fear from any creature who announced his coming and did not strike him by surprise?

"Come in!" called Happy Jack.

There was no answer. Then he knew that his throat had refused to give body to the words he tried to speak. He went to the door and drew it open and, white against the darkness of the hall, he found himself looking down into the face of his pseudo-mother, Mrs. John Neilan.

VII

"Happy's Gift Promise"

She was wrapped to the throat in a black dressing gown, and her white hair, quite disordered, floated like a mist about her face. But, at sight of Happy Jack, her eyes brightened.

"You!" said Happy Jack. "You?"

He would rather have faced the guns of ten hard fighters at that moment than the pair of eyes which one glimpse of him had so brightened. Suddenly she was clinging to him.

"Johnny!" she was pleading. "You're not going? You're not going?"

"Me?" muttered Happy Jack. "Me? Why should I go?"

"Your hat and your coat . . . at this hour. . . ."

"I couldn't sleep. Being all sort of filled up with happiness about being home, I thought I'd step out and take a walk in the snow to get quieted down again. You see?"

She stroked his big arm gently, as though to make sure of him by the sense of touch, not trusting to her eyes or ears.

"And that's all?" she pleaded.

"Sure!"

She drew back at that, laughing a little.

"I guess I'm a goose," she said, "but I haven't been able to sleep, either. Do you know what I've been doing? I've been standing at the window, half expecting, any minute, to see you slip out and go to the stable for your horse. You see, when you talked about the freedom of being your own master in the world, the idea stayed with me. And I didn't see how you could be happy here with us. And then . . . then I came up to make sure of you."

She laughed again, but this time happily.

"And here I am," said Happy Jack, wretched to the bottom of his heart as he studied the aged, kindly face. No matter what charges could be brought against Neilan, there was nothing to be said against his wife. And in the final accounting, how black would be the record of his trick upon this woman! "Here I am, and here to stay."

He forced a smile to cover the lie and give it reality.

"And happy, dear?"

"Aye," said Happy Jack. "I'm happy."

"When you opened the door you fairly growled at me. 'You!' you said, in such a voice! As though I were an armed man, you know. And, Johnny, won't you take off that hat and coat for just a minute? It makes me nervous to see you dressed to go."

He obeyed without a word and turned to find her nodding and smiling.

"When you were a boy, dear," she said, "you'd have growled at me for being so foolish."

"Was I as bad as that?"

"Not bad! Oh, no. But just headstrong. I suppose every boy with the makings of a man in him is that way now and then. But you remember the checked suit I bought for your birthday, the one you burned because you were ashamed to wear it? That was one of the things I couldn't understand in the old days. But, oh, Johnny, how much more I can understand now!"

"Did I do that?" muttered Happy Jack. "Did I burn the suit? The one you gave me for a birthday present?"

"But don't tell me you've forgotten! It was your thirteenth birthday, you know. The last one. . . ."

She stopped, and her eyes filled. And Happy Jack threw back his head and opened his shirt at the throat. He was stifling. What would go on in the brain and the soul of the woman when she learned of the hoax that had been played?

"I remember," he said huskily.

"And now you're angry because I've brought it up! I didn't mean to. . . ."

"Hush!" gasped Happy Jack. "Don't talk like that! Angry? With you? D'you know where a gent like me ought to be when he's talking to a lady like you? Down on his knees! Down on his knees, thinking what a mean, sneaking coyote he is."

She ran to him and stopped him with a raised forefinger.

"That isn't a bit like my Johnny," she said. "I . . . I'm afraid you've had hard times, or you'd never have learned to talk like this."

"I was a brute of a hard-mouthed kid," said Happy Jack. "All I knew was pulling on the bit. But I've learned different. It was kicked into me."

"Who dared to strike you?"

"About a hundred, off and on," and Happy chuckled, "have taken a crack at me."

"My dear, my dear," murmured the mother. "But I have you safely home now."

Happy Jack laughed.

"I've growed big enough to . . . to take care of myself tolerable well," he declared. "But. . . ."

He stopped. She had uttered a little cry of horror and, reaching up, she pushed back his shirt and exposed his chest. A great ragged scar ran across it. And, drawing back the cloth a little more, she saw a broad spot, shining like silver.

"Johnny!" she gasped. "What . . . what made those marks on you?"

"Them?" said Happy Jack carelessly, but re-buttoning his shirt, nevertheless. "Well, you see, I've had little mixes now and then. And those are the marks."

"But on your chest . . . weren't you nearly killed?"

"Pretty near, a couple of times. But I come through, all right."

"And that's the world you called your world of freedom! A world of death is what it is!"

"Maybe. But, when a gent's knocking around, he's got to take what comes his way."

"Tell me this minute," demanded the mother,

"the names of the . . . the creatures who hurt you like that!"

"The long one," said Happy thoughtfully, "with the fancy lace work about the edges, that scar come from a little run-in I had with a hoss. Him and me had it out to see which was the better man. And he put me to bed. He got me off the saddle by running under a tree. And when I was down he come along and done a dance on top of me."

She covered her eyes, shuddering.

"And they killed the horrible brute, I hope."

"Killed him? Killed old Captain?" He started, almost in alarm, and then relaxed in a chuckle. "I should say not! Captain is the hoss I ride, and they's none better. He can turn around on a dime and jump like he had wings and dodge like a yearling calf. Besides, him and me are pals."

Mrs. Neilan looked at him as though he stood at a great distance and she had to peer hard to make him out.

"I never could understand in the old days," she said sadly, "and I guess I'll have to give up trying to understand now. But I'll never give up loving you, Johnny, dear, and keeping you! And . . . and that long straight scar below the ragged one, dear?"

"It don't make no pretty story," said Happy Jack. "But I'll tell you if it'll make you feel any easier. I was playing poker one night in a strange town with some strange gents. Playing poker with strangers is like eating in a strange cookhouse.

You got to keep watching your hand or you'll starve. Anyway, there was a Canuck down from Canada with a disposition like a branding-fire on a hot day. He was so plumb nacheral mean that he cussed his tobacco while he was rolling a cigarette, and he cussed the cigarette after the tobacco was in it, and he cussed the match while he was lighting the cigarette, and then he wound up by cussing the floor he dropped the match on. You know that kind?

"Well, he was sure a fine gent to sit across the table from at poker. If you made a bet ag'in' him, he looked at you like he was picking out the place where he was going to shoot you. He had me plumb nervous with his little ways and his hitching at a knife one minute and playing with a gun the next. Anyway, to make a short yarn of it, I come over three kings and a brace of jacks in his hand with three bullets and a pair of measly little deuces in mine. And I pretty near cleaned him out. Well, he sure went up in smoke. He was trembling all over, he was so mad. He passed a word or two at me, and then he reaches over the table with a grin and says he'll shake hands to show they's no hard feelings. And when he had my right hand, he pulls a knife with his left and slashes me. That's the way that happened."

"I hope they lynched him!" said Mrs. Neilan through her teeth, her eyes shining with anger.

"Nope, they took him to a hospital. I took care not to kill him, but I sure salted him away plenty. And the funny part was that it took all my winnings at that game to pay his hospital expenses."

"You paid them?"

"Think I was going to leave him to charity? Nope. I have my fun and pay my bills for it. I guess that's all you want to know about the scars?"

"I . . . I'm afraid to ask any more, Johnny. But there's a round, white one, about the size of a twenty-five-cent piece. . . ."

"That was at Morgan Run. They got me good that day!"

"Who are they?"

"I was doing a favor for a friend of mine that was a sheriff down south. Not that I play in with posses much. But a gang turned loose and did a couple of pretty bad jobs around the country. When they robbed a house, they burned it afterward to cover their tracks. And that ain't a pretty game. So I rode in the sheriff's party, and we took up with 'em at Morgan Run."

"And then . . . ?" she breathed.

"Then there was quite a little party, and they nicked me plenty. But we got 'em all."

"I want to know!"

"You'll never know from me," he said gloomily. "That's something I don't talk about. It . . . it's the only day in my life that I shot to kill. But the skunks got me cornered, and it was me or them! They didn't leave no other chance, and I had to work quick. But here I am, and their trails are all a blank. It was a bad day."

Mrs. John Neilan stared at him in profound wonder.

"And to think," she whispered, "that once I held all of you in my arms . . . so easily . . . so easily . . . Johnny, are you happy to be back with us here?"

"Don't I look it?"

"You have such big, fierce ways." The mother sighed as she spoke. "Sometimes even your own mother is afraid of you!"

"Heaven rest her! Do you think she is?"

"What do you mean?" asked Mrs. Neilan, worried.

"Nothing! But you're not really afraid?"

"I suppose not . . . really. Until you begin to talk about battles."

"You asked me, you know."

"I'll have to keep on asking you until I know about every one, but they won't be twice-told tales for me, Johnny. Only, I have to hear everything once. Because everything that you've done is a part of you. And everything that's a part of you is a part of me. And I have to understand myself, don't I?"

He chuckled at her reasoning.

"But will you prove you're happy here?"

"Any way I can."

"By making me a great gift?"

"It's Christmas," said Happy Jack, "and that's the time for giving, I guess!"

"Then promise me, dear, that you'll never again draw a weapon on any human being. Life is not worth being bought at the expense of another's life. Will you promise? Besides, I'm going to wall you about with such fences of peace that you'll never need a gun again! Will you promise, and make your old mother happy?"

After all, what did one more lie matter?

"I promise!" said Happy Jack.

"Heaven bless you for it! Now I'll go back to my bed and sleep . . . the first real sleep in twelve years, my dear."

VIII

"The Code of an Honest Man"

When she was gone, Happy Jack sank inertly into a chair. He remembered, once, having encountered a formidable enemy in a battle in which no shot was fired. But they merely passed and repassed each other half a dozen times in the little cattle town that day, and always when they were near there was a steady exchange of side glances and insulting smiles. That night the other had ridden suddenly out of town and, when word of his going was brought to Happy Jack by an attentive friend who knew the secret of the feud, Happy had collapsed on a chair as though from the exhaustion of a twenty-hour ride.

So it was now. Every nerve in his body seemed frayed by the strain of talking to Mrs. Neilan. And on his lips was still the tingle of the kiss with which she had left him. It was a living evidence of his lie. It was a brand for his guilt. Never again could he raise his head as an honest man and look his fellows in the face.

How it came about, Happy Jack was never to know. But it was as though a light were turned on in his brain and suddenly he was seeing everything clearly. He had raised his head and met, accidentally, the eyes of the boy pictured on the wall. And he knew as he examined those mischievous eyes that what he intended to do this night was exactly what the dead son would have done had he lived. Yes, it had been fortunate indeed that he had not lived, for surely he would have broken the heart of his mother and maddened his father. That episode of the burned birthday suit, and all it connoted of sullen pride and silly vanity, had not been thrown away upon Happy Jack. And, searching the face for signs of other weaknesses, he was not long in finding them. The eyes were too close together. The mouth was too loose, even for boyhood, and without promise of refinement. Such a daring deed of bravado as he had enacted on the day of his death in the log jam, that face was certainly capable of promising. But for any tenderness, generosity, faith, there was no room.

He, Happy Jack, the man without name, without a family, without a past save that of his own making, was beyond all shadow of question the better man of the two. This stealing in the night, this shameful imposture upon two old people, would have been in the line of the capabilities of the dead man. He, Happy Jack, was above it! He took from his pocket the thick bundle of bills. And he ran his fingers over them. Every one of them represented the wages that might be earned by a month or more of hard labor. Here, in his grip, was the cash valuation of two or three lifetimes of work, for himself and that widow and her three children. All in the grip of his one hand!

He flung it from him to the top of the bureau. He tore out another flyleaf, this time taking a little more care in the selection of the book to be mutilated, and he scrawled across the paper:

This is why I came, and the reason I'm leaving it behind me is because of I don't know what. But I'm not Johnny. You can lay to that. And I'm a pile sorry for having got up a lot of hopes that are not true. Yours to the end of time,

HAPPY JACK

And when the thing was done, he drew a great breath of relief. After all, it was a marvelously simple thing to do. Once he set his hand to it. It seemed to him that a hand fell from his shoulder, the invisible hand of Sandy Crisp which had impelled him first toward this cruel and wicked crime, and which had kept urging him on.

He remembered another thing out of the evening, something which at the time he had taken lightly enough, but which now loomed larger and larger in importance. It was his promise to Mrs. Neilan that he would never again draw his gun upon a human being. Great beads of sweat stood out on his forehead as he thought of it. And that he, Happy Jack, of all people should have made such a promise! It was madness. It was worse — it was suicide! A hundred men would welcome an opportunity to take him at a disadvantage and shoot to kill. Happy Jack without a gun? They would come flocking at the news like buzzards gathering above a dying bull.

Slowly he wiped off the perspiration. His own image from the mirror above the bureau looked forth at him, and he saw a drawn, anguished face.

And, as a matter of fact, he was confident that he was signing his death warrant as he drew out his Colt and placed it on the paper and the money below the paper. Mrs. Neilan would understand when she saw it. At least she would understand what a thousand good men in the southland could have told her before — that the word of Happy Jack was as good as gold.

Once more he turned toward the door of the room, and this time he passed through it, walking strangely light without the weight of the gun at his hip. But there was no other way. To be sure, once outside the house he would have to run the gantlet of Sandy Crisp and whatever men Sandy might have with him. But, if he wished to keep his plighted word, he dared not carry a weapon. His fingers would be too practiced in the art of whipping it forth, and in time of need they would act without his volition. The gun would suddenly appear in his hand and would be discharged before conscience and memory could stop him. Indeed, all the perils which he had previously faced in his life would be nothing compared with the troubles to which the good old woman had consigned him with the promise which she had exacted.

And so, going thoughtfully, and downheaded, along the hall, quite heedless now of the noise which his footsteps made — that being the difference between guilt and an innocent mind — he was quite unaware of a door swinging softly ajar behind him. It was not until he heard the voice, raised barely above a whisper, that he turned.

It was Mary Thomas, a figure to be guessed at rather than seen. Behind her, the shaded lamp, further obscured by the back of a chair pushed up against it, sent a broad film of light straight up toward the ceiling. But the radiance did not reach to her. It was rather the background against which she stood out.

The first thing he noted was the white gesture of her hand waving him toward her. The second thing he saw was that she had not prepared to retire. And that item might mean anything. It might be explained, perhaps, by the curious manner in which she had watched him all through the earlier part of the evening. He went to her at once, for there was no graceful escape.

"I knew it would be this way," she said, as soon as he was close enough. "But you mustn't do it. Come in here a moment!"

He obeyed without a word. She closed the door behind him and turned the key in the lock. And now, as she faced him, there was light enough to show her eyes dancing with excitement.

"You were going to leave?" she said at once. "You were going to leave forever?"

He hesitated. How much did she know?

"I think I understand," she said. "It was either one of two ways. You made a bet that you could do this cruel thing. Or else you were simply hungry and decided to do a bit of acting for the sake of a Christmas dinner."

He rubbed his big, bony knuckles across his chin and smiled at her rather foolishly.

"When did you find out?" he asked

She did not understand.

"It was perfectly clear to anyone with an eye to see. It was perfectly clear the moment you refused to open the packages that they gave you for Christmas. You wouldn't open them simply because they didn't belong to you."

"Hm," muttered the wanderer. "If I'd thought about it, I would have opened 'em!"

She shook her head, still smiling, still keeping back something whose suppression excited her.

"You've been listening for me to start out?"

"I heard you when you left your room before. But I was too late to stop you. I was afraid then that you had gone for good. But I peeked into your room and saw your coat, so I was sure that you had simply gone out for walk. I wanted to talk to you, you see? That's why I've been waiting and watching, and all the time the idea has been growing."

"Fire it at me," said Happy Jack. "I'm tolerable open to good ideas all the time."

"It's simply this, that if you go away now, you'll break Mrs. Neilan's heart. I know her. She isn't very well, and she isn't very strong. Such a shock as this would be about the end, I think."

"I don't quite foller the drift," said Happy Jack. "You know I ain't Johnny, and yet you seem to be figuring that I had ought to stay here?"

"Why not?" she said with a wide gesture. "Why not? Don't you like the place?"

"But what's that got to do with it? It ain't mine, lady!"

"It has everything to do with it. You can have it if you want it!"

He gaped at her.

"How far away is your own country, the place where people know you?"

"Oh, around about five days' stiff riding, I guess."

She clapped her hands, triumphant.

"Then it's settled. You'll stay!"

"Miss Thomas," he said soberly, "this sure is queer talk."

"It's right talk and true talk. No matter what made you come here, Providence was behind it. It was intended for the best. This is the place you belong. Johnny is dead. Everyone really knows that . . . everyone except the old folks. And they'll never believe. So let them have their belief, because they'd die without it. Let them have it and think that you are he."

"D'you think I'm low down enough to do a thing like that?"

"No. I think you're big and fine enough to do it. Oh, I know you're honest, and that it goes against the grain to think of such a thing as that which I suggest. But at bottom, isn't it a bit of charity?"

"Things that are built up on lies, lady, don't usually last particular long, from what I've seen. Some folks may call it charity, and some folks may call it another thing; but a lie is pretty apt to be a lie, and that's an end to it!"

He shook his head with such finality that the argument seemed ended on the spot. And still she persisted.

"The ranch has been like a graveyard. There has never been a smile or a laugh, so far as I can remember, until tonight. There has been no kindness, no thought for others, until you came. Oh, this evening it seemed to me that you were working a miracle. And that's why I'm asking you to stay."

"And you ain't joking?"

"Joking? I tell you in all seriousness that I really think it's a matter of life or death to them. Mr. Neilan has had no interest in life for years, and Mrs. Neilan has simply been living in the hope that Johnny would come back. And if you disappoint her, I know the effect. It will be murder, just as certainly as though you pressed a revolver against her temple and fired!"

He wavered.

"Is it square?" he said. "Is it square to even think about playing a trick like that?"

"Not for some people. But for you, yes. Because you're honest!"

"Are you sure of that?" he asked.

"Hasn't every word you've said to me gone to prove it?"

She had stepped close to him while she spoke, and now she made a gesture of such lasting trust in him, and smiled up at him so perilously near, that the sense of her went to the brain of Happy Jack and made his heart leap.

"I'm going to show you how much I'm worth a trust like that," he said at length. "Will you come with me for a minute?"

He led the way to his own room. He opened the door. He pointed to the telltale pile of money on top of the bureau with the long revolver weighing it down.

She went close to examine it, made sure of what it was, and then started back with a soft exclamation of dismay. And the frightened eyes which she turned on Happy Jack hurt the big man more than a blow.

"You see how it is, and you see how much I can be trusted," he said.

"That's what you came for?"

"Yep. That's what I came for."

"Someone else put it into your mind. You never thought of it by yourself."

"How come you figure that?"

"Why, simply because you couldn't go through with it. You did all the hard part of the work, and then, when you had merely to walk out of the house with the money, you stopped and left it there. Why, if I thought you were honest and to be trusted before, I know it now!"

Happy Jack shook his head. Such reasoning as this was beyond him.

"Besides," she was saying suddenly, "it isn't only for the sake of the old folks. I'm partly selfish about it. I've dreaded every vacation, because every vacation brought me back to the ranch. But if there were . . . were a human being here who knew how to smile . . . why, it would be wonderful to come back to the mountains, because I love them!"

Happy Jack caught his breath. Her color had mounted as she spoke. And, though she could never be really beautiful, she was so pretty at that moment, so clear of eye, so wonderfully fresh in her young womanhood, that Happy Jack believed until that moment he had never known a woman worth looking at.

"I got few rules to live by!" he said after a moment of staring at her, "but one of 'em is never to refuse a girl what she asks for. And if you really mean what you say. . . ."

"I'll shake on it," broke in Mary Thomas.

He took her hand and pressed it gently.

IX

"Bad-Luck Tidings"

The bedroom of Mr. and Mrs. Neilan was on the first floor of the house with a big window opening onto the verandah, and the wife had barely finished detailing to her smiling husband the account of her interview with the wanderer, when a light tapping came against that window.

"How come anybody to be rapping at the window?" growled John Neilan. "And at this time of night!"

"It's only the wind shaking the pane," said his wife. "There can't be anyone out there in the storm!"

"Hark at that! There is someone."

It was unmistakable this time — three strong taps, equally spaced — and John Neilan, slipping out of bed into a capacious bathrobe, tucked his old feet into slippers and picked up the Colt which he always kept at hand near his bedside.

"John," cautioned Mrs. Neilan, "you aren't going to answer that knock with a gun in your hand?"

"Why not?"

"It's Christmas Day! That's why. No good will

337

come of it. I know! Surely this day of all days is for gentleness!"

"Gentleness . . . stuff!" grunted Neilan.

He went to the window and cast it up suddenly, at the same time stepping to one side in case some enemy attempted a direct attack by leaping into the room. But there appeared at the window the gray head of Chip Flinders, the oldest of their cowpunchers. He was obviously in a state of the most intense alarm, his jaw set hard and his eyes glancing hastily from side to side.

"What fool business is this?" grumbled Neilan.

"I didn't dare come around the front way," said Chip Flinders, his voice husky with fear. "He might of seen me!"

"Who might have seen you?"

"Him!" and he pointed above his head.

The rancher regarded Chip a moment from beneath the shadow of scowling brows. "Come in!" he growled at length.

And Chip stepped through the window and stood turning his hat uneasily in his hands and looking from side to side at the carpet, so as to avoid looking at Mrs. Neilan, who was sitting bolt erect in the bed, hugging a cloak around her shoulders.

"Now," said the rancher, "talk straight and talk quick. You ain't the kind to come around packing fool yarns to me, Chip. What's got into your head tonight?"

"I figured I knew him the minute I clapped eyes on him," said the cowpuncher hurriedly, "but I couldn't place him, and I begun figuring hard. But the harder I figured, the farther away I stayed from getting at him. I was plumb in bed and lying there almost asleep when it popped into my head. I seen the whole thing over again, and I knew him."

"Knew who, idiot? Who are you talking about?"

"Him that calls himself your son. And he's no more your son than I am!"

There was a faint cry of alarm from the bed.

"It isn't true!" moaned Mrs. Neilan. "I tell you, John, I'd swear it's Johnny. He . . . he's promised never again to use a gun just because I asked him. Isn't that proof?"

Chip Flinders suddenly began to laugh.

"Excuse me, ma'am," he said. "You mean to say Happy Jack said he wouldn't pull a gun again in a fight? Why, lady, he could just about as soon stop drawing his breath as stop drawing his gun. His Colt is his third hand. It's his brains. He does his thinking with it, they say down south."

"Happy Jack," said Neilan. "You call him Happy Jack?"

"Don't listen to him, John," pleaded the wife. "Ah, I knew this would bring bad luck! But don't talk to him any longer!"

"Hush up!" growled Neilan. "I'm going to get at the truth of this. Maybe Johnny went by the name of Happy Jack down south. What of it?"

Chip Flinders shook his head.

"Tell your story. Take your time," said Neilan.

"I'll wait and listen patient till you're all through. This is tolerable important, Chip. If you're wrong, you're done with me. If you're right, I'll see that you don't lose none by opening my eyes to an impostor. Now take a breath and get your brain to working and start in."

Chip Flinders obeyed these instructions to the letter, bowed his head a moment in thought, and then looked up.

"You remember when I got restive about five years back?" he said.

"The time you quit and went south to do some prospecting?"

"Sure. That's the time."

"It was a fool thing to do. You came back broke . . . nothing left of all your savings."

"Right enough. I come back broke, but I sure got my money's worth in experiences."

"When a gent's got gray hair, it's time for him to let somebody else do the collecting of experiences."

"Maybe. But this experience that I had is sure something you can be glad of, Mr. Neilan."

"Huh!" grunted the rancher, "go ahead, and I'll see."

"It was down in the town of Lesterville," began Chip Flinders. "I'd made a little stake up working a vein that pinched out on me just when I thought I'd struck it sure enough rich. I come down into Lesterville and put eight hundred in the bank, which was a tidy little stake and would see me get all fixed and started for another flyer at the mountains and the mines. Left me about three hundred dollars, and I started out to liquor up and have a large time, generally and all around.

"Which I was doing pretty good in a small way when there was a bunch of shooting started in town, and a lot of folks begun to rear and tear around. And pretty soon we got word that Bill Tucker's gang had just passed through, stuck up the cashier in the bank, and cleaned out the safes with a dust cloth. He didn't leave a penny behind him.

"I ain't a fighting man, but when I heard that and figured all was gone up in smoke, it sure hit me hard. I run out and tossed a saddle on my bronc and tore around and got to the center of town in time to join in with the posse that was starting. Sheriff Brown was running the party. I guess you've heard about Brown even away up here; but down there he still is pretty much looked up to. He'd a pile rather fight than eat. I seen him sitting his hoss and giving directions about how some of the boys should start in one direction and some should start in another. But every now and then he'd stop and turn around and ask a question of a gent that was sitting a hoss beside him, like he wanted to have that gent check up on what he was doing and say it was all right.

"It seemed to me pretty queer that a man like Brown would have to ask advice of anybody, even a judge, so I took a good look at the stranger. And they was a lot to see. He was only a kid, not much more'n twenty, I guess. But he was sure

341

built for keeps. Big wide shoulders and a thick chest, and always grinning and laughing and treating this like it was the beginning of a fine party. I turned to a gent near by me, and I asked him who that was.

" 'You don't know him?' he says, turning around and looking at me sort of queer.

" 'No,' says I. 'I sure don't. Who is he?'

" 'Before this here party is over you'll find out,' he says. 'That's Happy Jack, son, and you can lay to it that the trail he makes Tucker run will be the hottest that skunk ever traveled over. And that's the straight of it! That's Happy Jack. A plumb nacheral fighting man, son. The kind you heard your dad talking about that used to frolic around in the days of 'Forty-Nine. Well, Happy Jack is a ringer for that kind. He makes a gun talk Spanish when he feels like it.'

" 'Regular killer?' says I.

" 'Nope. Fighter, I said. Not killer. He don't fight to get notches on his gun.'

"Well, after that I sure watched Happy Jack close. When the sheriff was ready to start, he took most of us boys with him, but Happy Jack picked out half a dozen gents and rode off another way.

"I asked where he was going, and somebody told me that he was going to try to head off Tucker by a short cut across the mountains. But the gent that told me said they wasn't no chance of him doing it, that short cut being plain murder on a hoss.

"Anyway, Happy Jack started off and disappeared, and the rest of us buckled down and started to foller Sheriff Brown. We headed straight up a valley out of Lesterville. We rode hard, too, I'll tell a man! They was fifty-two gents started that trail, by my way of counting. When he got up the valley, they was only eighteen left. I had that Molly pinto, and that was the only reason I was left in the running. Sheriff Brown sure used up hossflesh when he hit a trail.

"And it done him some good, too, for pretty soon, away off in the moonlight, when we rounded a hill, we seen Tucker's men scooting away. When they seen us, they let out a yell that we could hear, the whole bunch of 'em, and they lit out as hard as they could ride. They was weighted down by a lot of gold. But our hosses were all plumb fagged by the hard work they'd done already. First we lost ground, and then we picked it up. On the open we could run faster than Tucker's men, but when it come to climbing, they sure had us beat.

"Looked like we could go on forever and never get no closer to 'em. And our hosses was beginning to roar, they were so plumb tired. We was all about to give up the fight, when all at once a shooting started right ahead of us up the valley, and Sheriff Brown, he lets out a yell.

" 'It's Happy Jack!' he hollers. 'It's Happy Jack, boys, and he's sure made the short cut. He must of turned his men and hosses into goats to get up there!'

"But there wasn't no doubt about it. Pretty

soon, down come the Tucker gang . . . eleven instead of the fourteen we'd first counted, and we knew that Happy Jack had counted for three of 'em.

"Tucker tried to rush us. But eleven ag'in' eighteen wasn't no easy chance for him. We give him some quick fire. We emptied a couple of saddles and, when they turned to run up the valley again . . . there being no manner of ways for them to climb the sides of that ravine . . . we give it to 'em again, and even in the moonlight we shot good enough to drop another of 'em.

"You can count for yourself. That left eight gents all ready to fight for their lives, and all heading up the valley straight for Happy Jack. They was bad ones, that gang of Tucker's. Nothing they wouldn't do. They'd burned and murdered and tortured and robbed. A choice lot of devils they was, every one! And now they had to fight for their lives.

" 'How many men did Happy get through the mountains by the short cut?' hollers the sheriff. 'How many? But Lord help 'em if they can't turn Tucker back before he gets to close quarters!'

"And he hollers: 'Ride, boys! Ride!'

"And thinking about Happy and the rest of the boys . . . which couldn't of been more'n two or three that he'd got through the short cut . . . we sure did punish our hossflesh to get up in time to help.

"But, when experts are fighting, it don't take long to end a scrap. We heard a crackling and a booming and a smashing of guns up the valley. And then came a couple of yells that made your heart stop beating. And then all at once there was a dead silence. There wasn't even a whisper. Just that cold, white moonshine a-pouring down on the valley.

" 'They've busted through!' called out Brown. 'Lord help Happy and the rest. Tucker must of busted through!'

"Up the valley we go like a shot. Pretty soon we get near the place. We see one of Tucker's men lying on his back with his arms throwed out. Then we come on three strung out one after another. And we knew that they'd dropped while they was rushing a big bunch of rocks right ahead of us. We galloped for them rocks. Right on the top of them we seen another of Tucker's men fallen on his face. And there was a second inside the rocks. That made six we found dead or wounded bad.

"What we seen next was sure a funny picture. It was Happy Jack sitting there in the moonshine with his back against a rock smoking a cigarette, with two dead men at his feet. We come to him with a yell.

" 'Are you hurt bad?' asked Brown, putting his arms around Happy like Happy was his own kid.

" 'They drilled me,' says Happy, quiet as you please. 'But I think that I'll pull through, right enough. Mind that poor devil there, though, will you? I think he's got a spark of life in him. He needs help more'n me!'

"We turned that gent over. It was Tucker. And he was just kicking out.

" 'Carry me over to Jack,' he says.

"We done it. It sure rides hard not to do what a dying man asks, even when he's a murdering skunk like Tucker was. We carried him over, and he puts out his hand to Happy.

" 'If I'd had you with me, kid,' he says, 'I'd of beat the world. So long, and good luck!'

"And then he died.

" 'But where's the rest of the boys, Happy?,' says the sheriff, while we work like fury tying up Happy's wounds, and him never making a murmur.

" 'They didn't get here,' says Happy. 'The going was pretty rough.'

" 'You stood 'em off all alone?' says the sheriff.

" 'I had to,' says Happy and grins.

"And that was the honest truth. He'd done that fighting all by himself. And he'd won out. And that man, that Happy Jack, is the gent that's in your house tonight calling himself your son!"

"And why not?" asked Mrs. Neilan, her voice trembling. "Surely we'd be proud to have such a hero for a son!"

"Sure you would," and Chip Flinders nodded kindly. "But, you see, I asked about Happy Jack. He'd been brought up around Morgan Run, which was the name of the creek that run down the valley where he killed Tucker. Somebody passing through left a baby behind 'em, and that baby was raised by everybody in general and nobody in particular, and because of his grin they got to calling him Happy Jack. They remembered him since he was a baby, and Johnny didn't leave home till he was fourteen, pretty near."

Mrs. Neilan dropped her face in her hands. Her husband rose and strode to and fro in the room.

"He looks like Johnny," he said. "But he sure ain't got Johnny's mean streak in him. And . . . Chip, heaven help you if you're lying to me!"

"Do I look like I was lying?" said Chip. "And d'you think I'd talk ag'in' a gunfighter like Happy Jack if I didn't know that I was right? Ain't I taking my life in my hands by saying what I've said?"

"Them that bring bad-luck tidings don't get much thanks," said the rancher. "Almost I wish you hadn't told me. But what would Happy Jack be doing here?"

"He's trailed crooks and fought crooks and lived with crooks. And them that live free and easy are kind of apt to get free and easy. Ain't you got a pile of money in your safe down the cellar?"

Neilan started.

"Money? I should say! You think he come to make a play for that?"

"John, John!" moaned Mrs. Neilan. "Are you going to give him no chance to clear himself? Even if I swear that I know he's good and honest, even if he ain't my boy?"

"And I gave him the key, like an idiot!" groaned

347

the rancher. "If the money's gone, I deserve losing it!"

Gathering his revolver in a closer grip, he ran out of the room.

X

"The Lesser Danger"

Down into the cellar ran Neilan, as fast as his old legs would carry him, and one glance at the open door of the safe was enough. He whirled and labored back up the stairs with teeth set and his gun poised. Not that he had any real hope of finding Happy Jack in the house, but he was in a fighting humor, and the touch of the rough gun butt was soothing against his palm.

He started straight for the room which Happy had slept in. But a whisper of voices in the hall, as he approached the top of the stairs, gave him pause.

Flat against the steps he dropped and, pushing the revolver ahead of him, he raised his head to look. He saw Happy Jack and the girl standing side by side. What they said he could not make out. But what happened he could easily see. In the hand of Happy Jack there was a thick wad of greenbacks, and he transferred the entire bundle of money to the hands of the girl. Then, with a wave of the hand, he turned away down the hall.

The master of the house waited to see no more. He whirled and scurried down the stairs as fast as he could run, blessing the age which had withered him to such lightness that his footfall made no sound on the boards.

He whisked into the safety of his room and confronted his wife and Chip.

"You're right, Chip," he said, "and I'm sure thanking you for what you told me. He done it. The safe's open, and the money's gone. And then I sneaked up to find him in his room, thinking he mightn't of gone yet. And he hadn't. He was still here. He was in the hall talking to the girl. And what d'you think the fox has done?"

"Talking to Mary?" breathed Mrs. Neilan.

"Aye, he's bought her out. That's the gratitude she returns us for giving her a home! I seen him put the money in her hands. Don't you see how he figures? Suppose he's trailed and caught? He'll pass it off easy. He'll say that coming here was just a joke. He played the joke, and he left before morning. We say he busted open the safe and done burglary. He says: 'Then where's the money I took?' And they's no money on him! Why? Because he's left it with the girl! And afterward she's to slip away and send him the stuff, or half of it. She's always hated us. I've seen it in her quiet ways and the look she gives us now and then. And now she's going to have money enough to start her out in life!"

He ground his teeth in his fury.

"We'll change that! We'll teach her, the vixen! And if being caught with stolen goods means the penitentiary in this state, I'm sure going to see that she lands there!"

350

"John!" broke in his wife, wringing her hands. "Won't you listen to reason? Won't you please listen to me? There must be some explanation. If you'll only wait, you'll find out that neither Happy Jack nor Mary means anything wrong!"

"Are you plumb losing your mind?" exclaimed her irate husband. "Didn't I see the door of the safe open? Didn't I see him making her a Christmas present of the money? He's leaving the house right now!"

He raised his hand to hush them. And in the breathless interval of silence, all three could hear the soft thud of a closing door. Neilan roused himself suddenly; in the space of a few seconds he had thrust his legs into trousers, his feet into shoes which he did not pause to button, and huddled a coat over his thin shoulders.

"You're not going to follow him?" cried his wife. "Oh, John. I wish I'd never been born!"

"Hush up!" commanded her husband. "There he goes now!"

Peering through the window, they saw the tall figure of Happy Jack striding through the starlight across the snow.

He went slowly, realizing that he had gone out to face the second great danger which he had confronted tonight. But in the first event he had imperiled his honor and, now that this was safe, he looked forward to his meeting with Sandy Crisp as a lesser thing. Had he been able to bring his revolver with him, the adventure would have been an actual pleasure. But the promise to Mrs.

Neilan bound him to helplessness in that respect.

Approaching the outskirts of the pines, he slackened his pace still further. Somewhere in that covert Crisp was waiting and, perhaps, Shorty was with him. The pines shut out the starlight and the haze of the westering moon after he had taken a few steps past the verge. He paused now, and whistled softly, raising his head so that the notes would travel as far as possible down the wind, which hummed and purred and whined through the upper branches.

After that he went on again, whistling a short note every few steps, until he came into a little clearing. He had hardly entered it when a hand fell without warning upon his shoulder and, staring about, he found himself face to face with Crisp, with Shorty grinning in the background.

"You got the stuff?" asked Sandy eagerly. And he rushed on, without waiting to hear an answer, as though he took success for granted: "But why didn't you go by the stable and get your hoss?"

But the larger man shook his head.

"I ain't got the stuff," he said simply.

"You didn't get the key?"

"No," lied Happy Jack.

But Sandy Crisp began to chuckle softly.

"That'd make a good Christmas story," he declared, "but I ain't no ways in the humor for hearing yarns. It's too cold, and we been waiting for you till we're all froze up! Don't lie, Happy. D'you think that we let all that party run along without watching? Not us! I slipped up and watched through the window. It was dead easy. And I seen with my own eyes when the old fool give you the key. So pony over the stuff, Happy, and we'll be on our way as soon as you can get your hoss. I don't blame you for wanting to hog the whole lot of it. But I'm onto your game, Happy."

Still Happy shook his head.

"You want to know what happened, Sandy," he said.

"Sure I do," said the other. "But what's that?"

"Where?"

"I heard somebody break through the snow . . . that sort of crunching sound, anyways."

"Maybe a branch fell. They ain't anybody out here. Nobody knows I left the house."

"Go look over there behind that brush, Shorty, and see!"

Shorty obeyed, but his survey of the gloom behind the thicket was a most cursory one. He came back with the report: "All clear. Nobody there."

"All right," said Sandy. "Now go on with your yarn, Happy. And make it quick."

"I got the key," said Happy Jack, "and I went down from my room and opened the safe and took out the loot."

"That sounds like straight stuff!" and the outlaw grinned as he moistened his lips.

"And then," went on Happy, "old Mrs. Neilan come in and talked to me. She sure is a fine old lady, Sandy."

"So you give her back the money!" Sandy sneered. "Come straight, now, Happy. Maybe I know more'n you think!"

"I didn't give her the money," said Happy Jack. "But, when she got through talking and left, I sure done a pile of thinking. And I seen that it was as all a bum play, Sandy. I was playing the part of a sneaking coyote with folks that trusted me. You say that old Neilan is hard. Maybe he is, but he sure showed me a white hand all the way through. Anyway, I got to thinking, and finally I made up my mind that they wasn't enough money in this game to buy me off. I've lived straight, Sandy, up to now, and from now on I figure on going extra straight. I gave that money to the girl, Mary Thomas, to put back in the safe, because I wouldn't trust myself to handle that much coin. I might weaken at the last minute, thinking how many years' pay was in the roll!"

"Just like a fairy story, you being the Fairy Prince!" Crisp was still sneering. "Go on. I'm trying to listen. But I sure got a limit to my patience, Happy. What you figure on doing now?"

"There's an old man and an old woman in that house, Sandy, that figure I'm their boy. Well, you know I ain't. But I've made up my mind that if I can give 'em any happiness by playing the part, I'm willing to try! I'm going back there and live like I belong in that family."

There was a moment of silence. The wind had dropped into a lull, and the hard breathing of

Sandy Crisp was audible.

"Of all the lies I've ever heard," he said at last, "this is the father and the grandfather of the lot, and I've sure heard some fine liars working in their prime days. But, d'you think I'm fool enough to believe you, Happy?"

Happy Jack shrugged his shoulders.

"That ain't worrying me none."

"And you expect me to believe, too, that because your holster is empty you ain't got a gun, maybe?"

"I promised Mrs. Neilan that I wouldn't carry a gun, Sandy, and I'm living up to the promise!"

Sandy Crisp choked and then broke into loud, indignant laughter.

"Am I dreaming, maybe?" he cried at length. "Am I having a funny dream? Pinch me, Shorty, so's I can wake up! Why, Happy, you fool, you're getting weak-minded. Don't you think I know you wouldn't come out and face me with that lie and without a gun?"

"I've told you straight," said Happy Jack quietly.

"Then," said the outlaw savagely, "you might of shot yourself first and saved me the trouble!"

"Wrong, Sandy. I know you're a hard one, but even you won't pull a gun on a gent that has bare hands!"

"Won't I? You don't know me, Happy. Not by a long ways!"

He swayed a little from side to side, very much as though the wind were unsteadying him, and yet at that moment there was not a breath. The dull moon haze fell softly into the clearing. The figures of the men stood out big and black and half obscured.

"I'm going to give you one more chance, Happy," said the outlaw. "Are you going to come across with that coin, or do you aim to start in pushing daisies?"

"I'm done talking," said Happy Jack, and turned on his heel.

He had almost reached the edge of the shadow when Sandy Crisp shouted: "Happy!"

Slowly he turned. The gun was already gleaming in the hand of Sandy, and the exclamation of Happy was drowned in the report that followed. Happy Jack slipped sidewise into the snow.

"Turn him over. See if he's dead!" exclaimed Sandy Crisp. "And then we'll make a break for. . . ."

The last of his sentence was blotted out in a sudden fusillade from that same thicket which Shorty had been ordered to search the moment before. Shorty, with a yell of agony, leaped high in the air and landed running. In an instant he had disappeared among the farther trees. Sandy Crisp had doubled over at the sound of the first shot and fled with wolfish speed into the covert.

The uncertain light, and arms and hands numbed by the wait in the cold of the night, accounted for that poor shooting. John Neilan and Chip Flinders started out of their hiding place cursing their erratic aim. Chip still was firing shot after shot through the trees beyond and shouting at the top of his lungs to the cowpunchers in the far-off bunkhouse. But, long before any response came, they heard the rapid crunching of the hoofs of galloping horses beating away through the snow.

In the meantime, John Neilan had dropped on his knees in the snow and with frantic efforts had turned the body of Happy Jack. He lay face up at length, a flow of crimson covering one side of his head. And suddenly his eyes opened and he stared about him.

"All right, Sandy!" he muttered. "You'll get yours for this, you hound!"

"It's not Sandy!" cried Neilan. "It's John Neilan! Chip! Chip! He's dead!"

The eyes had closed again.

But he was not dead. The scurrying crowd of half-dressed cowpunchers, coming in answer to those alarms of guns and shouts, lifted Happy Jack and carried him toward the house — carried him tenderly, in obedience to the frantic directions of John Neilan, freely interspersed with terrific curses directed at those who stumbled under the burden.

Halfway to the house they were met by a flying figure. It was Mary Thomas, and at her coming John Neilan ran a pace or two to meet her and turned her back.

"It's all right," he kept saying. "There's nothing wrong. Just an accident! He's going to get well. He sure has got to get well!"

And so they brought him eventually back into the ranch house and into Neilan's own bedroom, where his wife was cowering against the walls with her face sheltered behind her hands.

But when she saw what they had brought to her, she rose nobly to the occasion. Not even Mary Thomas could share in the direction of what was to be done. With quick, quietly delivered orders, in five minutes she had every man busy with a different task, one kindling a fire, another running for bandages, a third washing the wound, and a fourth standing by in reserve.

Hardly a word other than orders was spoken until well on into the night. In fact the dawn of the Christmas Day was beginning to appear when the doctor, who had been summoned, arrived.

His examination was quickly ended.

"It's not fatal," he said. "The bullet traveled almost the whole length of the side of the skull. He may not waken for two hours more. That's all."

A faint cry from Mary Thomas made him turn.

"Is this his wife?" he said kindly, as she dropped on her knees beside the bed.

"You're speaking sort of previous, Doc," said John Neilan. "But I dunno how it'll turn out."

"How did it happen?" asked the doctor.

"That's a long story. The main thing is the ending. My boy is going to get well."

"John," whispered Mrs. Neilan, "what d'you mean?"

"Why," said John Neilan, scratching his head,

"ain't it all pretty clear. Why, you yourself said that there was Providence in it. And I guess there is. This is Christmas Day, ain't it? And ain't Happy Jack sure meant to be our gift? Besides, he's lacking a last name, and I figure that he'll take kindly to the name of Neilan."

"Heaven be praised," said Mrs. Neilan, "for making you see the light!"

And as she spoke a red radiance fell across the room. The Christmas sun was rising through a clear, clear sky.

The employees of G.K. Hall hope you have enjoyed this Large Print book. All our Large Print titles are designed for easy reading, and all our books are made to last. Other G.K. Hall books are available at your library, through selected bookstores, or directly from us.

For information about titles, please call:

(800) 257-5157

To share your comments, please write:

Publisher
G.K. Hall & Co.
P.O. Box 159
Thorndike, ME 04986